ANGRY BIRDS™
FURIOUS FOWL

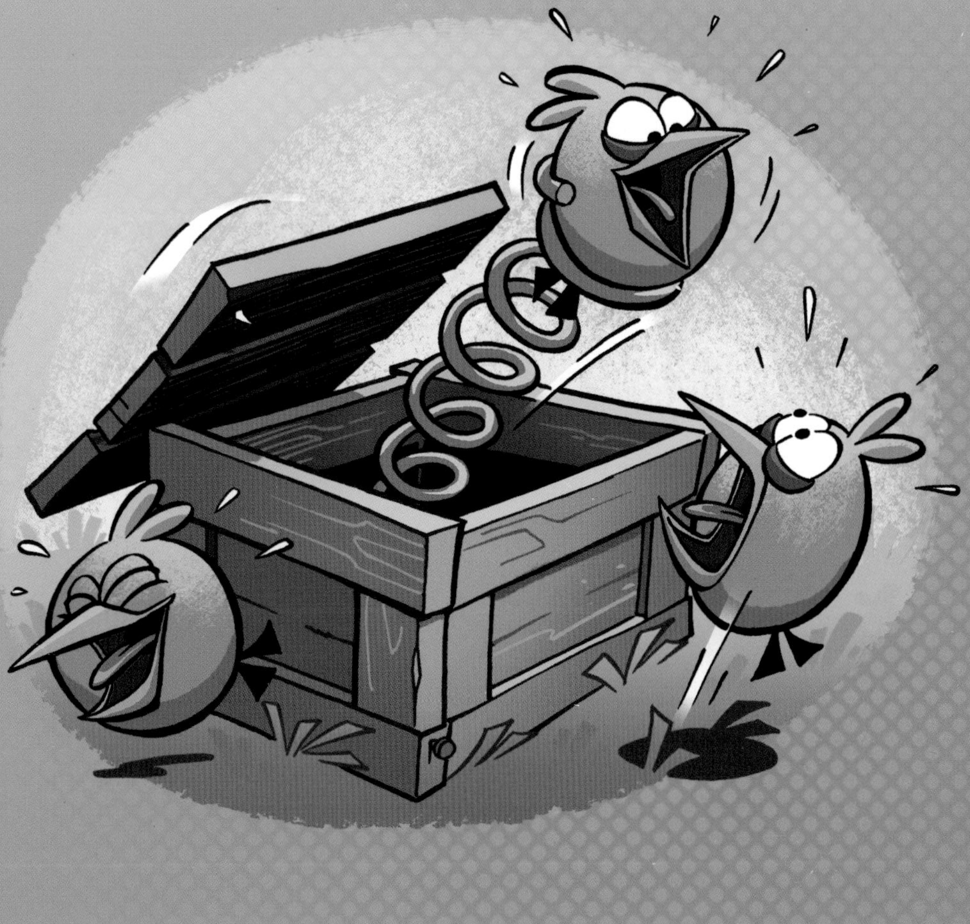

ANGRY BIRDS™
FURIOUS FOWL

THE MARTIAN

WRITTEN BY: PAUL TOBIN
ART BY: ANTONELLO DALENA
COLORS BY: PAOLO MADDALENI
LETTERS BY: PISARA OY

PEACE AND HARMONY

WRITTEN BY: KARI KORHONEN
ART BY: ANTONELLO DALENA
COLORS BY: PAOLO MADDALENI
LETTERS BY: PISARA OY

EDITORIAL ASSISTANCE BY: PETER ADRIAN BEHRAVESH
SERIES EDITS BY: DAVID HEDGECOCK
COLLECTION EDITS BY: JUSTIN EISINGER & ALONZO SIMON
COLLECTION DESIGN BY: NEIL UYETAKE & MARCONI TORRES
PUBLISHED BY: GREG GOLDSTEIN

COVER ART BY: PACO RODRIQUEZ
COVER COLORS BY: DIGIKORE

Thanks to Jukka Heiskanen for her hard work and invaluable assistance.

For international rights, contact licensing@idwpublishing.com

ISBN: 978-1-68405-153-3

21 20 19 18 2 3 4 5

ROVIO

Mikael Hed, Chairman of the Board • Laura Nevanlinna, Publisher, CEO • Jukka Heiskanen, Editor-in-Chief, Comics • Juha Mäkinen Editor, Comics • Henrik Sarimo, Graphic Designer • Nathan Cosby, Freelance Editor

KAIKEN ENTERTAINMENT

IDW®
www.IDWPUBLISHING.com

Greg Goldstein, President & Publisher • Robbie Robbins, EVP & Sr. Art Director • Chris Ryall, Chief Creative Officer & Editor-in-Chief • Matthew Ruzicka, CPA, Chief Financial Officer • David Hedgecock, Associate Publisher • Laurie Windrow, Senior Vice President of Sales & Marketing • Lorelei Bunjes, VP of Digital Services • Eric Moss, Sr. Director, Licensing & Business Development

Ted Adams, Founder & CEO of IDW Media Holdings

Facebook: facebook.com/idwpublishing • Twitter: @idwpublishing • YouTube: youtube.com/idwpublishing
Tumblr: tumblr.idwpublishing.com • Instagram: instagram.com/idwpublishing

Originally published as ANGRY BIRDS COMICS QUARTERLY: FURIOUS FOWL and ANGRY BIRDS COMICS QUARTERLY: MONSTERS AND MISTLETOE.

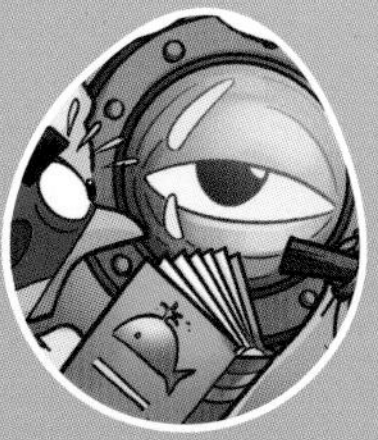

MOBY PIG

WRITTEN BY: PAUL TOBIN
ART BY: MARCO GERVASIO
COLORS BY: DIGIKORE
LETTERS BY: PISARA OY

ART APPRECIATION

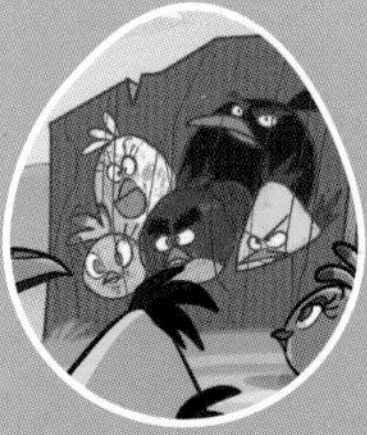

WRITTEN BY: JEFF PARKER
ART BY: ANTONELLO DALENA
COLORS BY: PAOLO MADDALENI
LETTERS BY: PISARA OY

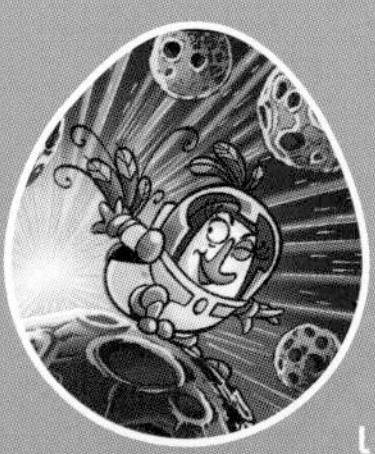

THE JOURNAL

WRITTEN BY: PAUL TOBIN
ART BY: COMICUP STUDIO
ROUGHS BY: JORDI ALFONSO
CLEANUPS BY: TONY FERNANDEZ
INKS BY: LORENA RUFIAN
COLORS BY: GLORIA CABALLÉ
LETTERS BY: PISARA OY

HUGGABLE YOU

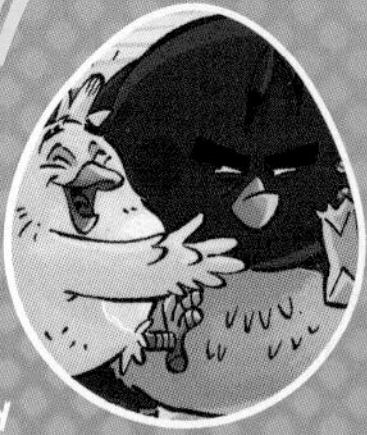

WRITTEN BY: KARI KORHONEN
ART BY: COMICUP STUDIO
ROUGHS BY: JORDI ALFONSO
CLEANUPS BY: TONY FERNANDEZ
INKS BY: LORENA RUFIAN AND SONIA ALBERT
COLORS BY: GLORIA CABALLÉ
LETTERS BY: PISARA OY

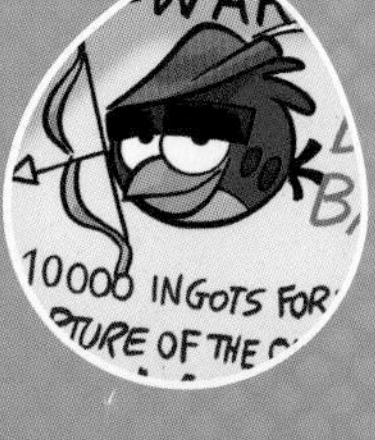
10000 INGOTS FOR

RED HOOD

WRITTEN AND DRAWN BY: MARCO GERVASIO
INKS BY: ALESSANDRO ZEMOLIN
COLORS BY: NICOLA PASQUETTO
LETTERS BY: PISARA OY

BOMBS AWAY

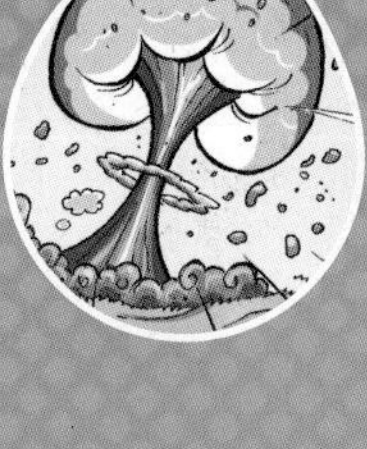

WRITTEN BY: JEFF PARKER
ART BY: UMBERTO SACCHELLI
COLORS BY: DIGIKORE
LETTERS BY: PISARA OY

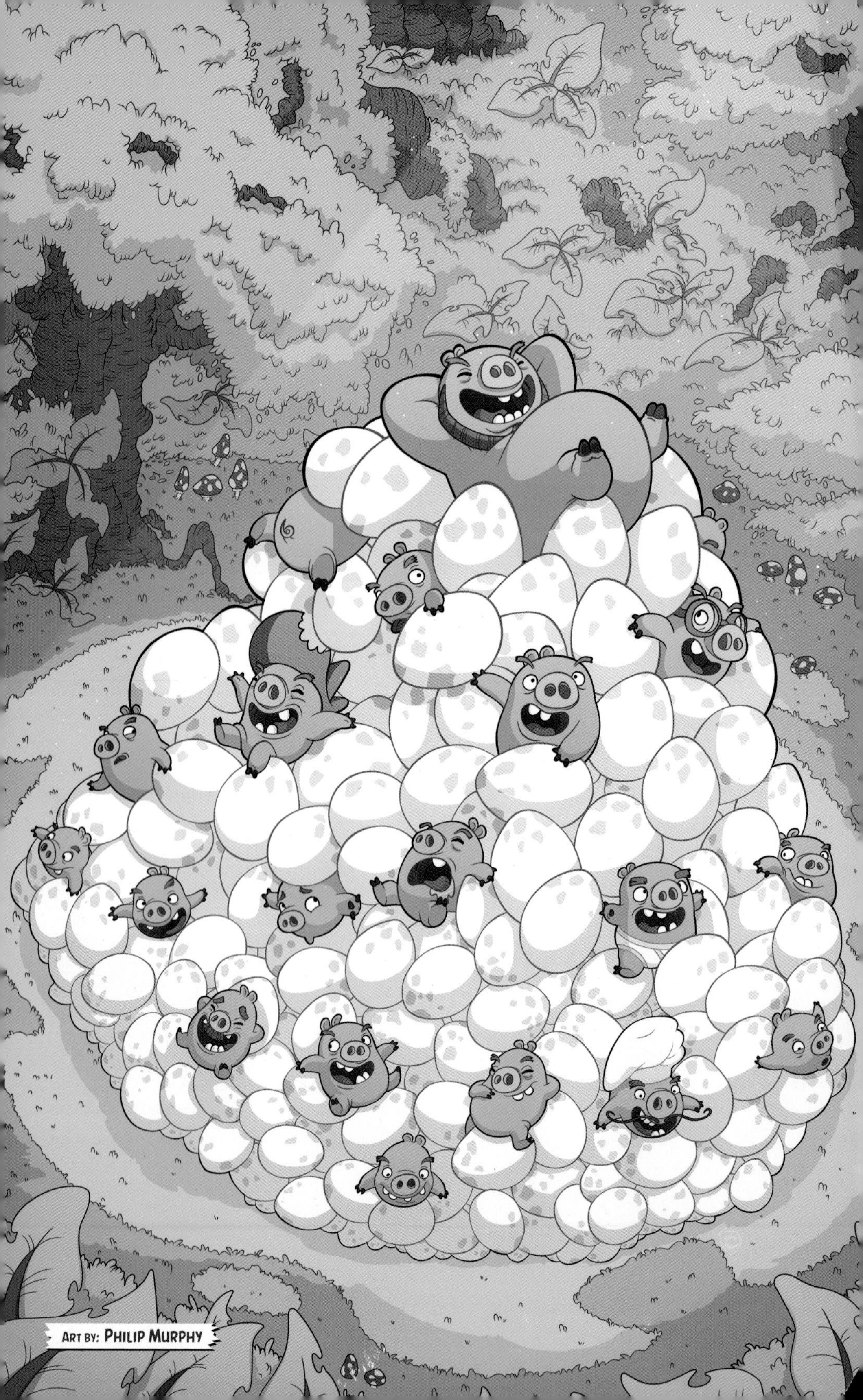
ART BY: PHILIP MURPHY

SO, TELL ME, WHAT BRINGS *CASTANOVA*, THE NUMBER ONE PLAY-WRIGHT IN ALL OF BIRD VILLAGE, TO *OUR* PART OF TOWN?

SIMPLE! I'VE JUST FINISHED WRITING MY NEWEST EPIC, AND I'M LOOKING FOR THE *PERFECT* STAR TO CAST AS THE *LEAD!*

HMM. *NO.* WHERE IS THE INNER FIRE? I NEED SOMEONE WHOSE PASSION ERUPTS FROM WITHIN!

I NEED SOMEONE WHO RESONATES AND DETONATES! I NEED SOMEONE WHO EXPLODES!

BUT...

NO. WE NEED SOMEONE WITH GRIT AND MENACE. NOT SONGS AND FLOWERS.

LA LA LA LA LA LA LA LA

WACH

WACH WACH

NO MIMES!

WHO WAS *THAT?* I COULDN'T EVEN *SEE* HIM!

THAT'S NO GOOD. THE AUDIENCE NEEDS TO *LINGER.* WE NEED TO *DWELL* ON THE *INTENSITY* OF THE ACTOR'S EXPRESSION, THE *ADAMANT FORCE* OF THEIR *GAZE!*

WE NEED SOMEONE WHO... WHO...

ANGRY BIRDS™
FURIOUS FOWL

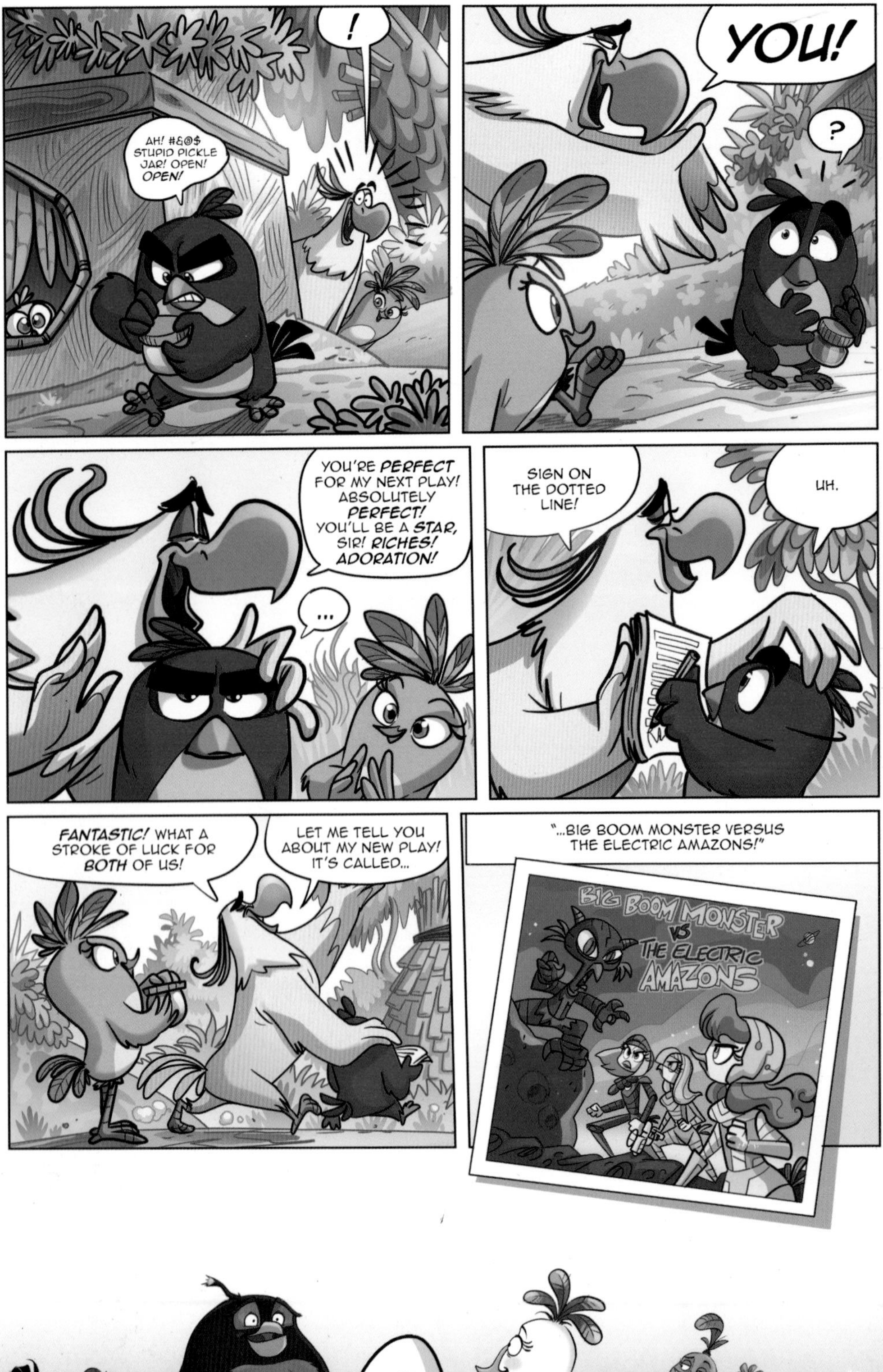
AH! #&@$ STUPID PICKLE JAR! OPEN! OPEN!
!
YOU!
?
YOU'RE PERFECT FOR MY NEXT PLAY! ABSOLUTELY PERFECT! YOU'LL BE A STAR, SIR! RICHES! ADORATION!
...
SIGN ON THE DOTTED LINE!
UH.
FANTASTIC! WHAT A STROKE OF LUCK FOR BOTH OF US!
LET ME TELL YOU ABOUT MY NEW PLAY! IT'S CALLED...
"...BIG BOOM MONSTER VERSUS THE ELECTRIC AMAZONS!"
BIG BOOM MONSTER VS THE ELECTRIC AMAZONS

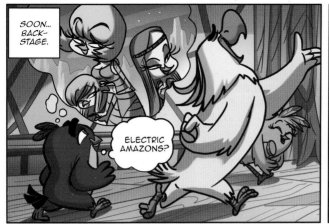

SOON... BACKSTAGE.

ELECTRIC AMAZONS?

OH, YES! *YES!* THEY'RE A *BIG* PART OF MY EPIC!

YOU'LL BE INTERACTING WITH *THEM* FOR QUITE SOME TIME!

COSTUMING

FOR NOW, LET'S GET *YOU* INTO *COSTUME!*

THERE! PRETTY IMPRESSIVE, RIGHT?

UH.

BUT I GUESS YOU'LL BE WANTING TO MEET YOUR CHARMING CO-STARS, THE ELECTRIC AMAZONS!

HERE THEY ARE!

WAVE WAVE WAVE

ANGRY BIRDS™
FURIOUS FOWL

SOON...
LUNCH TIME, EVERYONE! GRAB SOMETHING TO EAT, AND THEN WE'LL START REHEARSING!
ACTOR ENTRANCE ONLY
GRUMBLE GRUMBLE ELECTRIC AMAZONS GRUMBLE GRUMBLE
MAYBE I'LL GET A WATERMELON SALAD?
MANGO BURRITO?
OR, HMM, BIRD-SEED PIZZA?
?
?
AHHHHH!!!
?
OH, YEAH. I'M IN COSTUME.
WELL, I'M SURE IT'S JUST HATCHLINGS THAT WILL BE FOOLED. NO ADULT COULD POSSIBLY MISTAKE ME FOR A REAL ALIEN.
THAPP!
OOP
ALIEN! ALIEN INVASION!
RUN FOR YOUR LIVES!
THUMP! THUMP!
OUCH!
OOF!
HEY!
THAP THAP THAP
OW!
GRR!
THAP

SOON...

OKAY, THAT WAS WEIRD. MAYBE I SHOULDN'T HAVE WORN MY COSTUME OUTSIDE?

I'LL HAVE THREE *TOMATO TORNADO TACOS*, AND A—

SO-SO TACOS

?

AIEEEEEEE!!!

SO-SO TACOS

GAHHHH!

SQUILLRRRT

BLUURK

GARRRRR!

IT'S... IT'S SOME SORT OF... *SPACE ALIEN!*

AND IT'S GONE *BERSERK!*

RUN FOR YOUR LIVES!

NO! DON'T RUN!

RUB RUB

ATTACK! WE MUST DEFEAT THE CREATURE BEFORE IT DESTROYS US ALL!

?

YEAH! ATTACK!

ANGRY BIRDS
FURIOUS FOWL

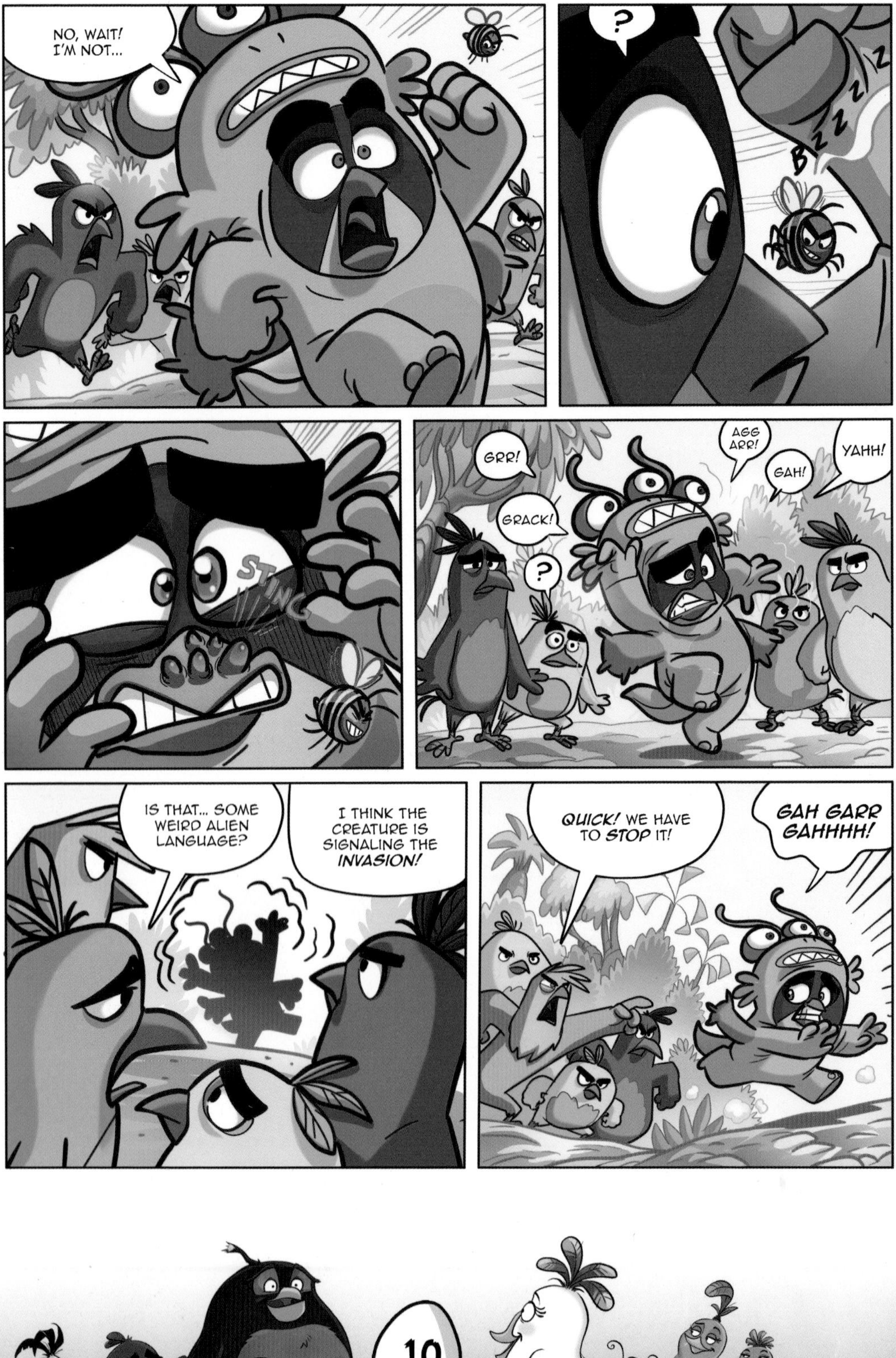
NO, WAIT! I'M NOT...
?
BZZZZZ
STING
GRR!
GRACK!
?
AGG ARR!
GAH!
YAHH!
IS THAT... SOME WEIRD ALIEN LANGUAGE?
I THINK THE CREATURE IS SIGNALING THE *INVASION!*
QUICK! WE HAVE TO *STOP* IT!
GAH GARR GAHHHH!

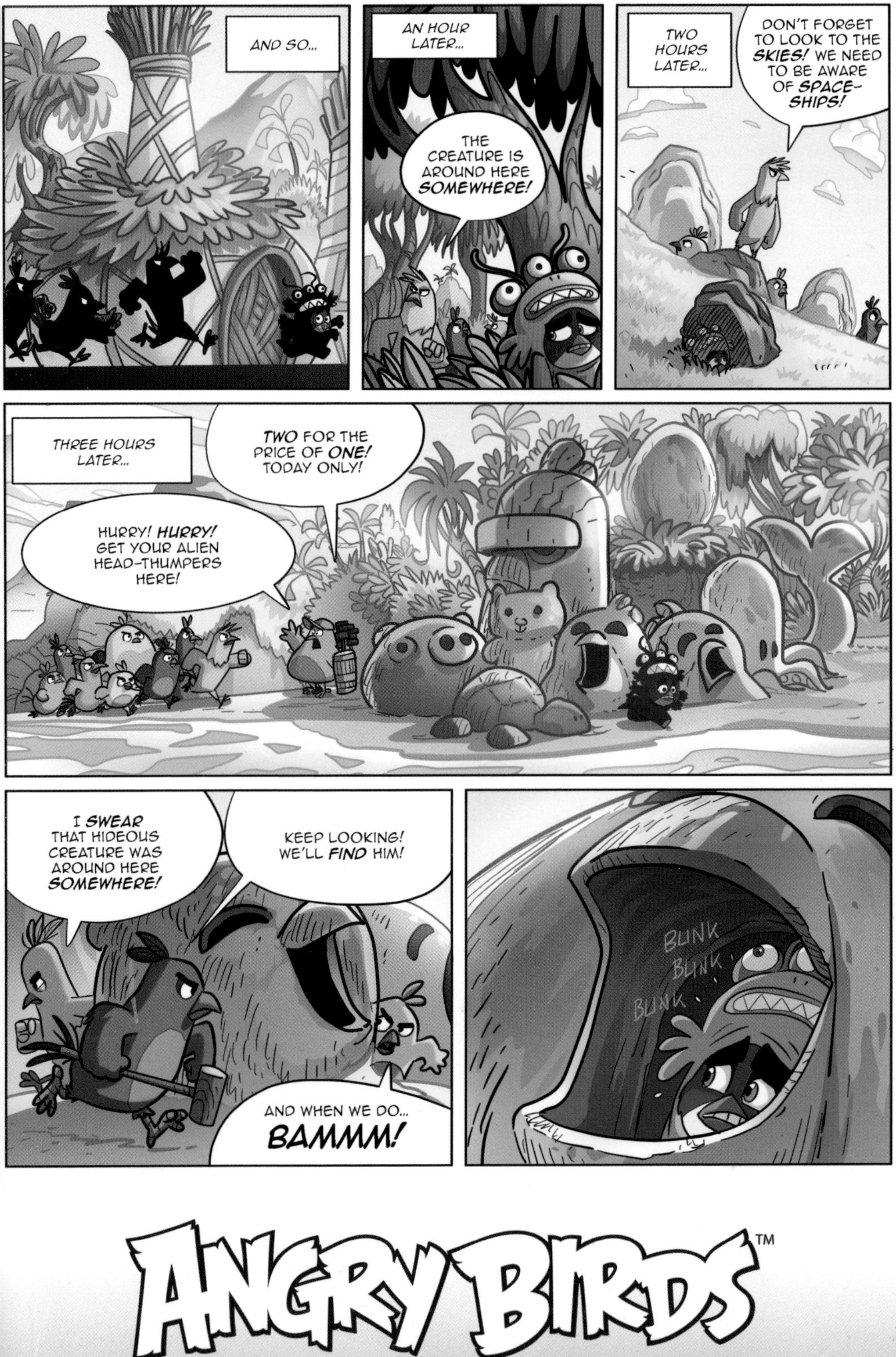
AND SO...
AN HOUR LATER...
THE CREATURE IS AROUND HERE SOMEWHERE!
TWO HOURS LATER...
DON'T FORGET TO LOOK TO THE SKIES! WE NEED TO BE AWARE OF SPACE-SHIPS!
THREE HOURS LATER...
TWO FOR THE PRICE OF ONE! TODAY ONLY!
HURRY! HURRY! GET YOUR ALIEN HEAD-THUMPERS HERE!
I SWEAR THAT HIDEOUS CREATURE WAS AROUND HERE SOMEWHERE!
KEEP LOOKING! WE'LL FIND HIM!
AND WHEN WE DO... BAMMM!
BLINK
BLINK
BLINK

ANGRY BIRDS™
FURIOUS FOWL

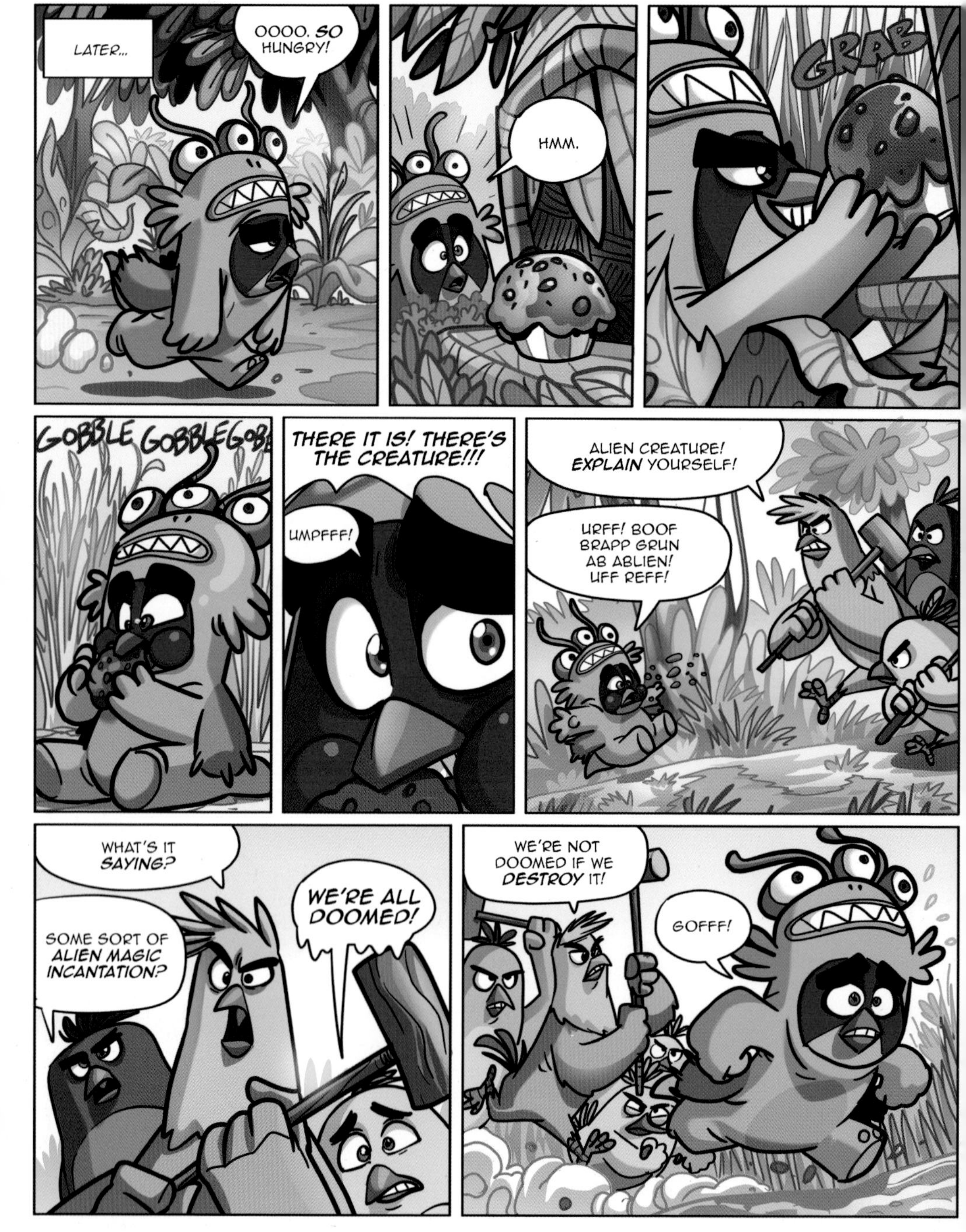
LATER...
OOOO. SO HUNGRY!
HMM.
GRAB
GOBBLE GOBBLEGOBB
THERE IT IS! THERE'S THE CREATURE!!!
UMPFFF!
ALIEN CREATURE! EXPLAIN YOURSELF!
URFF! BOOF BRAPP GRUN AB ABLIEN! UFF REFF!
WHAT'S IT SAYING?
SOME SORT OF ALIEN MAGIC INCANTATION?
WE'RE ALL DOOMED!
WE'RE NOT DOOMED IF WE DESTROY IT!
GOFFF!

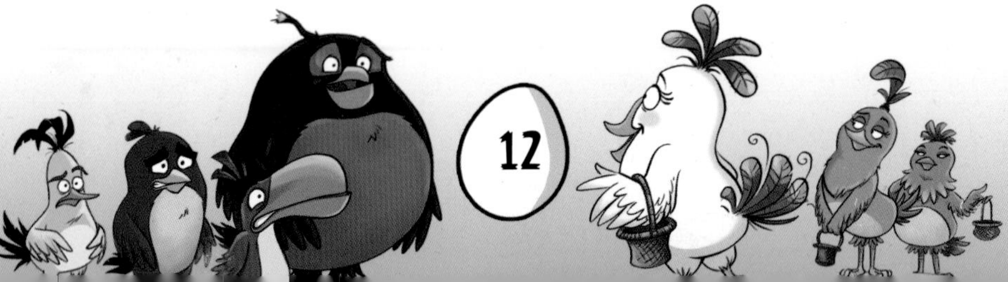

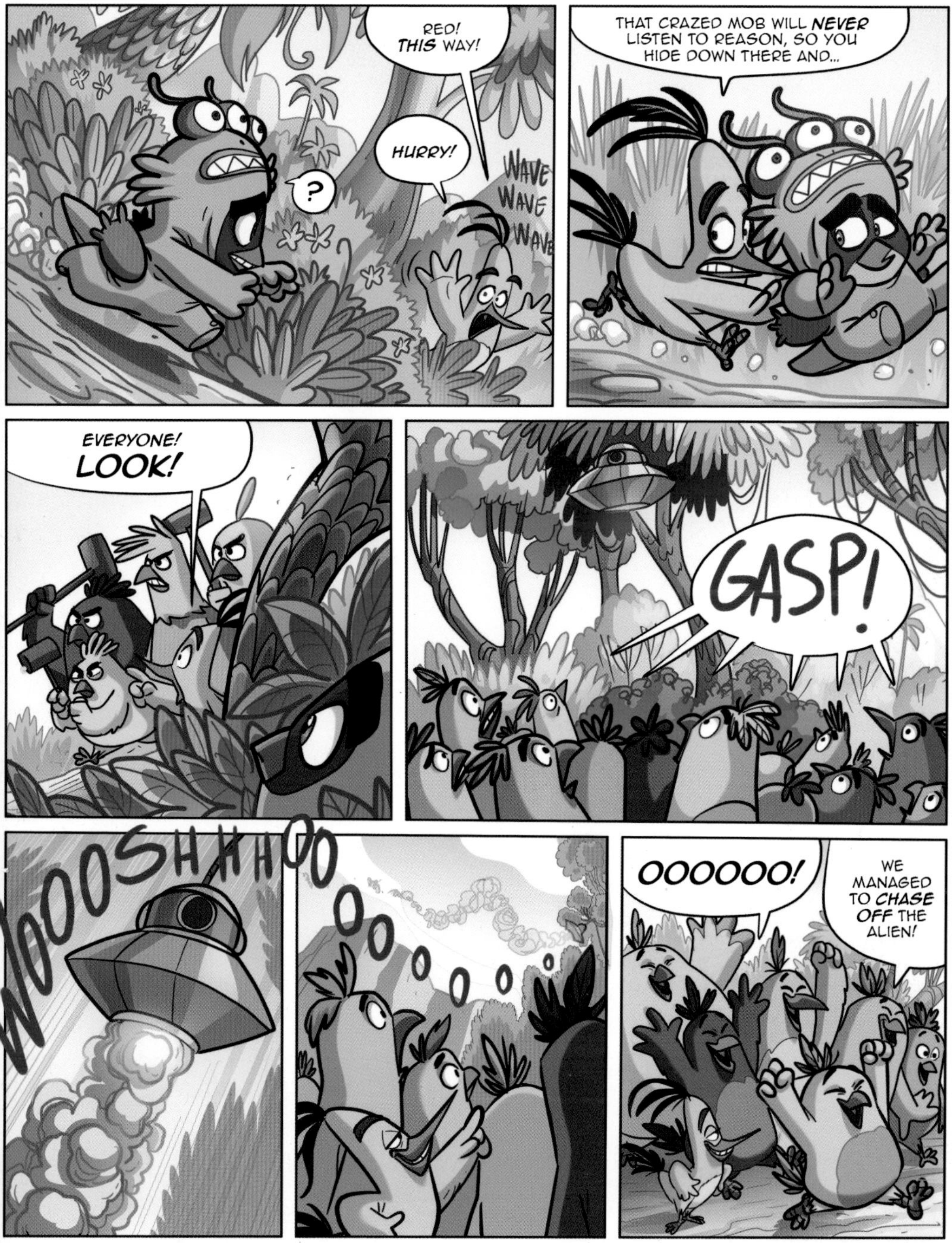
RED! **THIS** WAY!
?
HURRY!
WAVE WAVE WAVE
THAT CRAZED MOB WILL **NEVER** LISTEN TO REASON, SO YOU HIDE DOWN THERE AND...
EVERYONE! **LOOK!**
GASP!
WOOOSHHHOO
OOOOOO
OOOOOO!
WE MANAGED TO ***CHASE OFF*** THE ALIEN!

ANGRY BIRDS™

FURIOUS FOWL

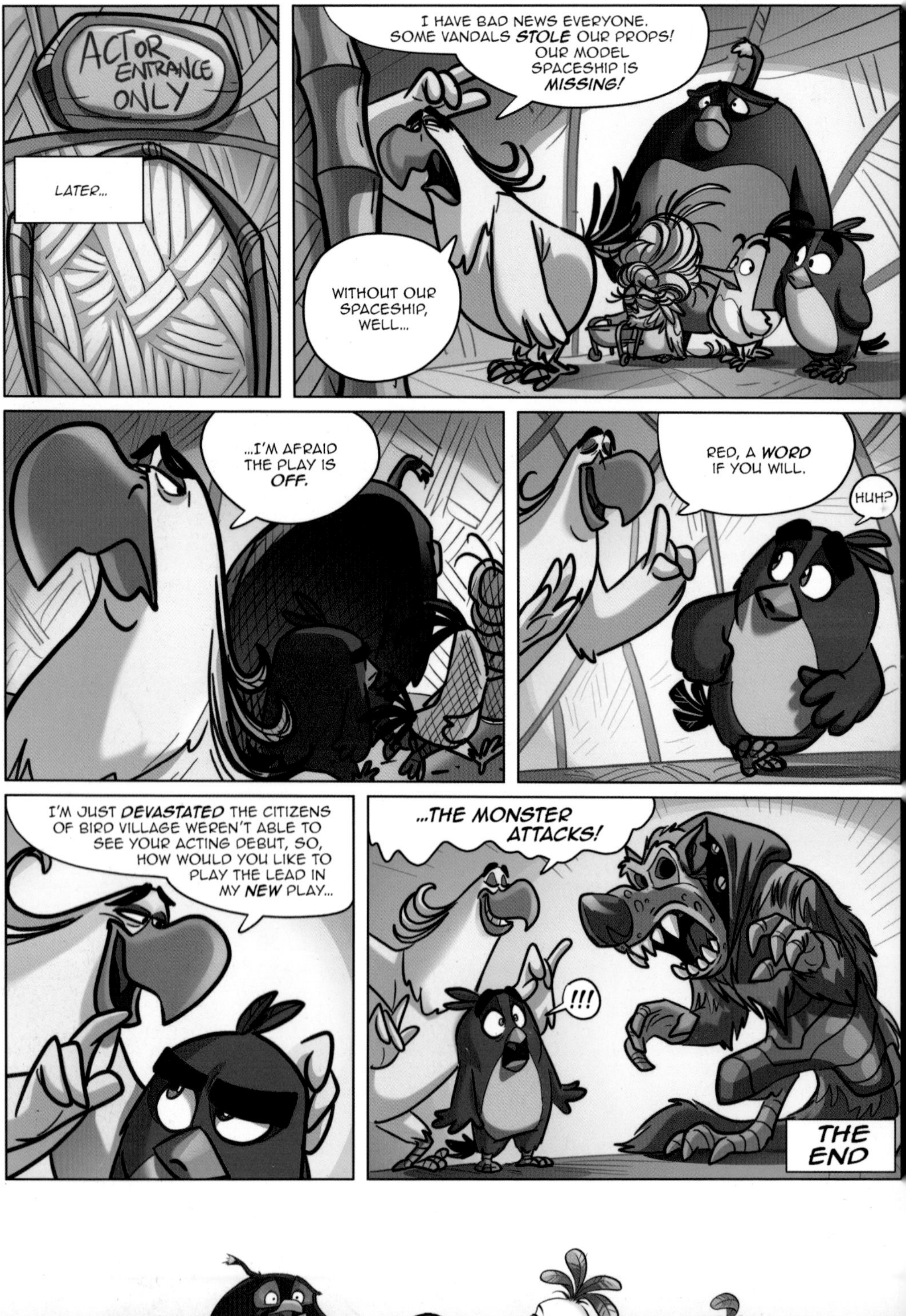
ACTOR ENTRANCE ONLY
LATER...
I HAVE BAD NEWS EVERYONE. SOME VANDALS STOLE OUR PROPS! OUR MODEL SPACESHIP IS MISSING!
WITHOUT OUR SPACESHIP, WELL...
...I'M AFRAID THE PLAY IS OFF.
RED, A WORD IF YOU WILL.
HUH?
I'M JUST DEVASTATED THE CITIZENS OF BIRD VILLAGE WEREN'T ABLE TO SEE YOUR ACTING DEBUT, SO, HOW WOULD YOU LIKE TO PLAY THE LEAD IN MY NEW PLAY...
...THE MONSTER ATTACKS!
!!!
THE END

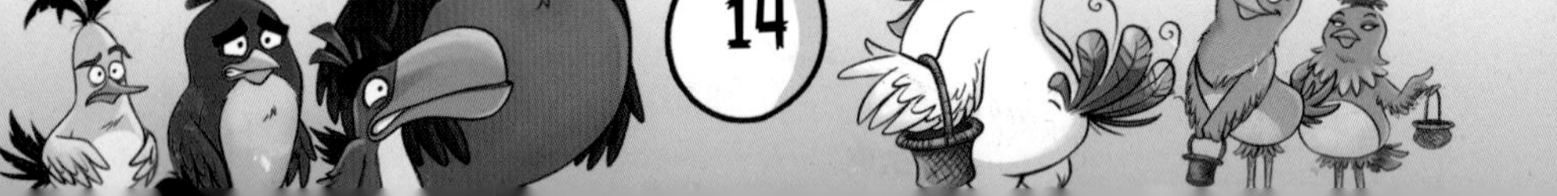

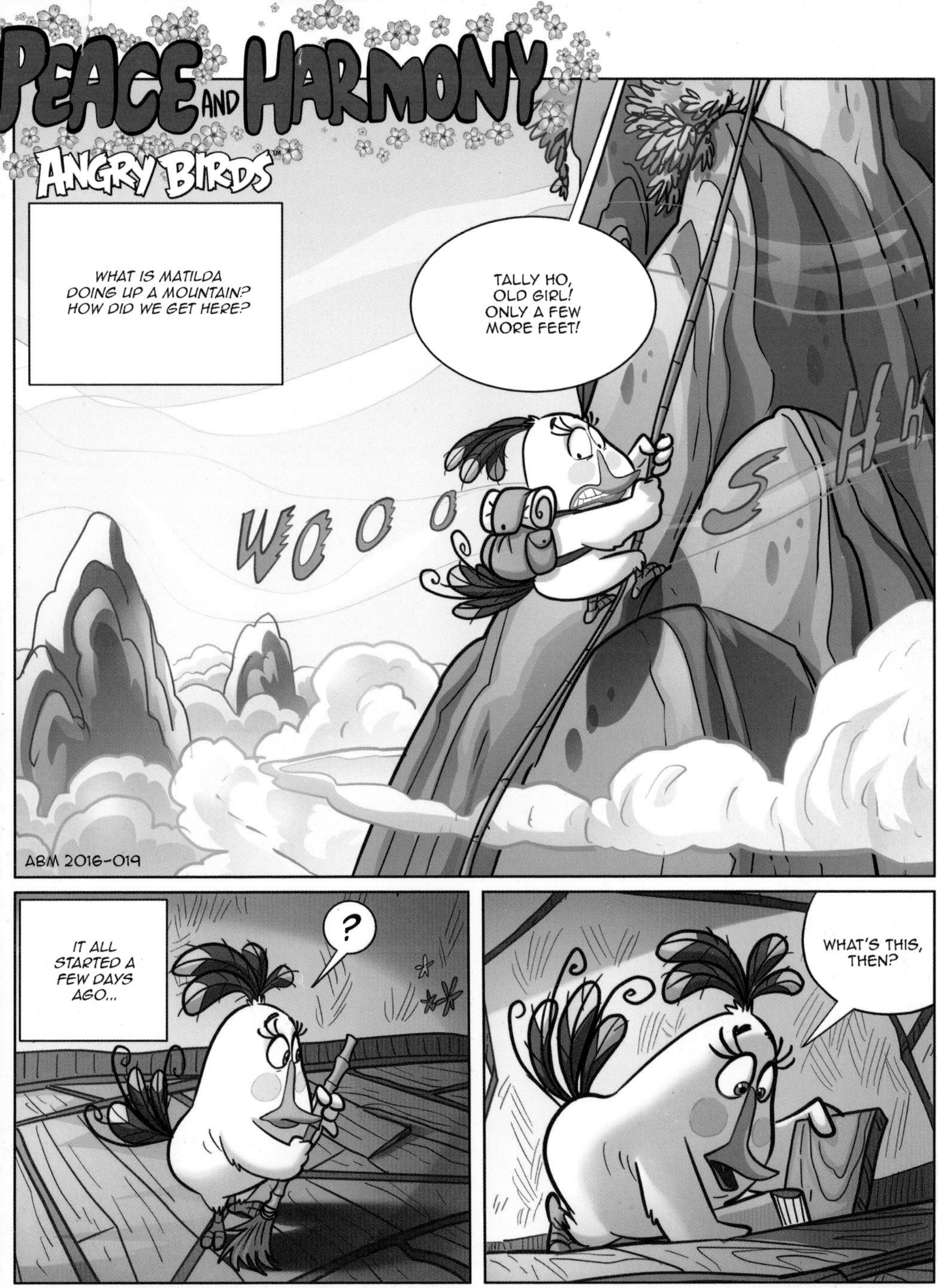
PEACE AND HARMONY
ANGRY BIRDS™
WHAT IS MATILDA DOING UP A MOUNTAIN? HOW DID WE GET HERE?
TALLY HO, OLD GIRL! ONLY A FEW MORE FEET!
WOOOSHH
ABM 2016-019
IT ALL STARTED A FEW DAYS AGO...
?
WHAT'S THIS, THEN?

ANGRY BIRDS™
FURIOUS FOWL

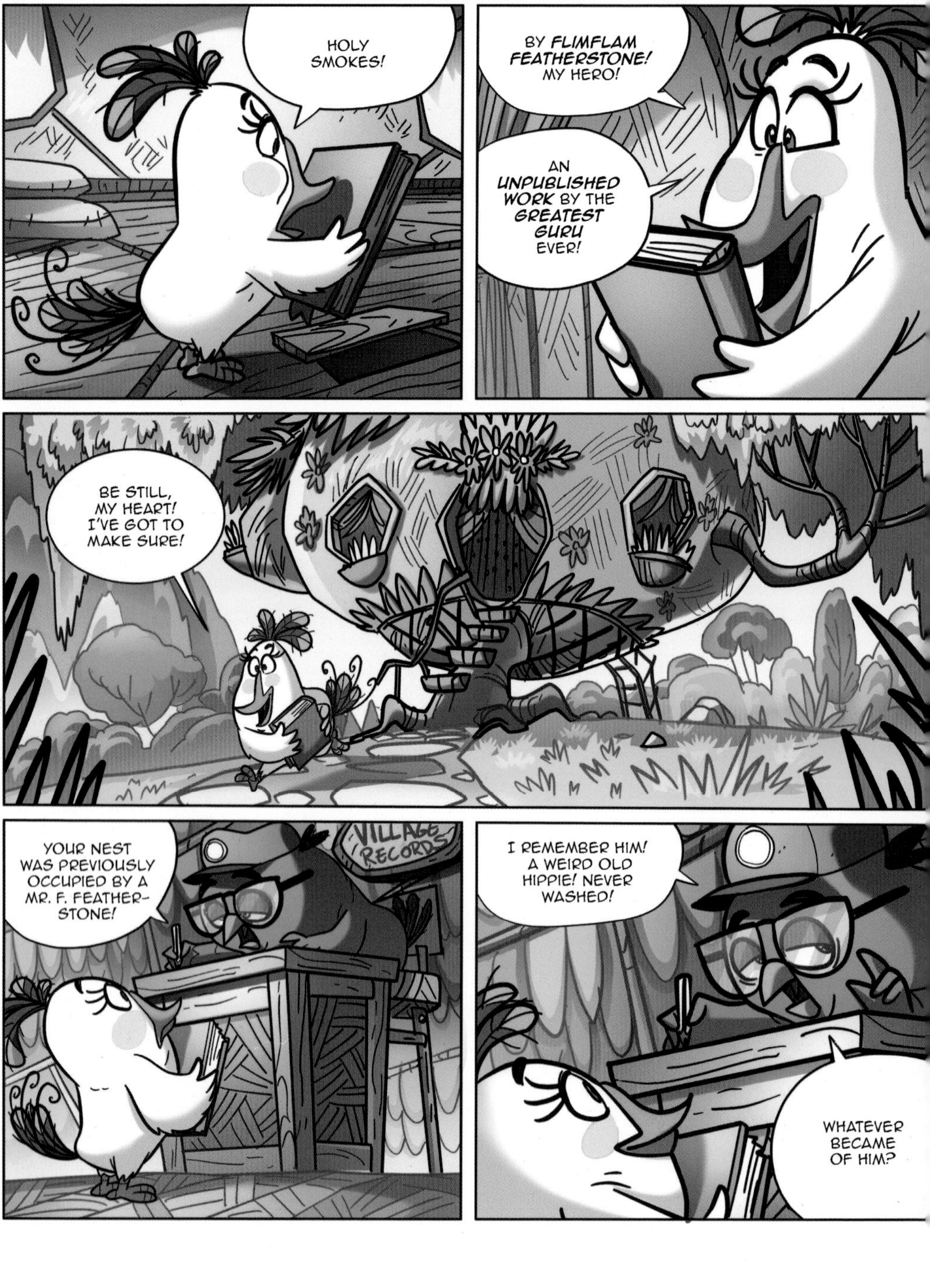
HOLY SMOKES!
BY **FLIMFLAM FEATHERSTONE!** MY HERO!
AN **UNPUBLISHED WORK** BY THE **GREATEST GURU** EVER!
BE STILL, MY HEART! I'VE GOT TO MAKE SURE!
YOUR NEST WAS PREVIOUSLY OCCUPIED BY A MR. F. FEATHER-STONE!
VILLAGE RECORDS
I REMEMBER HIM! A WEIRD OLD HIPPIE! NEVER WASHED!
WHATEVER BECAME OF HIM?

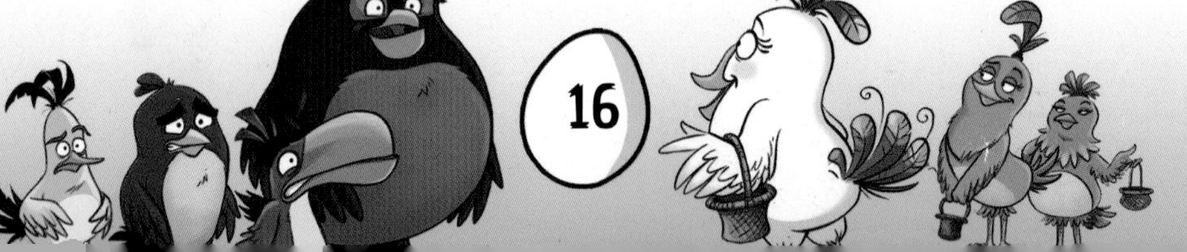

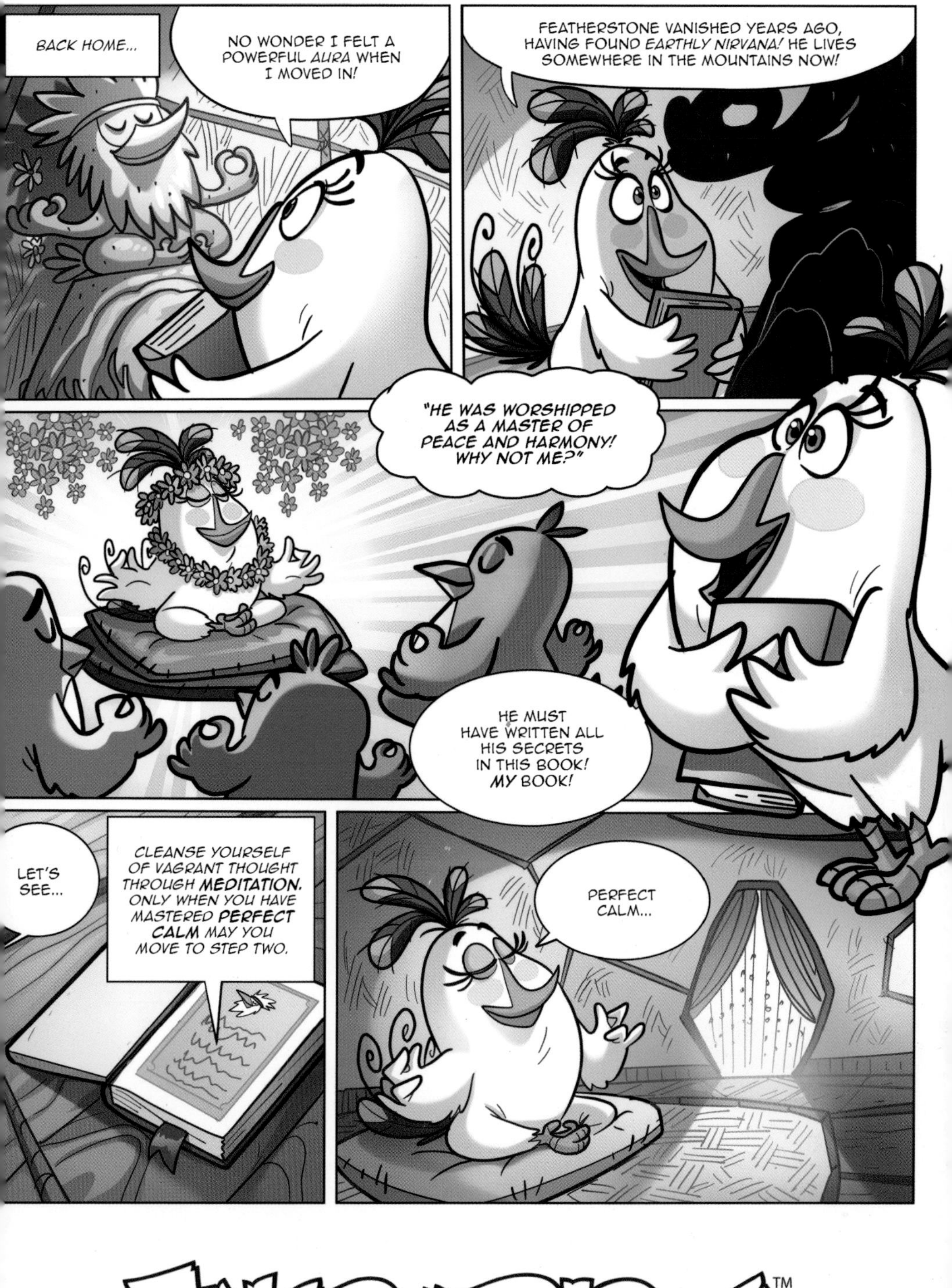
BACK HOME...
NO WONDER I FELT A POWERFUL *AURA* WHEN I MOVED IN!
FEATHERSTONE VANISHED YEARS AGO, HAVING FOUND *EARTHLY NIRVANA!* HE LIVES SOMEWHERE IN THE MOUNTAINS NOW!
"HE WAS WORSHIPPED AS A MASTER OF PEACE AND HARMONY! WHY NOT ME?"
HE MUST HAVE WRITTEN ALL HIS SECRETS IN THIS BOOK! **MY** BOOK!
LET'S SEE...
CLEANSE YOURSELF OF VAGRANT THOUGHT THROUGH **MEDITATION**. ONLY WHEN YOU HAVE MASTERED **PERFECT CALM** MAY YOU MOVE TO STEP TWO.
PERFECT CALM...

ANGRY BIRDS™
FURIOUS FOWL

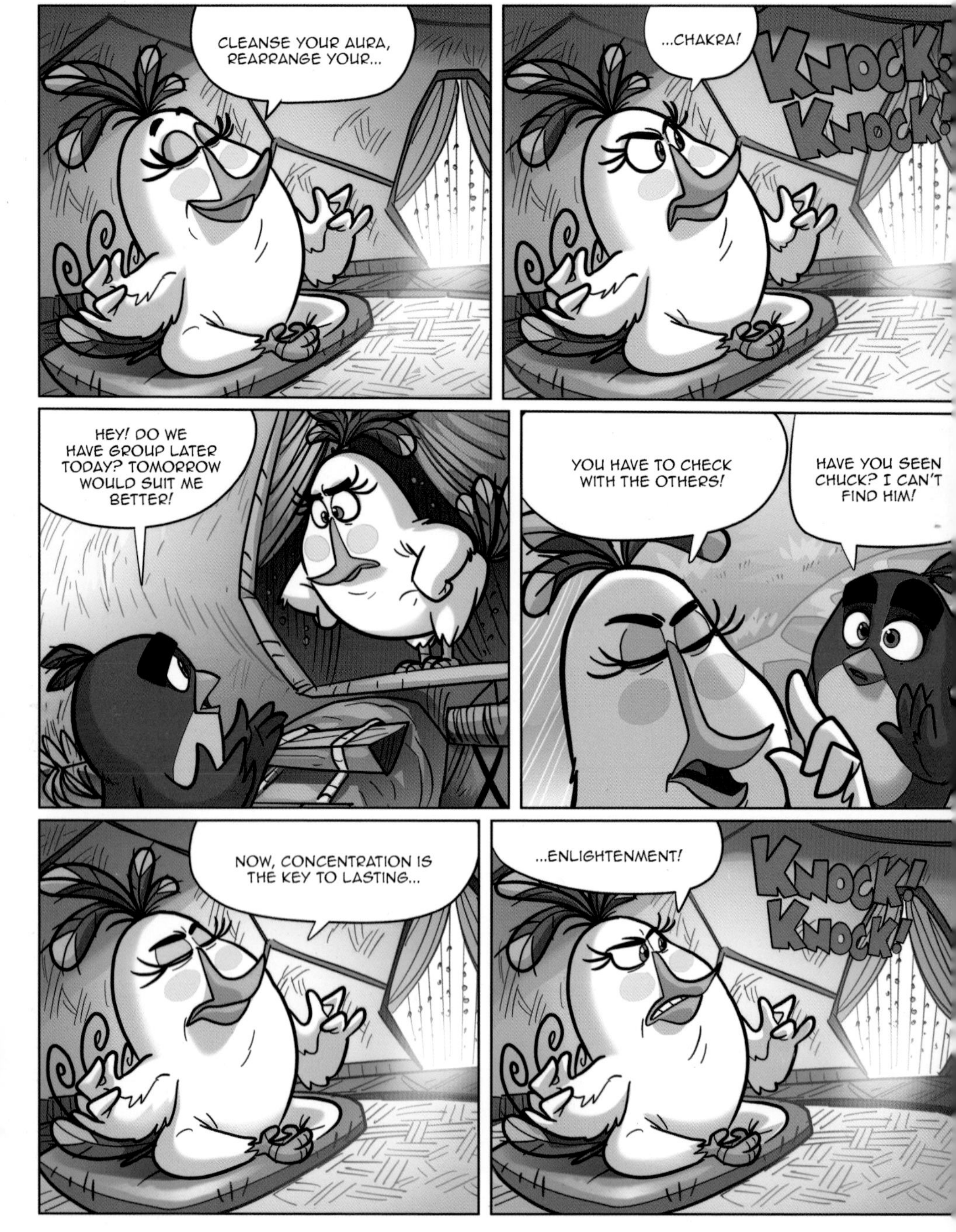
CLEANSE YOUR AURA, REARRANGE YOUR...
...CHAKRA!
KNOCK! KNOCK!
HEY! DO WE HAVE GROUP LATER TODAY? TOMORROW WOULD SUIT ME BETTER!
YOU HAVE TO CHECK WITH THE OTHERS!
HAVE YOU SEEN CHUCK? I CAN'T FIND HIM!
NOW, CONCENTRATION IS THE KEY TO LASTING...
...ENLIGHTENMENT!
KNOCK! KNOCK!

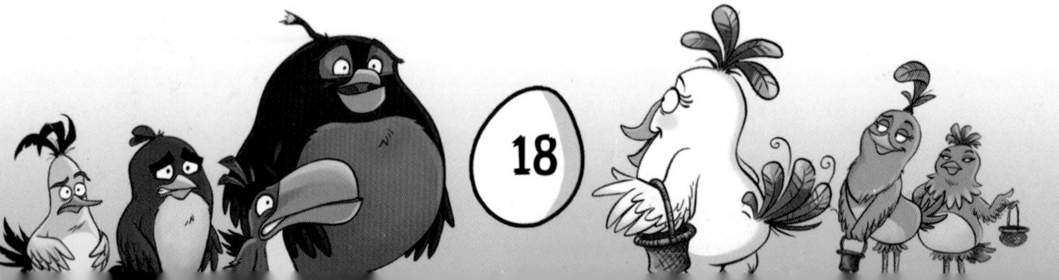

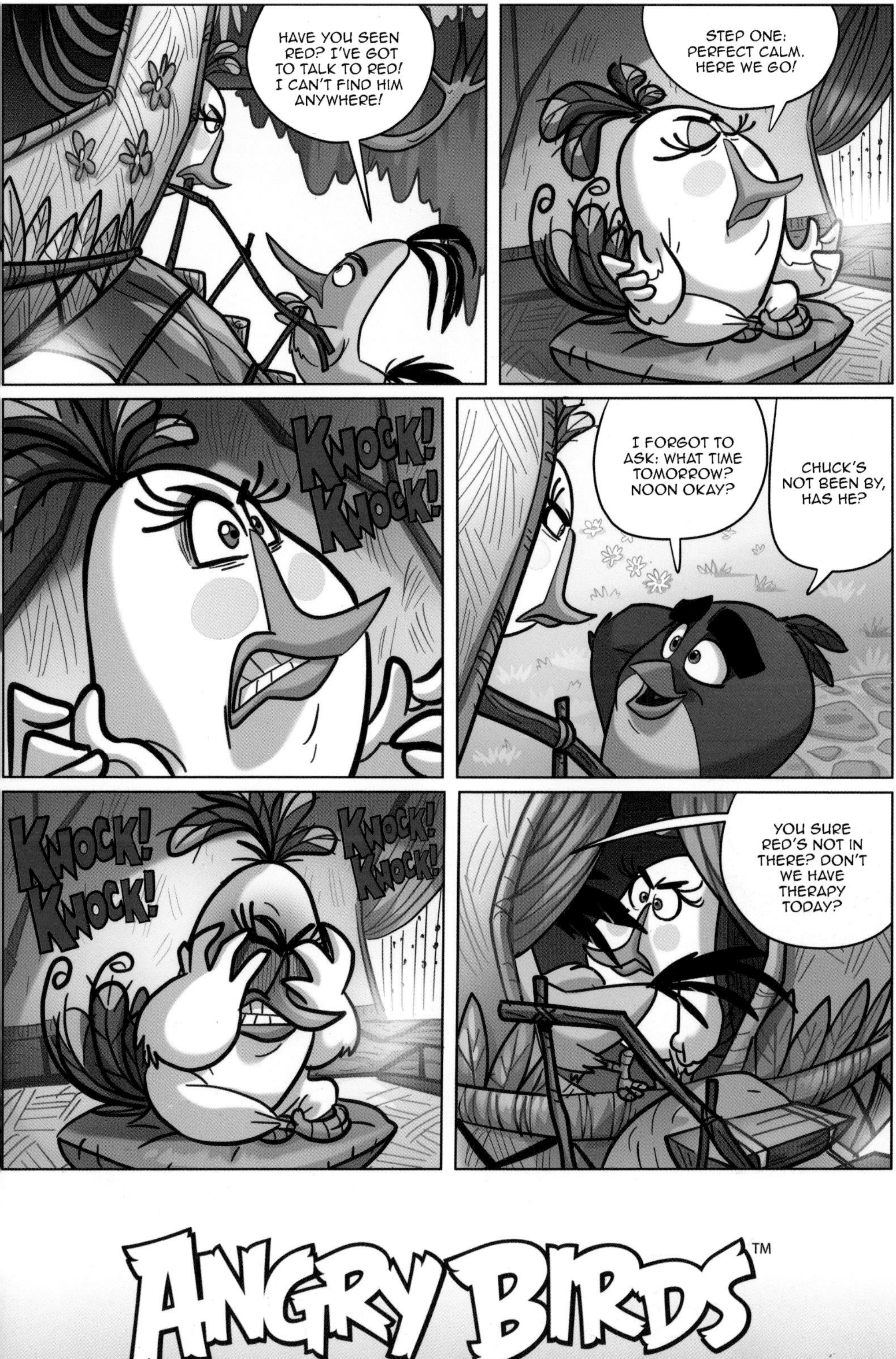
HAVE YOU SEEN RED? I'VE GOT TO TALK TO RED! I CAN'T FIND HIM ANYWHERE!
STEP ONE: PERFECT CALM. HERE WE GO!
KNOCK! KNOCK!
I FORGOT TO ASK: WHAT TIME TOMORROW? NOON OKAY?
CHUCK'S NOT BEEN BY, HAS HE?
KNOCK! KNOCK!
KNOCK! KNOCK!
YOU SURE RED'S NOT IN THERE? DON'T WE HAVE THERAPY TODAY?

ANGRY BIRDS™
FURIOUS FOWL

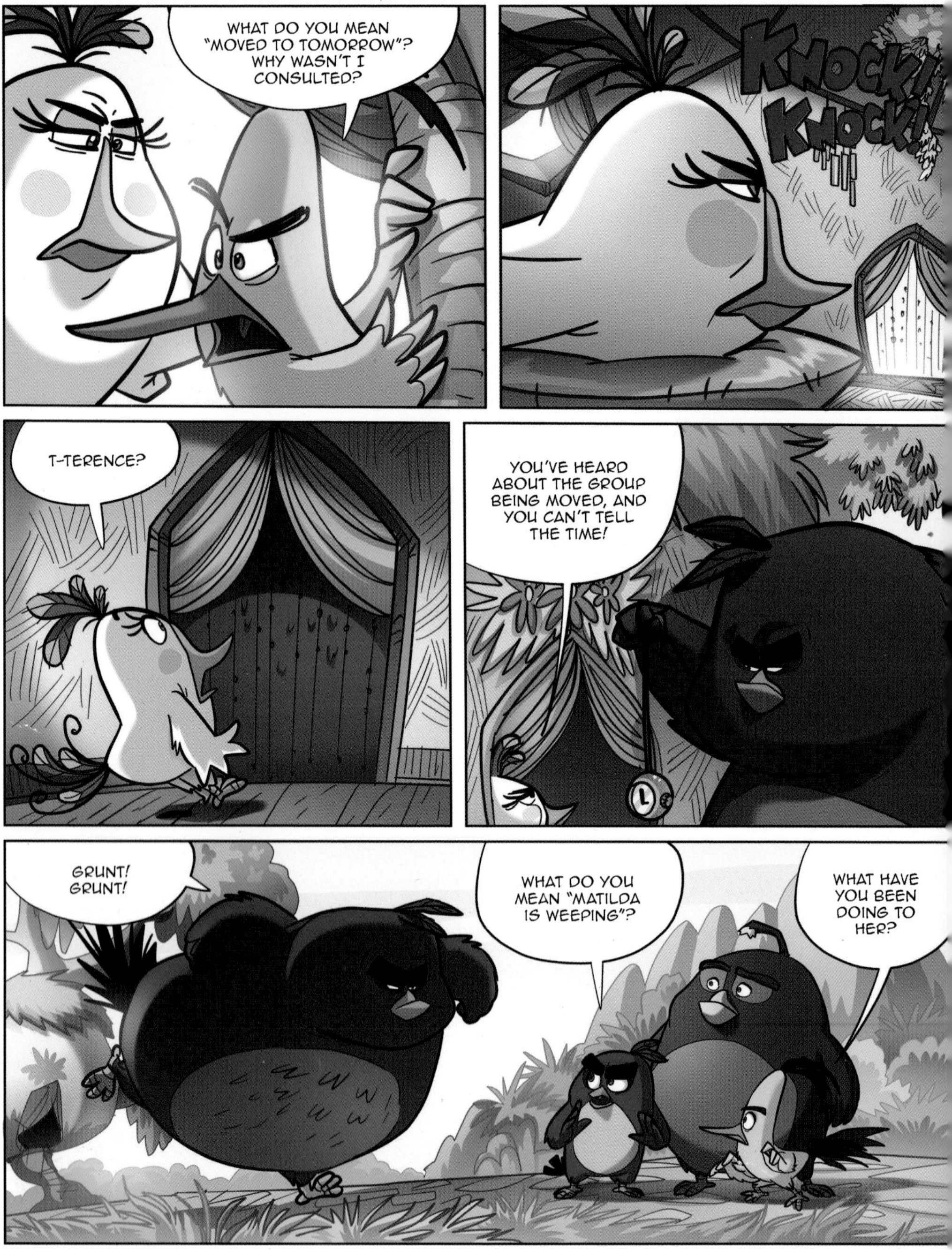
WHAT DO YOU MEAN "MOVED TO TOMORROW"? WHY WASN'T I CONSULTED?
KNOCK! KNOCK!
T-TERENCE?
YOU'VE HEARD ABOUT THE GROUP BEING MOVED, AND YOU CAN'T TELL THE TIME!
GRUNT! GRUNT!
WHAT DO YOU MEAN "MATILDA IS WEEPING"?
WHAT HAVE YOU BEEN DOING TO HER?

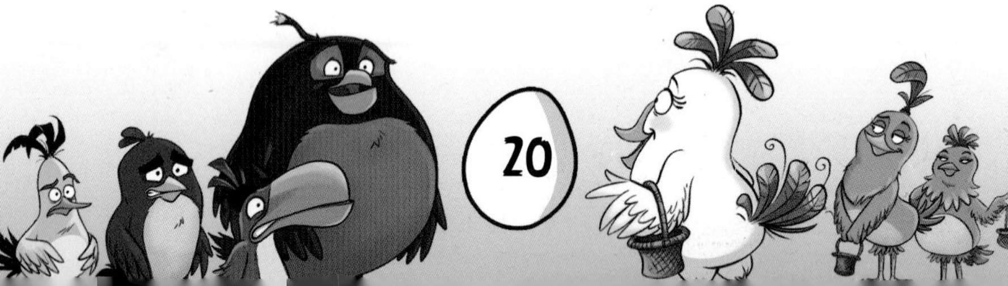

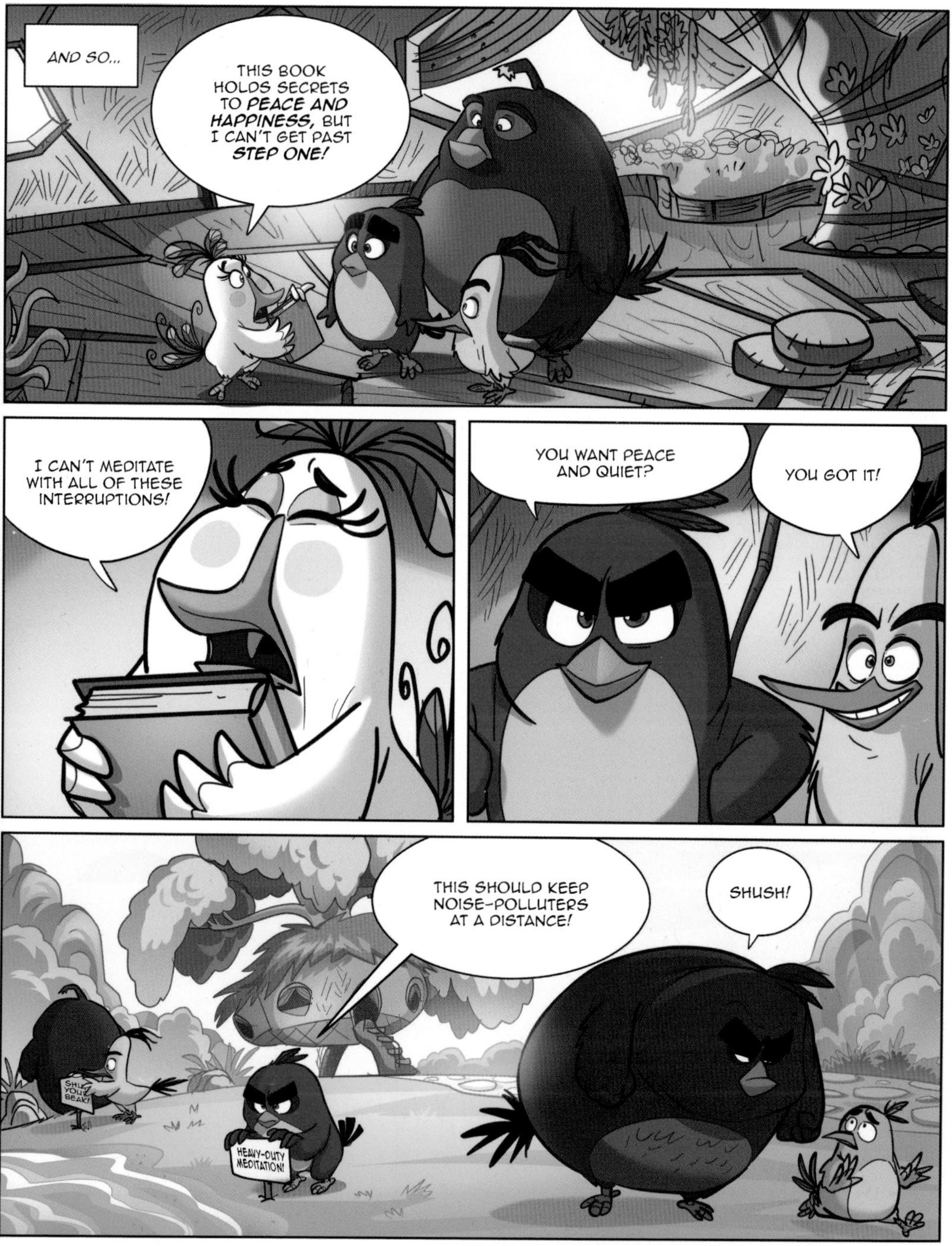
AND SO...
THIS BOOK HOLDS SECRETS TO **PEACE AND HAPPINESS,** BUT I CAN'T GET PAST **STEP ONE!**
I CAN'T MEDITATE WITH ALL OF THESE INTERRUPTIONS!
YOU WANT PEACE AND QUIET?
YOU GOT IT!
THIS SHOULD KEEP NOISE-POLLUTERS AT A DISTANCE!
SHUSH!
HEAVY-DUTY MEDITATION!

ANGRY BIRDS™
FURIOUS FOWL

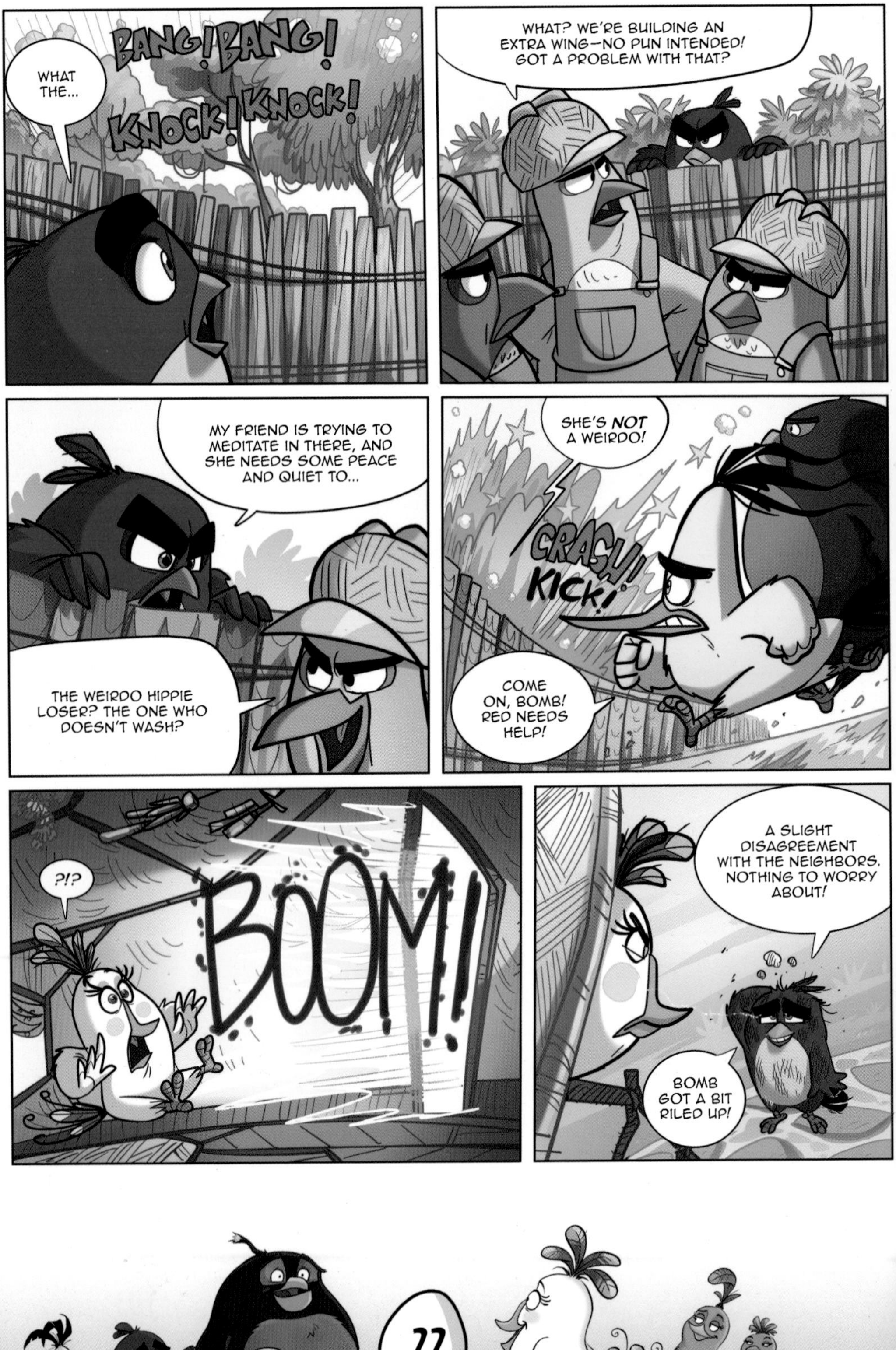

BANG! BANG!
KNOCK! KNOCK!
WHAT THE...
WHAT? WE'RE BUILDING AN EXTRA WING—NO PUN INTENDED! GOT A PROBLEM WITH THAT?
MY FRIEND IS TRYING TO MEDITATE IN THERE, AND SHE NEEDS SOME PEACE AND QUIET TO...
THE WEIRDO HIPPIE LOSER? THE ONE WHO DOESN'T WASH?
SHE'S ***NOT*** A WEIRDO!
CRASH! KICK!
COME ON, BOMB! RED NEEDS HELP!
?!?
BOOM!!
A SLIGHT DISAGREEMENT WITH THE NEIGHBORS. NOTHING TO WORRY ABOUT!
BOMB GOT A BIT RILED UP!

SOON...
SEE? THE BRANCH UP THERE!
RAP! RAP!
THAT RAPPING MUST BE DRIVING MATILDA *CRAZY* IN THERE!
HEY, STUPIDO! THAT'S THE WRONG BRANCH!
STUPIDO? YOU THINK THAT'S CLEVER, DON'T YOU? WHY I...
NOW SETTLE DOWN, BOYS, OR...
BOOM
JEEPERS !!!
JUST A SLIGHT DISAGREEMENT. NOTHING TO WORRY ABOUT!
BOMB PUT AN END TO IT ALL!
SOON...
WHY MUST YOU *ALWAYS* GRIND YOUR TEETH?!
SCREECH SCREECH

ANGRY BIRDS™
FURIOUS FOWL

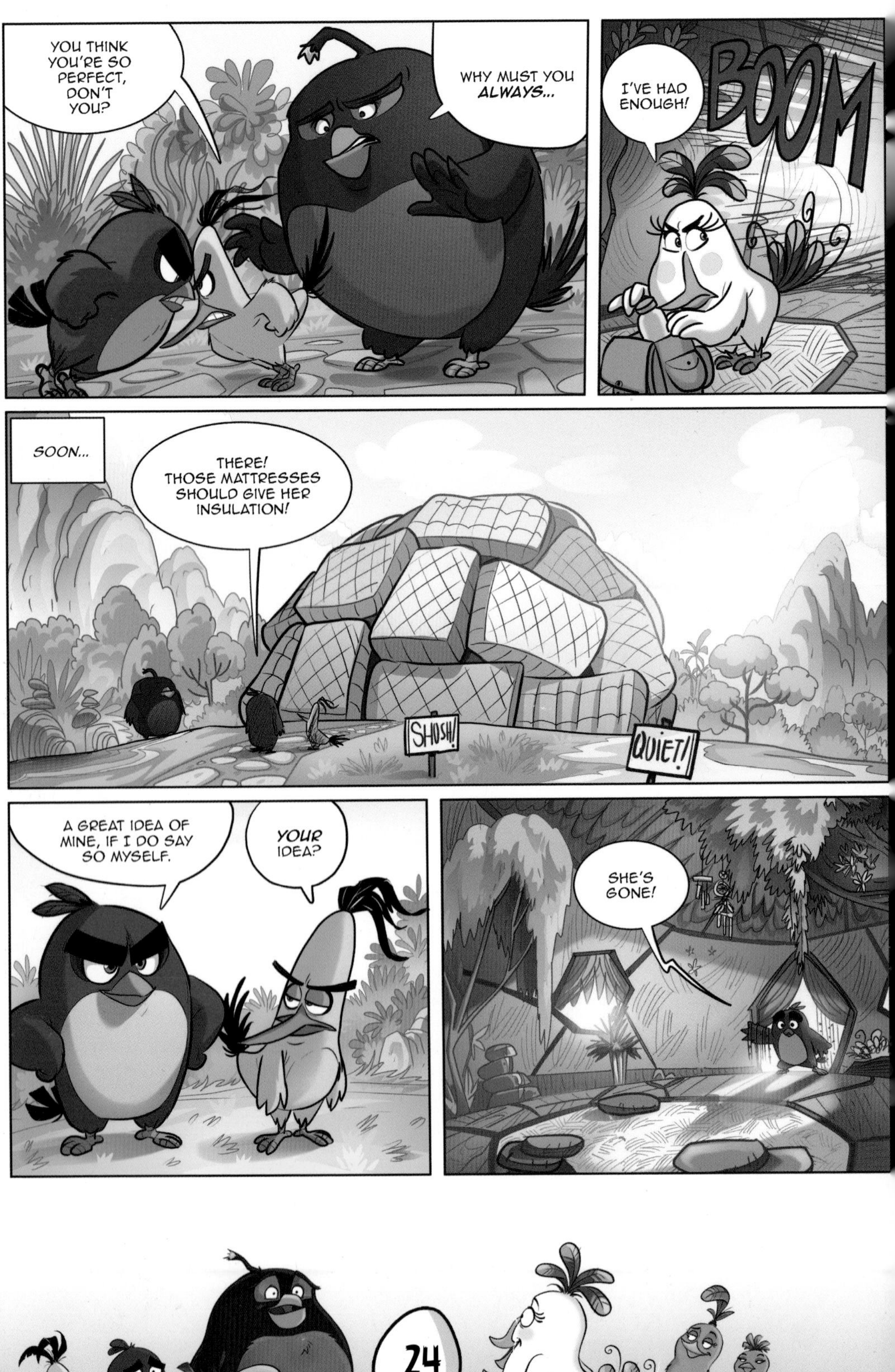
YOU THINK YOU'RE SO PERFECT, DON'T YOU?
WHY MUST YOU *ALWAYS...*
I'VE HAD ENOUGH!
BOOM
SOON...
THERE! THOSE MATTRESSES SHOULD GIVE HER INSULATION!
SHUSH!
QUIET!
A GREAT IDEA OF MINE, IF I DO SAY SO MYSELF.
YOUR IDEA?
SHE'S GONE!

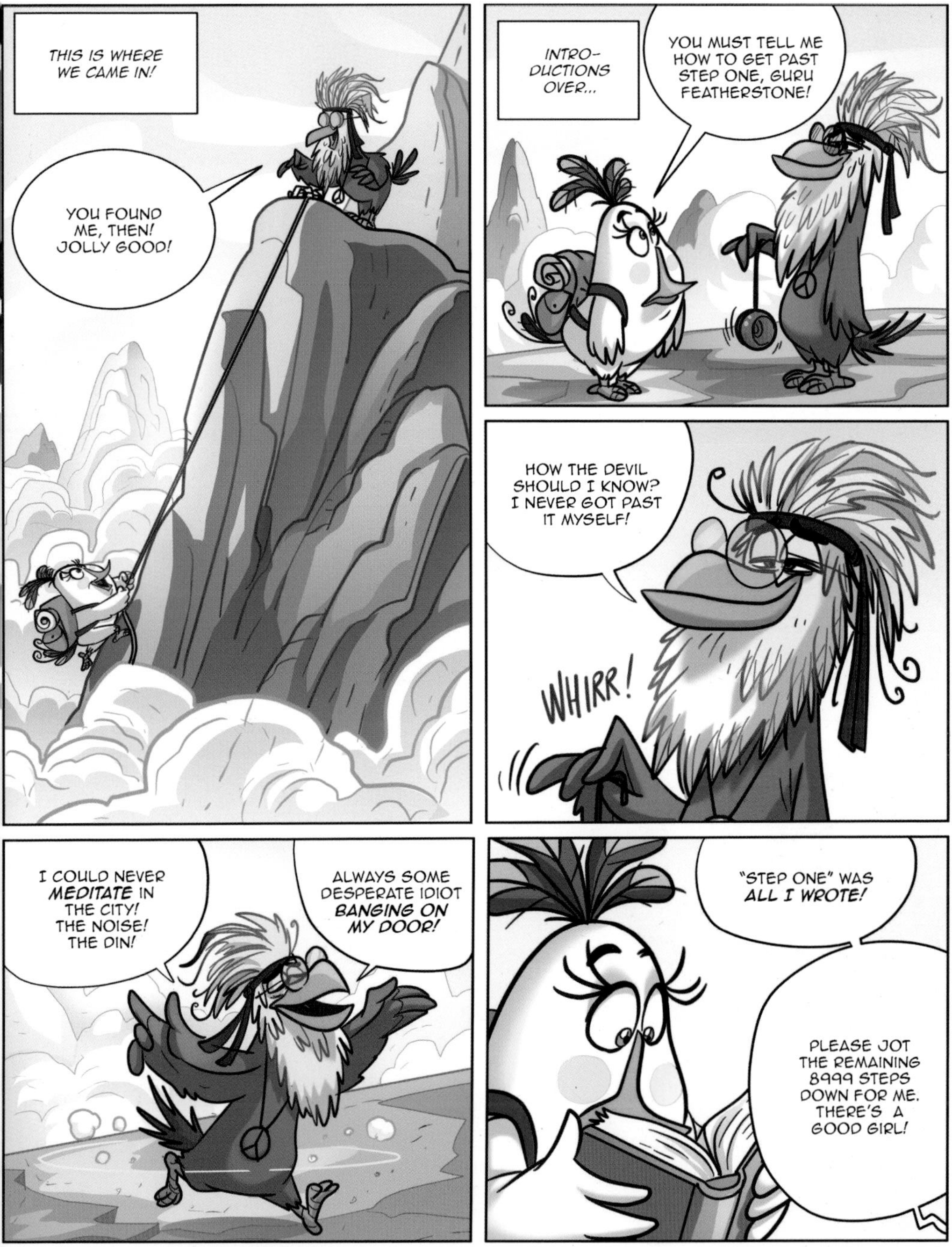
THIS IS WHERE WE CAME IN!
YOU FOUND ME, THEN! JOLLY GOOD!
INTRO-DUCTIONS OVER...
YOU MUST TELL ME HOW TO GET PAST STEP ONE, GURU FEATHERSTONE!
HOW THE DEVIL SHOULD I KNOW? I NEVER GOT PAST IT MYSELF!
WHIRR!
I COULD NEVER MEDITATE IN THE CITY! THE NOISE! THE DIN!
ALWAYS SOME DESPERATE IDIOT BANGING ON MY DOOR!
"STEP ONE" WAS ALL I WROTE!
PLEASE JOT THE REMAINING 8999 STEPS DOWN FOR ME. THERE'S A GOOD GIRL!

ANGRY BIRDS™
FURIOUS FOWL

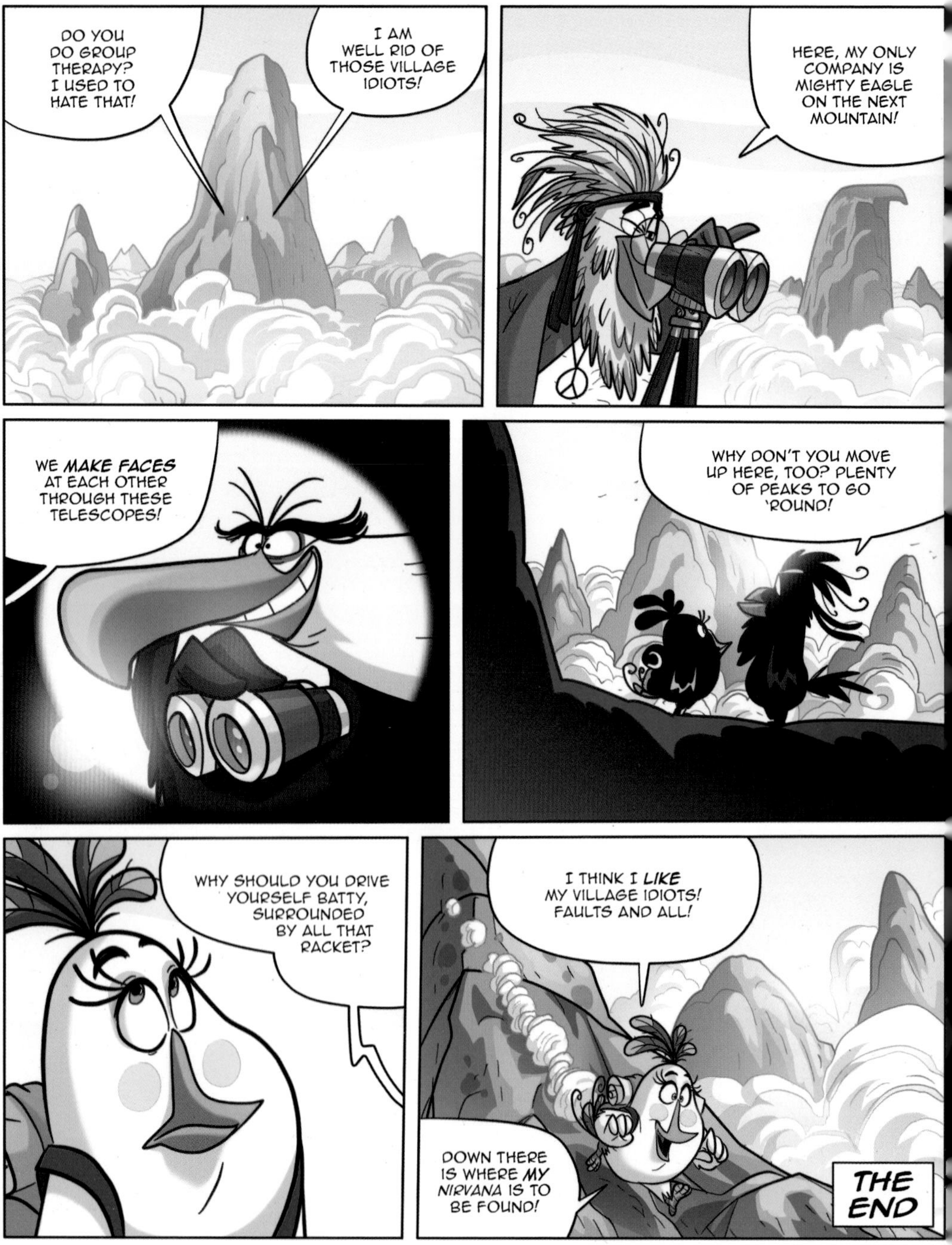
DO YOU DO GROUP THERAPY? I USED TO HATE THAT!
I AM WELL RID OF THOSE VILLAGE IDIOTS!
HERE, MY ONLY COMPANY IS MIGHTY EAGLE ON THE NEXT MOUNTAIN!
WE MAKE FACES AT EACH OTHER THROUGH THESE TELESCOPES!
WHY DON'T YOU MOVE UP HERE, TOO? PLENTY OF PEAKS TO GO 'ROUND!
WHY SHOULD YOU DRIVE YOURSELF BATTY, SURROUNDED BY ALL THAT RACKET?
I THINK I LIKE MY VILLAGE IDIOTS! FAULTS AND ALL!
DOWN THERE IS WHERE MY NIRVANA IS TO BE FOUND!
THE END

ANGRY BIRDS™
FURIOUS FOWL

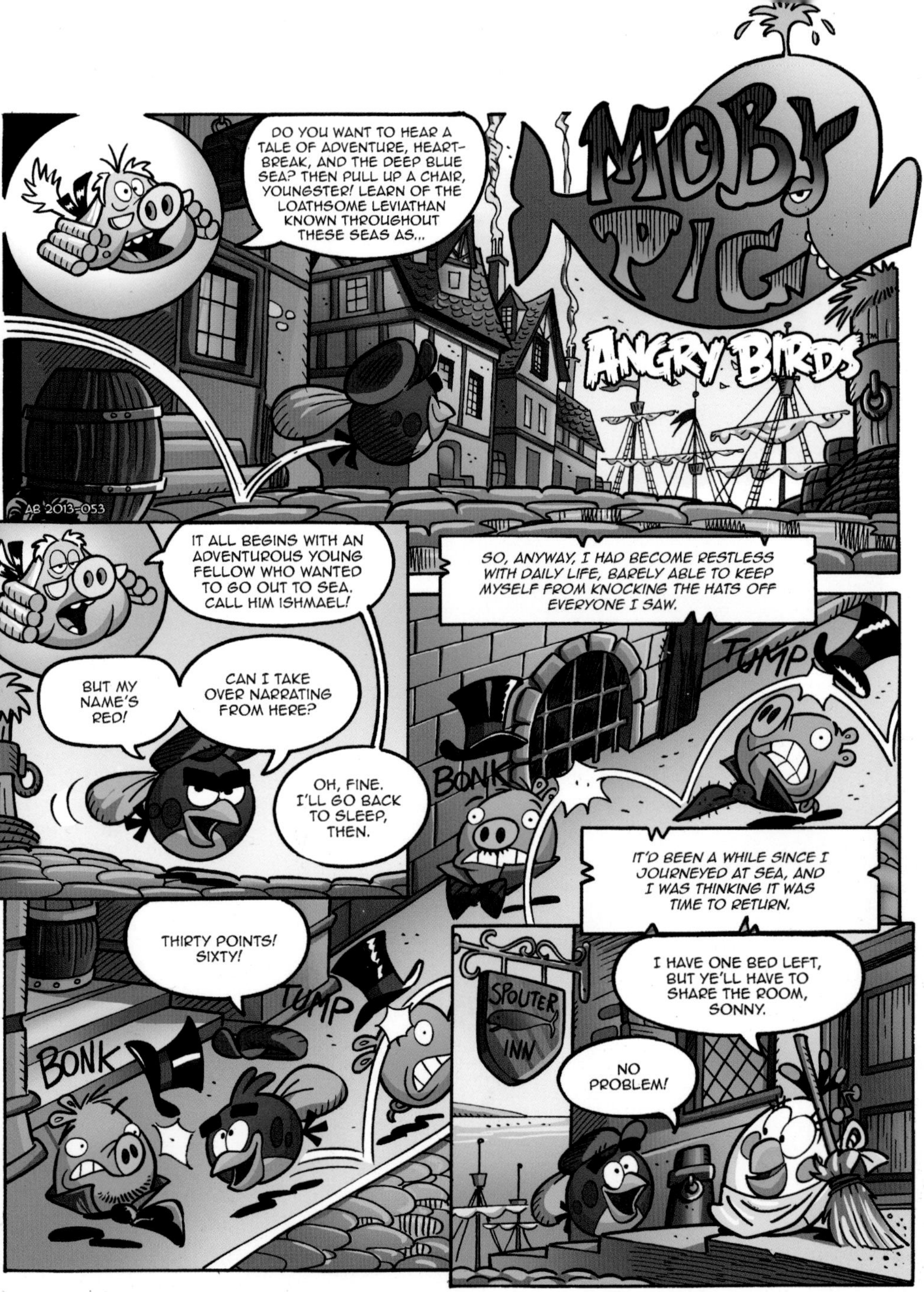
MOBY PIG
ANGRY BIRDS
DO YOU WANT TO HEAR A TALE OF ADVENTURE, HEART-BREAK, AND THE DEEP BLUE SEA? THEN PULL UP A CHAIR, YOUNGSTER! LEARN OF THE LOATHSOME LEVIATHAN KNOWN THROUGHOUT THESE SEAS AS...
AB 2013-053
IT ALL BEGINS WITH AN ADVENTUROUS YOUNG FELLOW WHO WANTED TO GO OUT TO SEA. CALL HIM ISHMAEL!
BUT MY NAME'S RED!
CAN I TAKE OVER NARRATING FROM HERE?
OH, FINE. I'LL GO BACK TO SLEEP, THEN.
SO, ANYWAY, I HAD BECOME RESTLESS WITH DAILY LIFE, BARELY ABLE TO KEEP MYSELF FROM KNOCKING THE HATS OFF EVERYONE I SAW.
TUMP
BONK
THIRTY POINTS! SIXTY!
TUMP
BONK
IT'D BEEN A WHILE SINCE I JOURNEYED AT SEA, AND I WAS THINKING IT WAS TIME TO RETURN.
SPOUTER INN
I HAVE ONE BED LEFT, BUT YE'LL HAVE TO SHARE THE ROOM, SONNY.
NO PROBLEM!

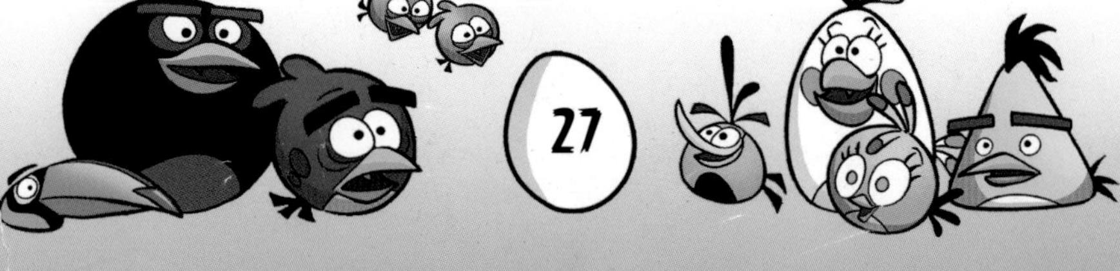

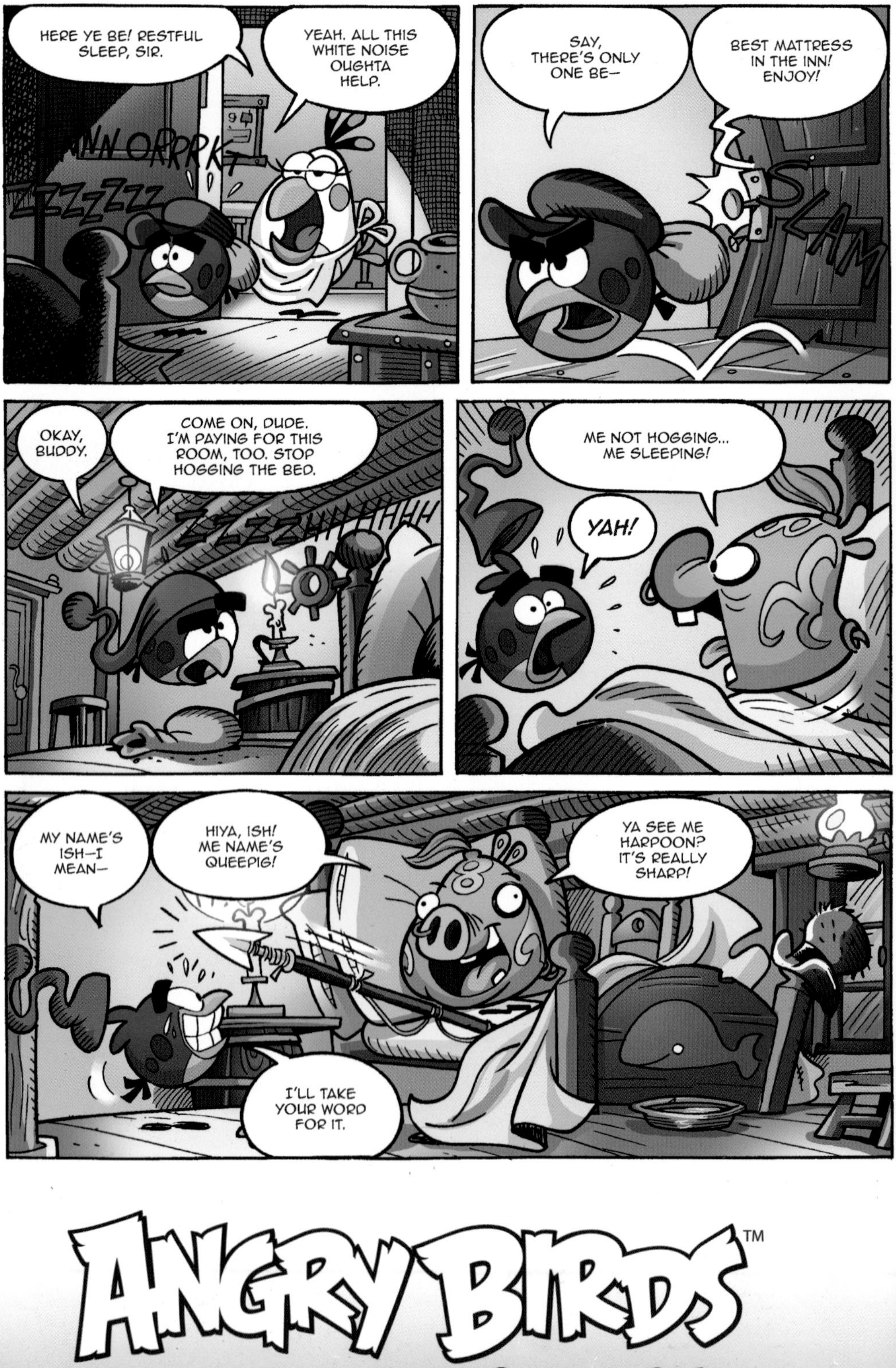
HERE YE BE! RESTFUL SLEEP, SIR.
YEAH. ALL THIS WHITE NOISE OUGHTA HELP.
SAY, THERE'S ONLY ONE BE—
BEST MATTRESS IN THE INN! ENJOY!
SLAM
OKAY, BUDDY.
COME ON, DUDE. I'M PAYING FOR THIS ROOM, TOO. STOP HOGGING THE BED.
ME NOT HOGGING... ME SLEEPING!
YAH!
MY NAME'S ISH—I MEAN—
HIYA, ISH! ME NAME'S QUEEPIG!
YA SEE ME HARPOON? IT'S REALLY SHARP!
I'LL TAKE YOUR WORD FOR IT.

ANGRY BIRDS™
FURIOUS FOWL

ME HIT ANYTHING WITH IT!

STOK

KWOONG

YOW!

SO, I'M GUESSING YOU'RE NOT A DENTIST.

ME A WHALER! TOMORROW ME GO ON SIX-MONTH VOYAGE ON BIG WHALING SHIP.

REALLY? IS THAT GOOD WORK? PLENTY OF VACATION TIME?

WHOLE JOB AM *ONE BIG* VACATION!

WHALERS TRAVEL WORLD! GO TO ISLANDS! HAVE LOT OF BIRTHDAY PARTIES!

REALLY? THAT SOUNDS LIKE THE KIND OF THING I'VE BEEN LOOKING FOR.

DO YOU THINK THERE'S ROOM FOR ANY MORE CREW ON THAT WHALING SHIP, QUEEPIG?

ALWAYS ROOM FOR MORE, 'CAUSE SO MANY CREW GET *KILLED* ON VOYAGE!

SPLONF

WAIT— KILLED?

BEST... JOB... EVER.

ZZZZZZHHHHKRRNH

29

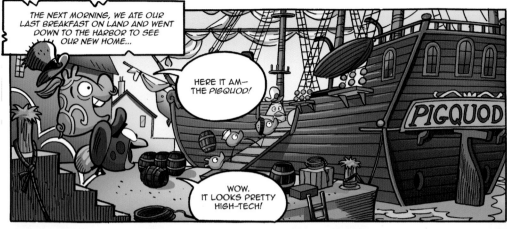

THE NEXT MORNING, WE ATE OUR LAST BREAKFAST ON LAND AND WENT DOWN TO THE HARBOR TO SEE OUR NEW HOME...

HERE IT AM—THE *PIGQUOD!*

PIGQUOD

WOW. IT LOOKS PRETTY HIGH-TECH!

AY, STARCHUCK! ME FRIEND ISH WANT JOB!

INDEED? EVER HUNTED WHALES, ISH?

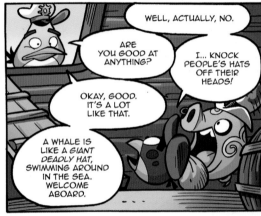

WELL, ACTUALLY, NO.

ARE YOU GOOD AT ANYTHING?

I... KNOCK PEOPLE'S HATS OFF THEIR HEADS!

OKAY, GOOD. IT'S A LOT LIKE THAT.

A WHALE IS LIKE A GIANT DEADLY HAT, SWIMMING AROUND IN THE SEA. WELCOME ABOARD.

THANKS, CAPTAIN. I'LL WORK HARD!

OH, HEH— I'M NOT THE CAPTAIN!

I'M THE FIRST MATE.

WE ANSWER TO THE ONE UP ON THE QUARTERDECK.

TOK

ANGRY BIRDS™
FURIOUS FOWL

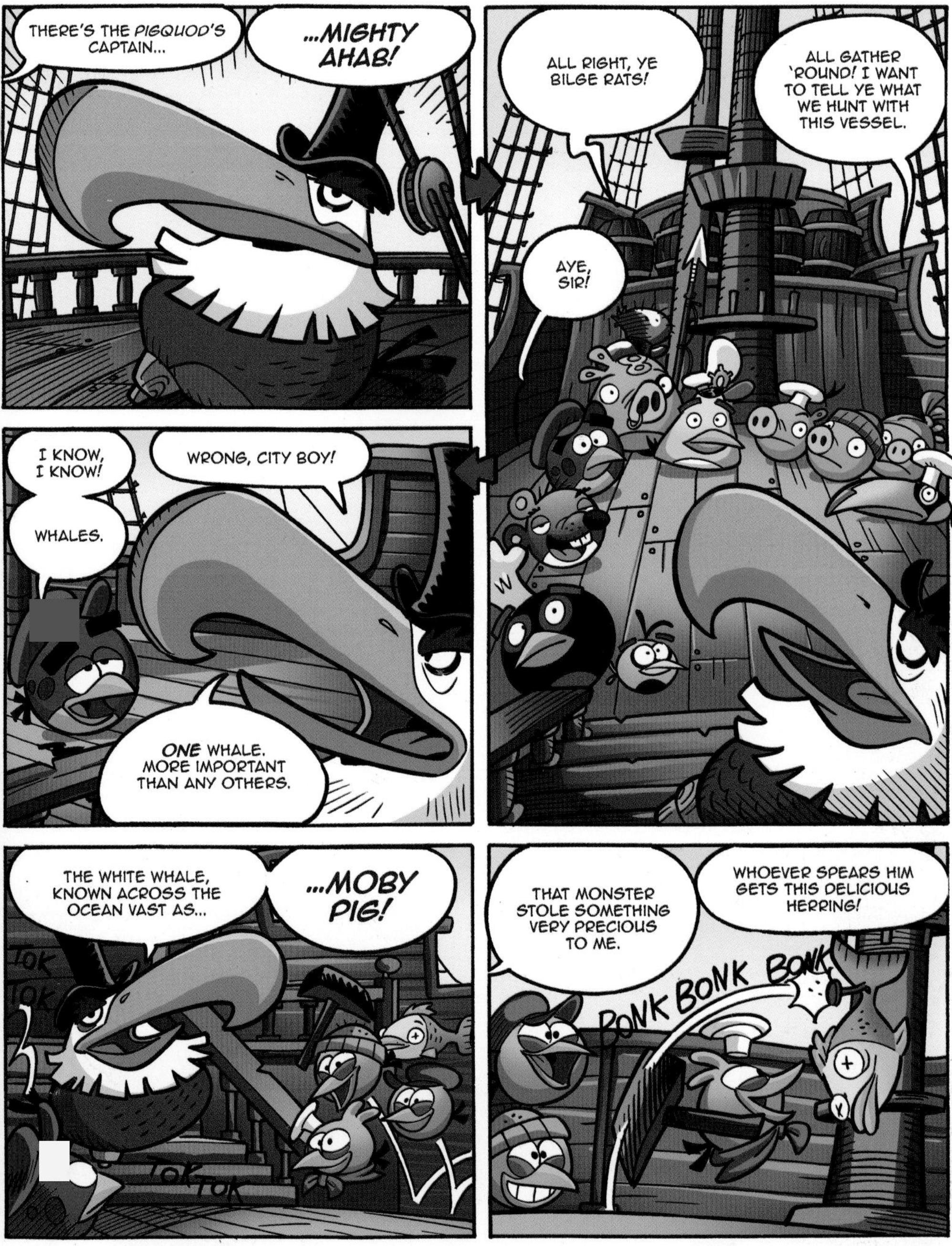
THERE'S THE *PIGQUOD'S* CAPTAIN...
...MIGHTY AHAB!
ALL RIGHT, YE BILGE RATS!
ALL GATHER 'ROUND! I WANT TO TELL YE WHAT WE HUNT WITH THIS VESSEL.
AYE, SIR!
I KNOW, I KNOW!
WHALES.
WRONG, CITY BOY!
ONE WHALE. MORE IMPORTANT THAN ANY OTHERS.
THE WHITE WHALE, KNOWN ACROSS THE OCEAN VAST AS...
...MOBY PIG!
TOK TOK
TOK TOK
THAT MONSTER STOLE SOMETHING VERY PRECIOUS TO ME.
WHOEVER SPEARS HIM GETS THIS DELICIOUS HERRING!
BONK BONK BONK

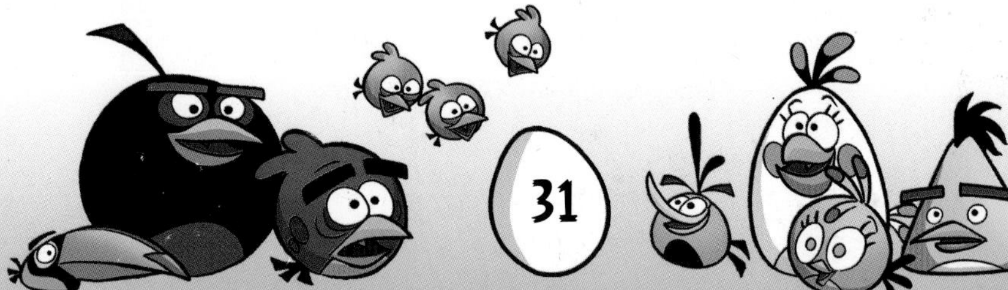

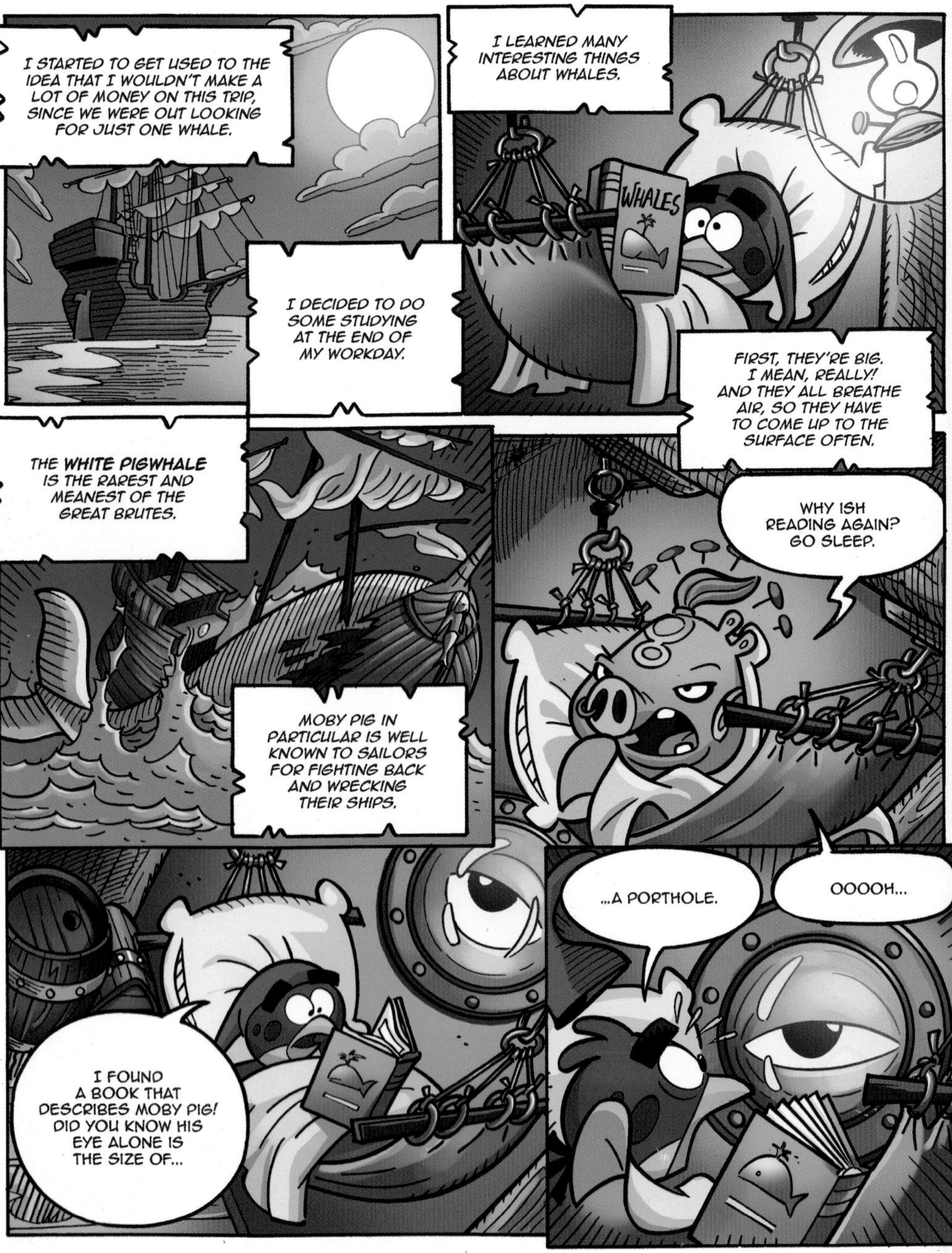
I STARTED TO GET USED TO THE IDEA THAT I WOULDN'T MAKE A LOT OF MONEY ON THIS TRIP, SINCE WE WERE OUT LOOKING FOR JUST ONE WHALE.
I DECIDED TO DO SOME STUDYING AT THE END OF MY WORKDAY.
I LEARNED MANY INTERESTING THINGS ABOUT WHALES.
WHALES
FIRST, THEY'RE BIG. I MEAN, REALLY! AND THEY ALL BREATHE AIR, SO THEY HAVE TO COME UP TO THE SURFACE OFTEN.
THE WHITE PIGWHALE IS THE RAREST AND MEANEST OF THE GREAT BRUTES.
MOBY PIG IN PARTICULAR IS WELL KNOWN TO SAILORS FOR FIGHTING BACK AND WRECKING THEIR SHIPS.
WHY ISH READING AGAIN? GO SLEEP.
I FOUND A BOOK THAT DESCRIBES MOBY PIG! DID YOU KNOW HIS EYE ALONE IS THE SIZE OF...
...A PORTHOLE.
OOOOH...

ANGRY BIRDS™

FURIOUS FOWL

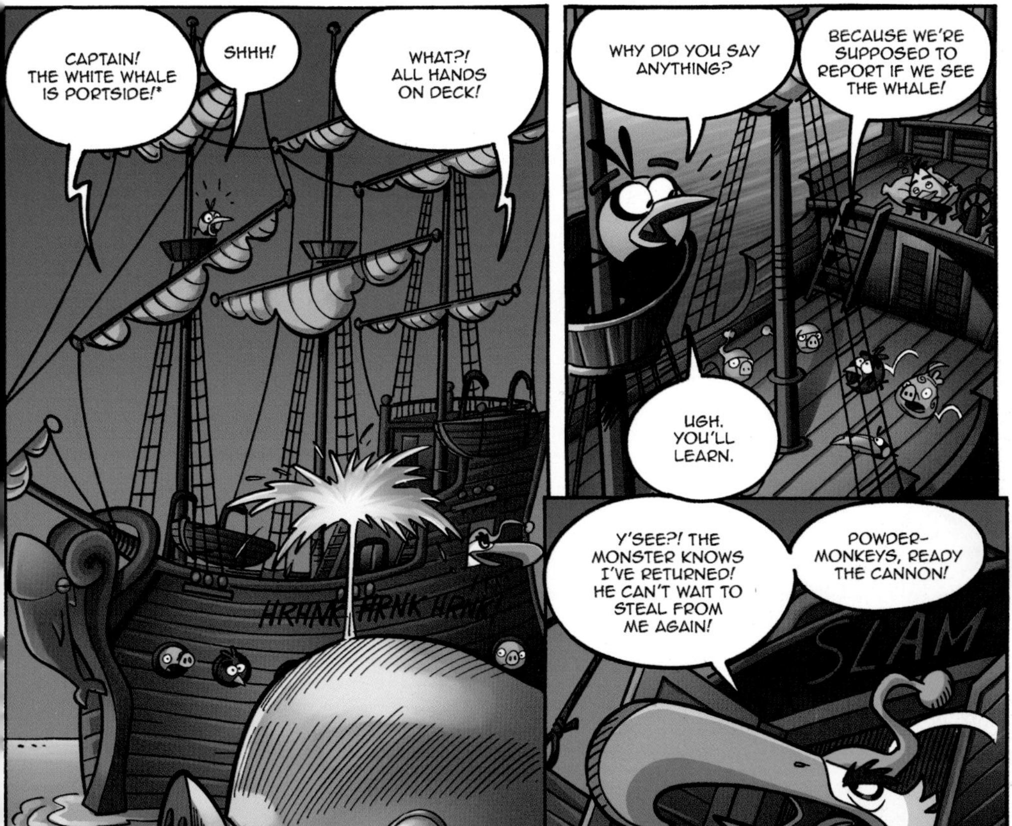
CAPTAIN! THE WHITE WHALE IS PORTSIDE!*
SHHH!
WHAT?! ALL HANDS ON DECK!
HRNK HRNK HRNK
*SAILOR TALK: LEFT OF THE SHIP!
WHY DID YOU SAY ANYTHING?
BECAUSE WE'RE SUPPOSED TO REPORT IF WE SEE THE WHALE!
UGH. YOU'LL LEARN.
Y'SEE?! THE MONSTER KNOWS I'VE RETURNED! HE CAN'T WAIT TO STEAL FROM ME AGAIN!
POWDER-MONKEYS, READY THE CANNON!
SLAM
TOK TOK TOK
YE MADE A MISTAKE COMING IN SO CLOSE, MOBY! YER IN ME GUN'S RANGE!
HERE—OOP—GOT IT—WAIT—NOPE—OKAY—HERE...

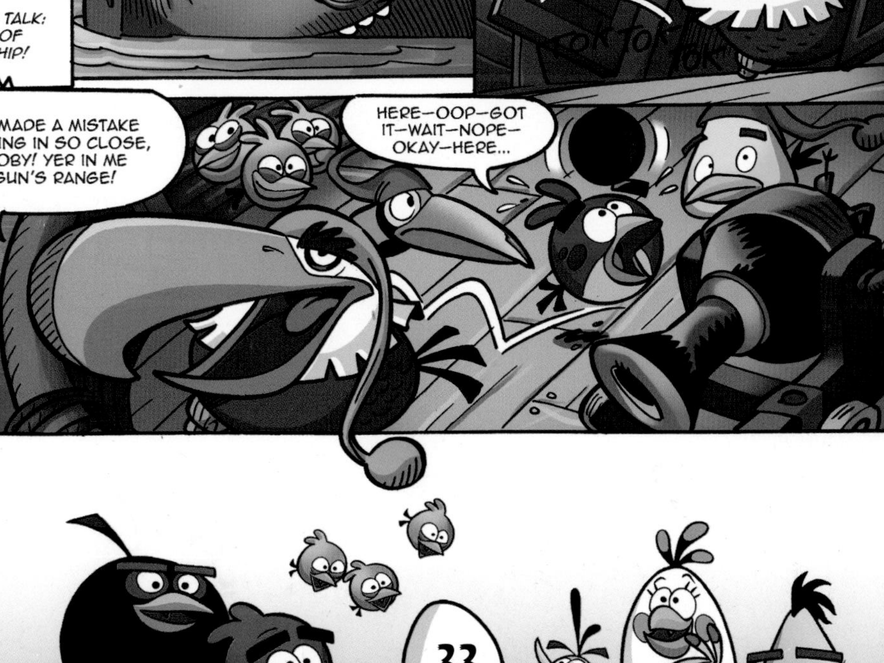

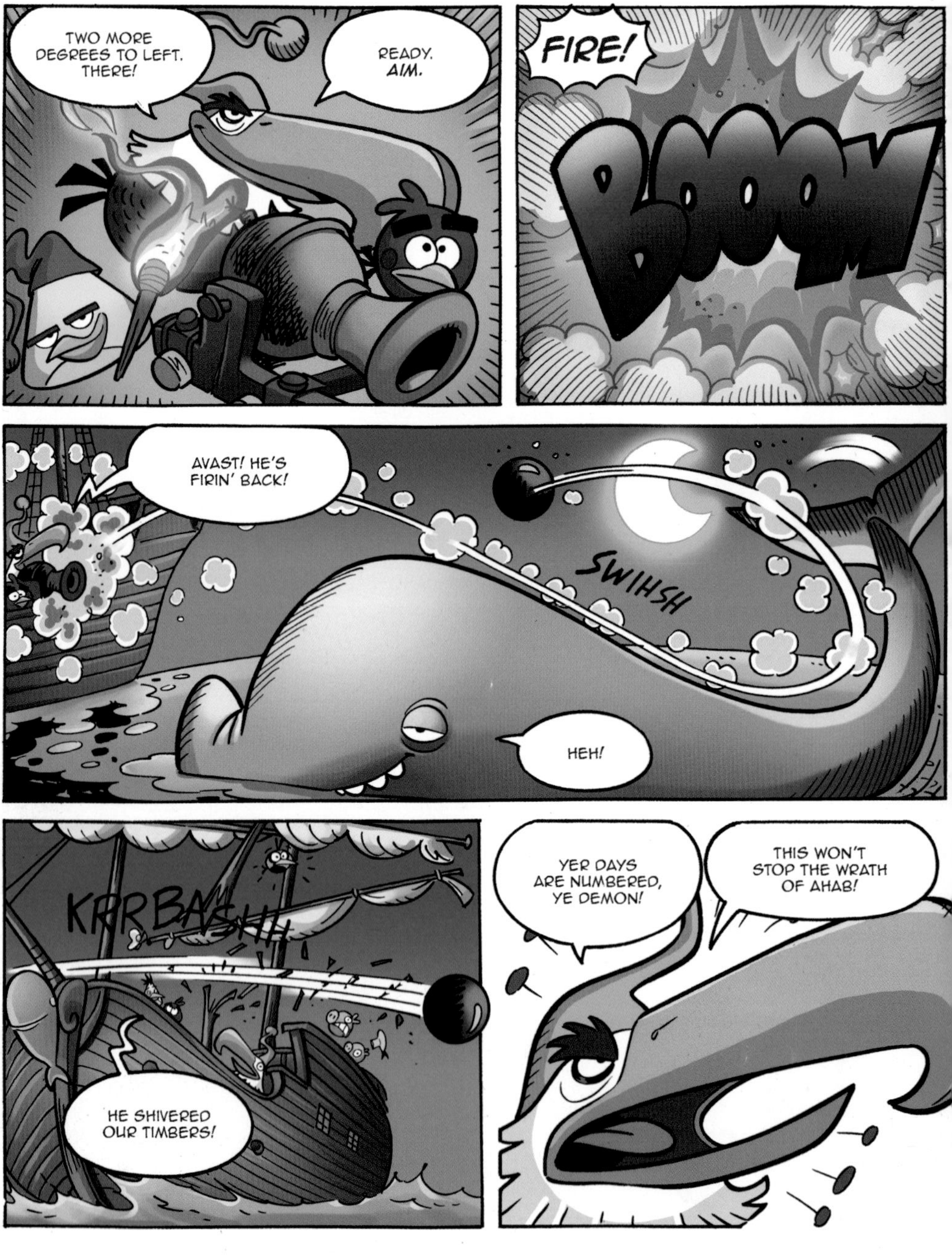
TWO MORE DEGREES TO LEFT. THERE!
READY. AIM.
FIRE!
BOOOM
AVAST! HE'S FIRIN' BACK!
SWIHSH
HEH!
KRRBASH!!
HE SHIVERED OUR TIMBERS!
YER DAYS ARE NUMBERED, YE DEMON!
THIS WON'T STOP THE WRATH OF AHAB!

ANGRY BIRDS™ FURIOUS FOWL

THE NEXT MORNING, WE SET OUT ON THE HUNT FOR THE WHITE WHALE AGAIN.
A LITTLE SLOWER THAN BEFORE.
AFTER MANY HOURS, MOBY PIG WAS SIGHTED!
I SEEN IT, I SEEN IT! 'TIS THE WHITE WHALE!
WE GOT NO WIND FOR SAIL. QUEEPIG, LOWER YOUR BOAT. WE'RE GOING AFTER 'IM!
ZOMP
YIPPEE!
ROW! ROW!
ROW YOUR BOAT!
THIS ALWAYS MAKES ME SLEEPY FOR SOME REASON...
WE LOST 'IM, CAP'N. BEST TO JUST GO BACK!
NO, HE'S HERE! I CAN SENSE HIM!

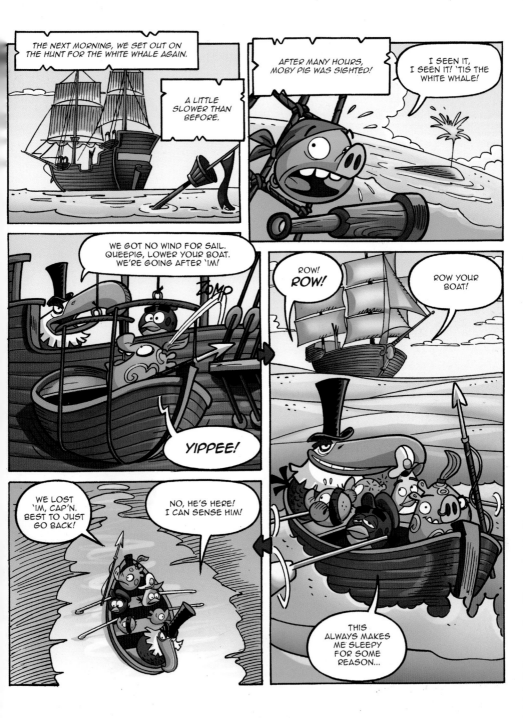

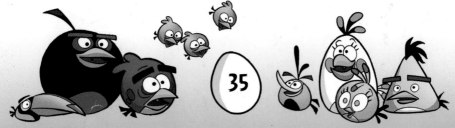

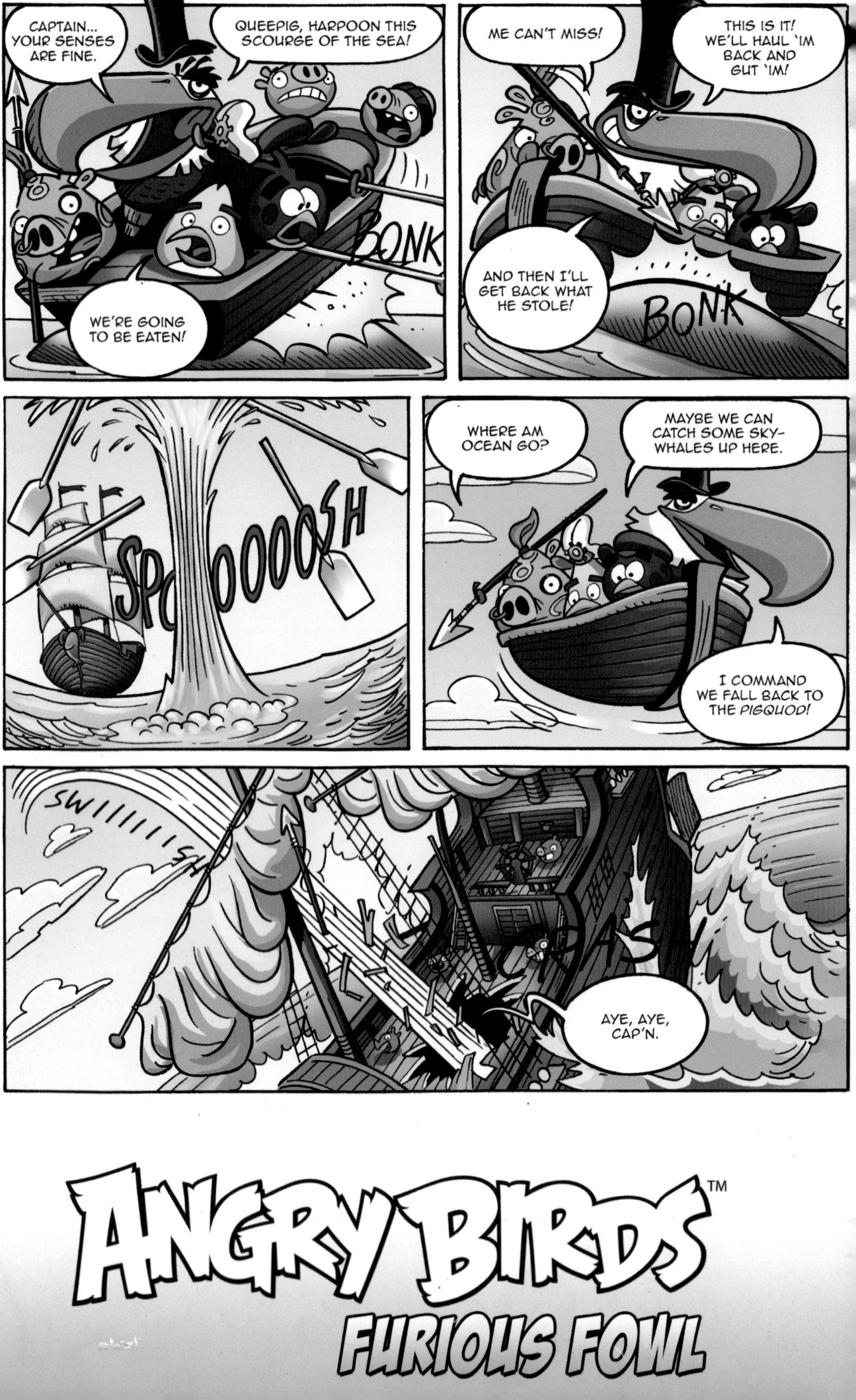
CAPTAIN... YOUR SENSES ARE FINE.
QUEEPIG, HARPOON THIS SCOURGE OF THE SEA!
BONK
WE'RE GOING TO BE EATEN!
ME CAN'T MISS!
THIS IS IT! WE'LL HAUL 'IM BACK AND GUT 'IM!
AND THEN I'LL GET BACK WHAT HE STOLE!
BONK
SPO OOOOSH
WHERE AM OCEAN GO?
MAYBE WE CAN CATCH SOME SKY-WHALES UP HERE.
I COMMAND WE FALL BACK TO THE *PIGQUOD*!
SWIIIIIISH
CRASH
AYE, AYE, CAP'N.

ANGRY BIRDS™
FURIOUS FOWL

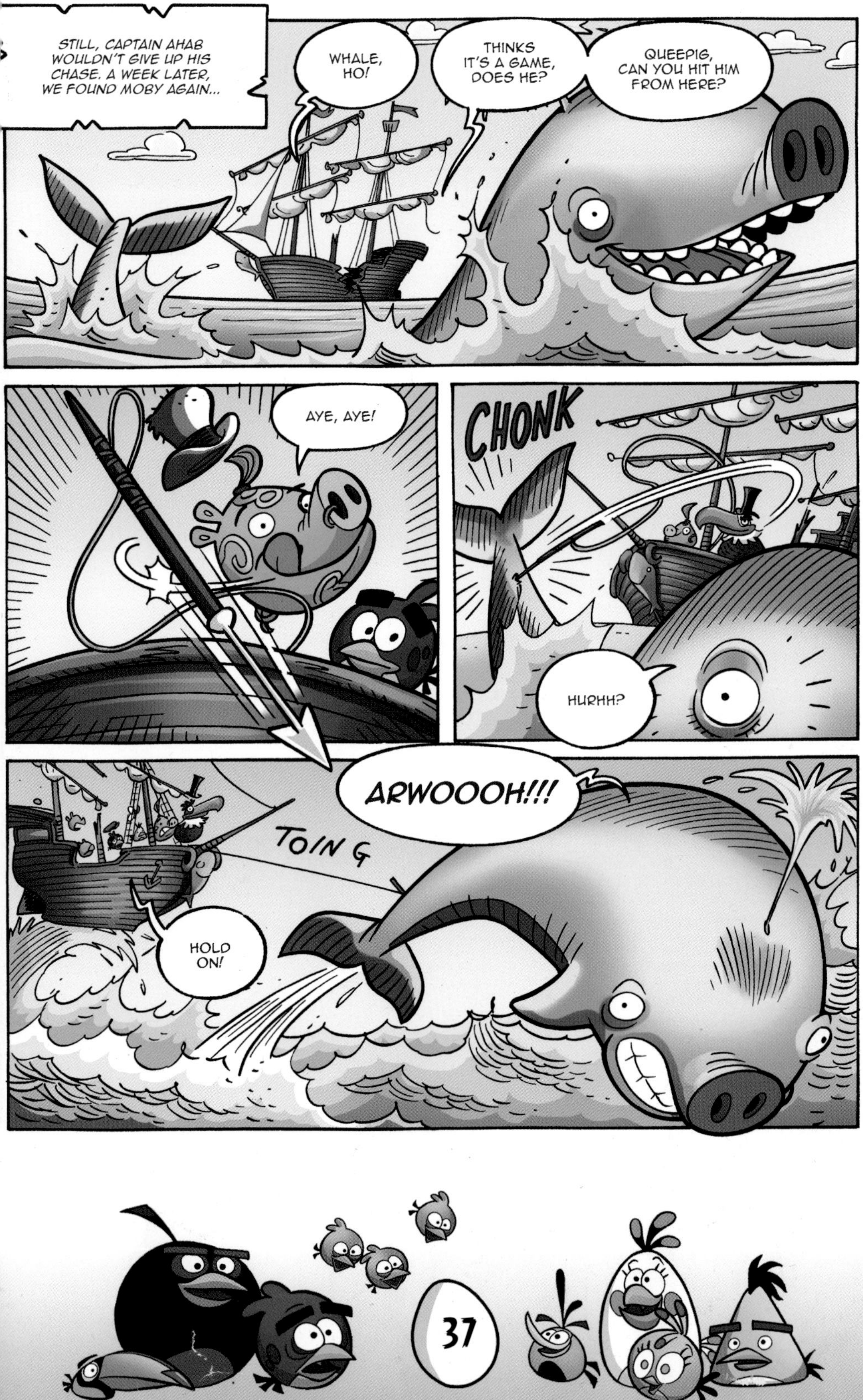
STILL, CAPTAIN AHAB WOULDN'T GIVE UP HIS CHASE. A WEEK LATER, WE FOUND MOBY AGAIN...
WHALE, HO!
THINKS IT'S A GAME, DOES HE?
QUEEPIG, CAN YOU HIT HIM FROM HERE?
AYE, AYE!
CHONK
HURHH?
ARWOOOH!!!
TOING
HOLD ON!

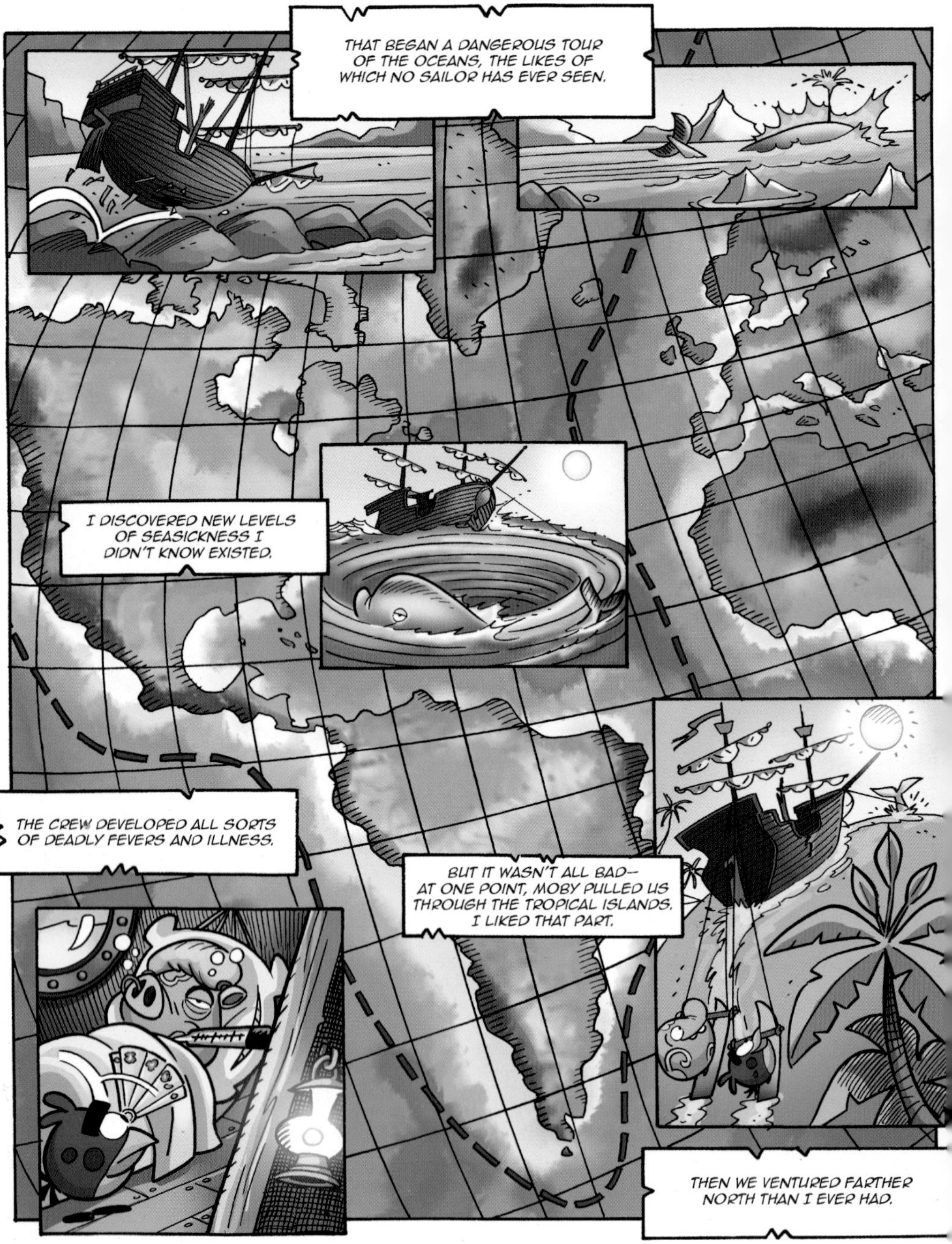
THAT BEGAN A DANGEROUS TOUR OF THE OCEANS, THE LIKES OF WHICH NO SAILOR HAS EVER SEEN.
I DISCOVERED NEW LEVELS OF SEASICKNESS I DIDN'T KNOW EXISTED.
THE CREW DEVELOPED ALL SORTS OF DEADLY FEVERS AND ILLNESS.
BUT IT WASN'T ALL BAD— AT ONE POINT, MOBY PULLED US THROUGH THE TROPICAL ISLANDS. I LIKED THAT PART.
THEN WE VENTURED FARTHER NORTH THAN I EVER HAD.

ANGRY BIRDS™

FURIOUS FOWL

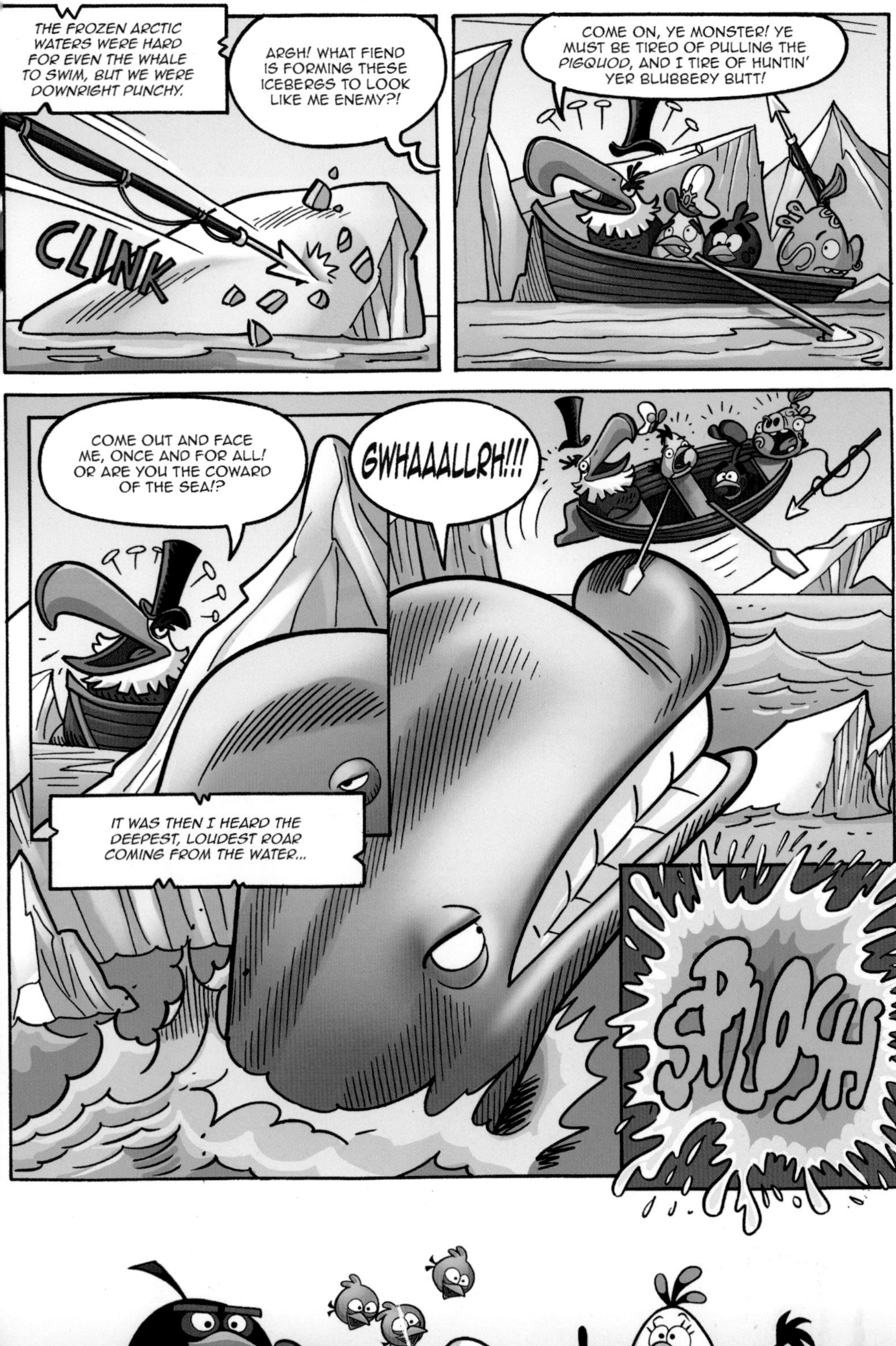
THE FROZEN ARCTIC WATERS WERE HARD FOR EVEN THE WHALE TO SWIM, BUT WE WERE DOWNRIGHT PUNCHY.
ARGH! WHAT FIEND IS FORMING THESE ICEBERGS TO LOOK LIKE ME ENEMY?!
CLINK
COME ON, YE MONSTER! YE MUST BE TIRED OF PULLING THE PIGQUOD, AND I TIRE OF HUNTIN' YER BLUBBERY BUTT!
COME OUT AND FACE ME, ONCE AND FOR ALL! OR ARE YOU THE COWARD OF THE SEA!?
GWHAAALLRH!!!
IT WAS THEN I HEARD THE DEEPEST, LOUDEST ROAR COMING FROM THE WATER...
SPLOOSH

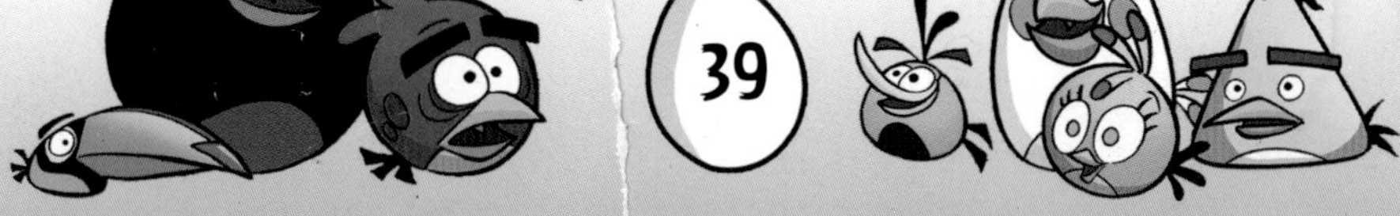

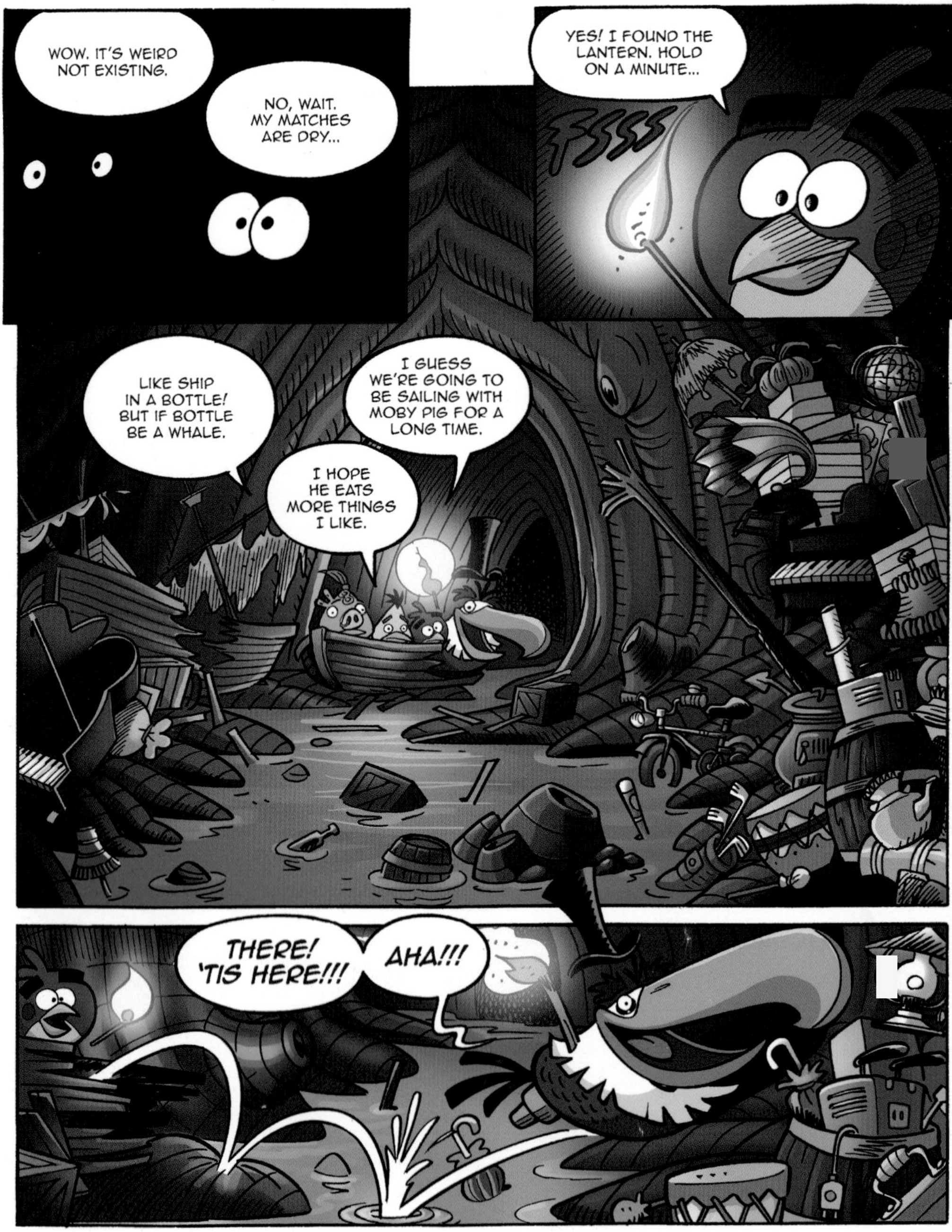
WOW. IT'S WEIRD NOT EXISTING.
NO, WAIT. MY MATCHES ARE DRY...
YES! I FOUND THE LANTERN. HOLD ON A MINUTE...
FSSS
LIKE SHIP IN A BOTTLE! BUT IF BOTTLE BE A WHALE.
I GUESS WE'RE GOING TO BE SAILING WITH MOBY PIG FOR A LONG TIME.
I HOPE HE EATS MORE THINGS I LIKE.
THERE! 'TIS HERE!!!
AHA!!!

ANGRY BIRDS™
FURIOUS FOWL

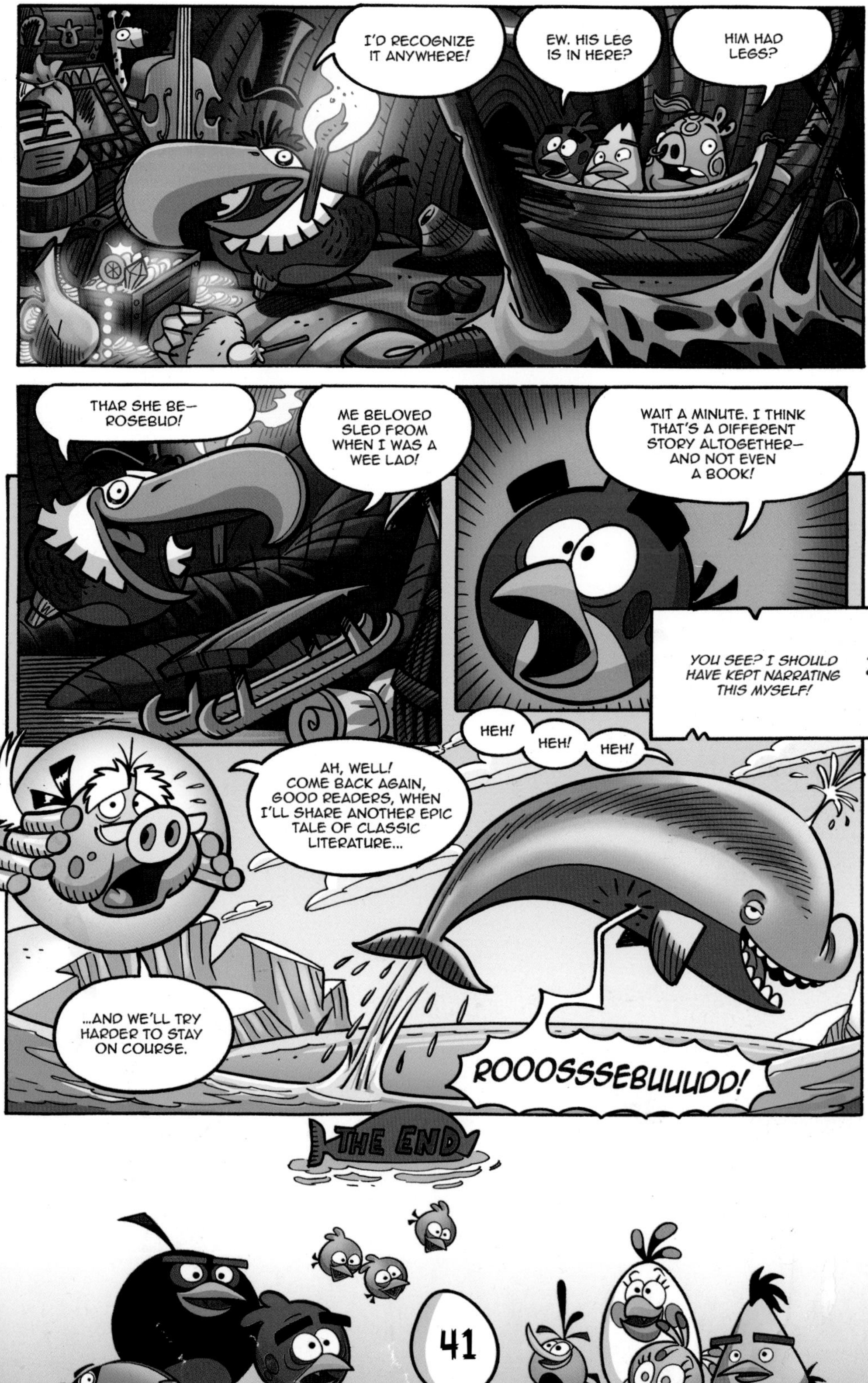
I'D RECOGNIZE IT ANYWHERE!
EW. HIS LEG IS IN HERE?
HIM HAD LEGS?
THAR SHE BE— ROSEBUD!
ME BELOVED SLED FROM WHEN I WAS A WEE LAD!
WAIT A MINUTE. I THINK THAT'S A DIFFERENT STORY ALTOGETHER— AND NOT EVEN A BOOK!
YOU SEE? I SHOULD HAVE KEPT NARRATING THIS MYSELF!
HEH!
HEH!
HEH!
AH, WELL! COME BACK AGAIN, GOOD READERS, WHEN I'LL SHARE ANOTHER EPIC TALE OF CLASSIC LITERATURE...
...AND WE'LL TRY HARDER TO STAY ON COURSE.
ROOOSSSEBUUUDD!
THE END

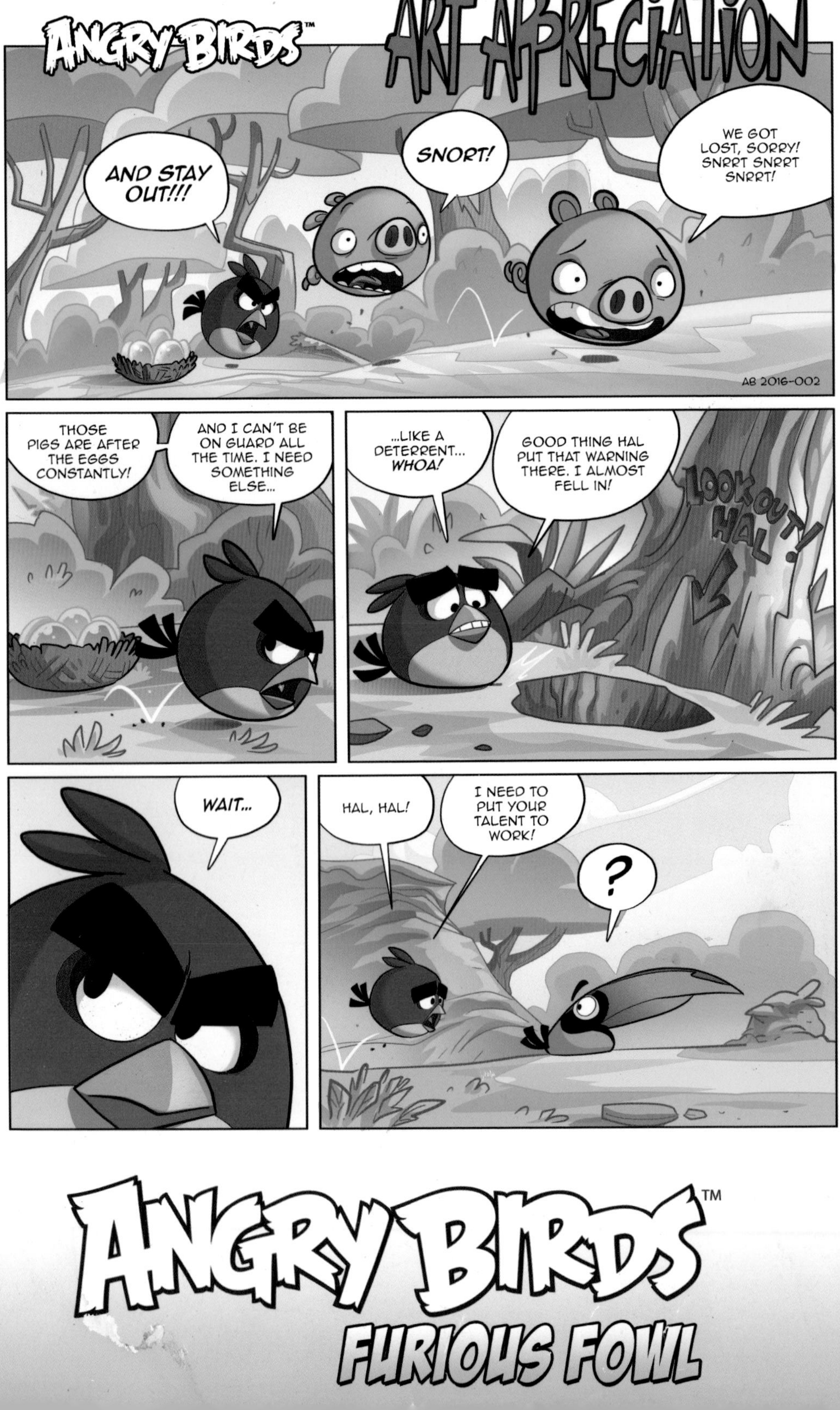
ANGRY BIRDS
ART APPRECIATION
AND STAY OUT!!!
SNORT!
WE GOT LOST, SORRY! SNRRT SNRRT SNRRT!
AB 2016-002
THOSE PIGS ARE AFTER THE EGGS CONSTANTLY!
AND I CAN'T BE ON GUARD ALL THE TIME. I NEED SOMETHING ELSE...
...LIKE A DETERRENT... WHOA!
GOOD THING HAL PUT THAT WARNING THERE. I ALMOST FELL IN!
LOOK OUT HAL!
WAIT...
HAL, HAL!
I NEED TO PUT YOUR TALENT TO WORK!
?

ANGRY BIRDS™

FURIOUS FOWL

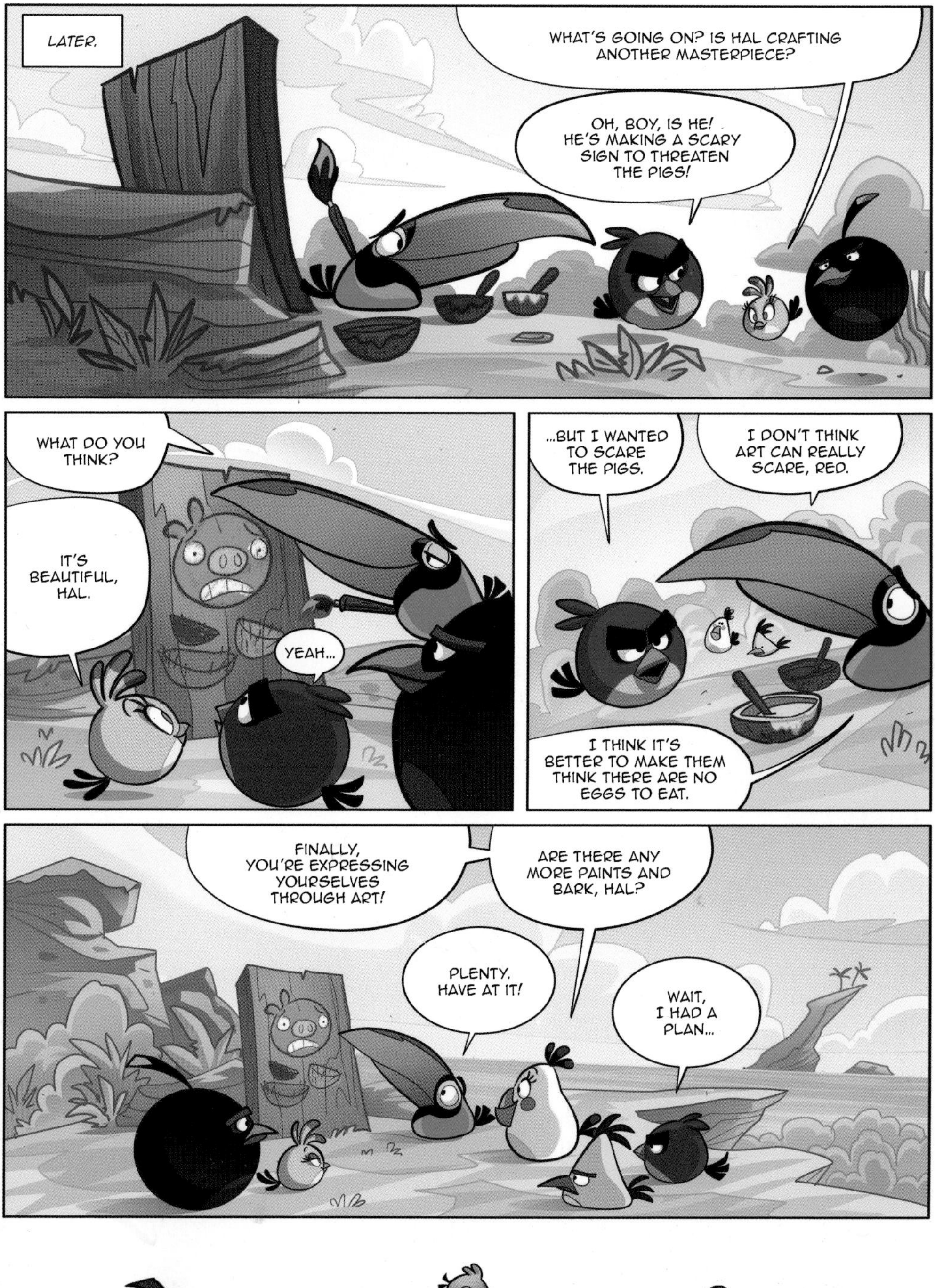
LATER.
WHAT'S GOING ON? IS HAL CRAFTING ANOTHER MASTERPIECE?
OH, BOY, IS HE! HE'S MAKING A SCARY SIGN TO THREATEN THE PIGS!
WHAT DO YOU THINK?
IT'S BEAUTIFUL, HAL.
YEAH...
I DON'T THINK ART CAN REALLY SCARE, RED.
...BUT I WANTED TO SCARE THE PIGS.
I THINK IT'S BETTER TO MAKE THEM THINK THERE ARE NO EGGS TO EAT.
FINALLY, YOU'RE EXPRESSING YOURSELVES THROUGH ART!
ARE THERE ANY MORE PAINTS AND BARK, HAL?
PLENTY. HAVE AT IT!
WAIT, I HAD A PLAN...

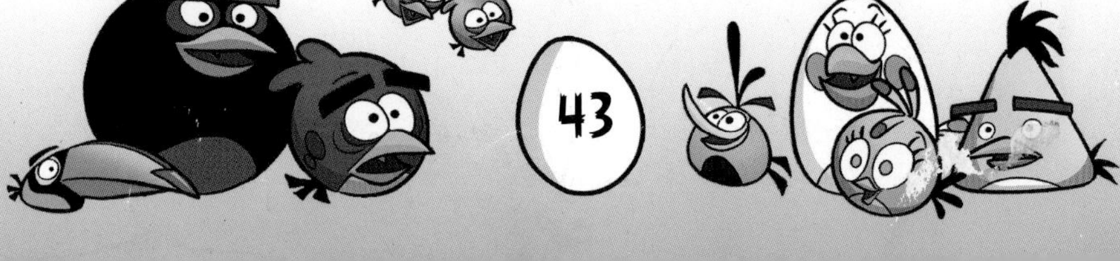

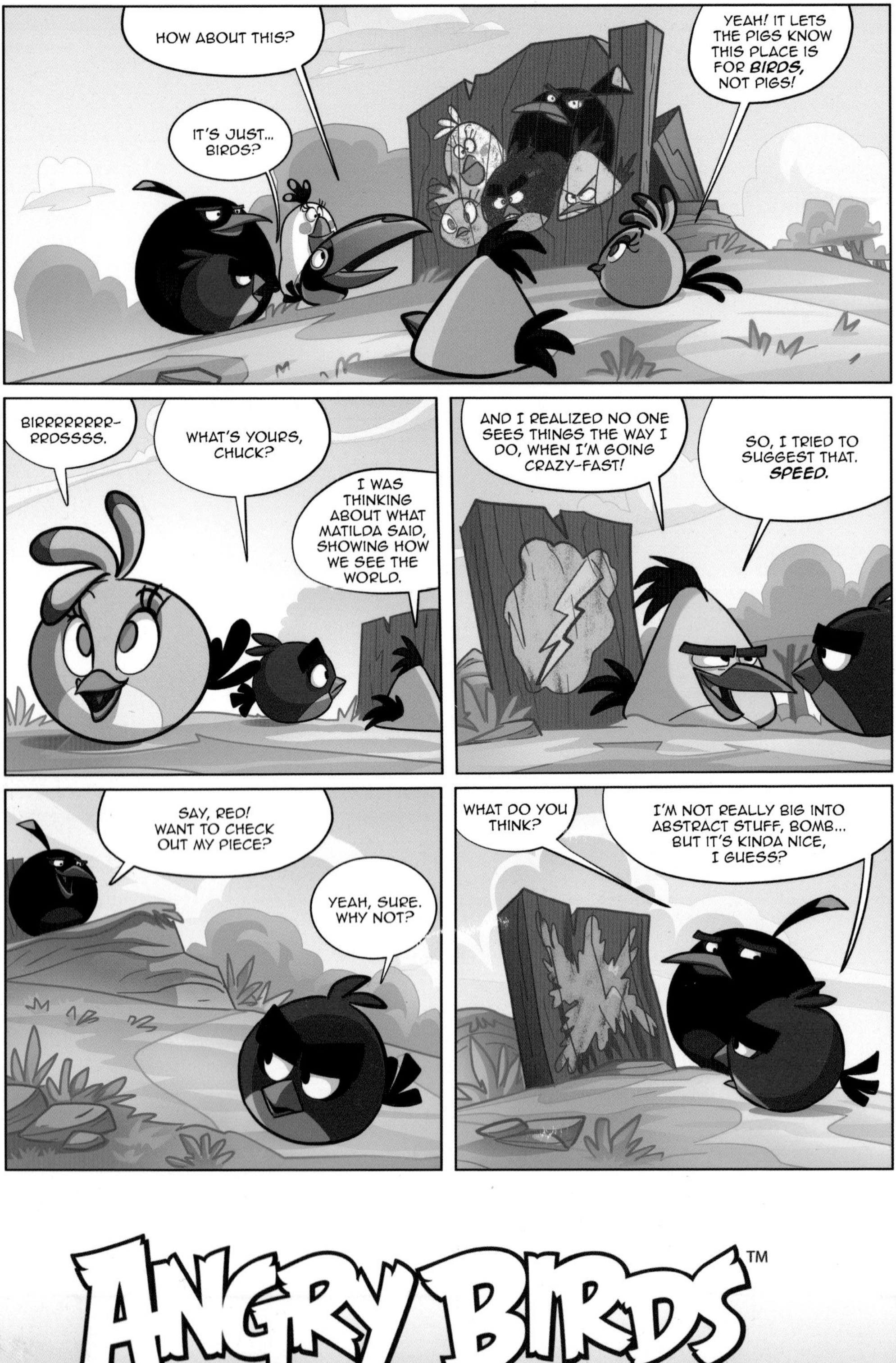
HOW ABOUT THIS?
IT'S JUST... BIRDS?
YEAH! IT LETS THE PIGS KNOW THIS PLACE IS FOR BIRDS, NOT PIGS!
BIRRRRRRRR-RRDSSSS.
WHAT'S YOURS, CHUCK?
I WAS THINKING ABOUT WHAT MATILDA SAID, SHOWING HOW WE SEE THE WORLD.
AND I REALIZED NO ONE SEES THINGS THE WAY I DO, WHEN I'M GOING CRAZY-FAST!
SO, I TRIED TO SUGGEST THAT. SPEED.
SAY, RED! WANT TO CHECK OUT MY PIECE?
YEAH, SURE. WHY NOT?
WHAT DO YOU THINK?
I'M NOT REALLY BIG INTO ABSTRACT STUFF, BOMB... BUT IT'S KINDA NICE, I GUESS?

ANGRY BIRDS™

FURIOUS FOWL

HMF! I PUT A LOT OF EMOTION INTO THIS! THAT'S MY EXPLOSIVE RAGE, RIGHT THERE ON THE CANVAS!
BUT SURE, SAY IT'S KINDA NICE. CRITICS!
I JUST KNOW WHAT I LIKE!
KIDS, WATCH OUT!
YOU WATCH OUT!
WE'RE DOING ART!
LOOK DOWN, RED!
YOU'RE STANDING IN OUR MASTERPIECE!
MAYBE WE SHOULD BUILD A MUSEUM AROUND IT!
OH, FOR BEAK'S SAKE.
DON'T LOOK! I'M NOT DONE YET.
I'M ONLY... HEY!!!
WHAT, WHAT?! DID I DO SOMETHING WEIRD?

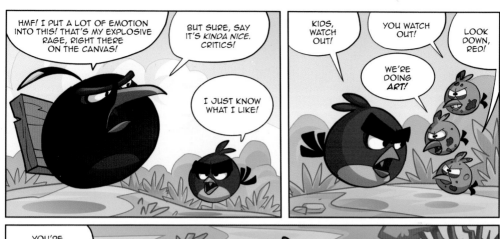

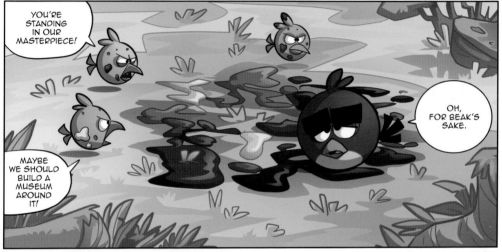

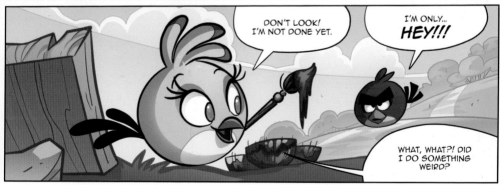

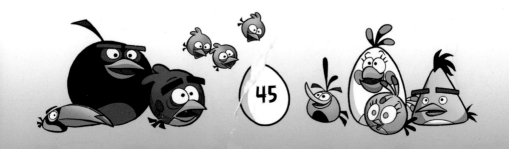

NO... IT'S... IT'S REALLY GOOD.

MATILDA WAS COACHING ME TO THINK ABOUT DIFFERENT MOODS, AND... I JUST TRIED TO PUT IN ALL OF THEM.

I NEVER REALLY THOUGHT ABOUT PAINTING WHAT'S IN ME.

I MEAN, WHERE DO I START?

JUST DIVE IN, HUH?

I LIKE THE WAY THIS PAINT FLOWS...

OOH! THAT WAS AN ACCIDENT, BUT I LIKE IT!

GONNA WORK WITH IT!

HOW DO I KNOW WHEN I'M DONE?

OH, HEY, GANG. WHAT DO YOU THINK?

IT'S...

IT'S, UM, WELL, YOU KNOW...

...NICE? NO, THAT'S NOT THE WORD...

ANGRY BIRDS™
FURIOUS FOWL

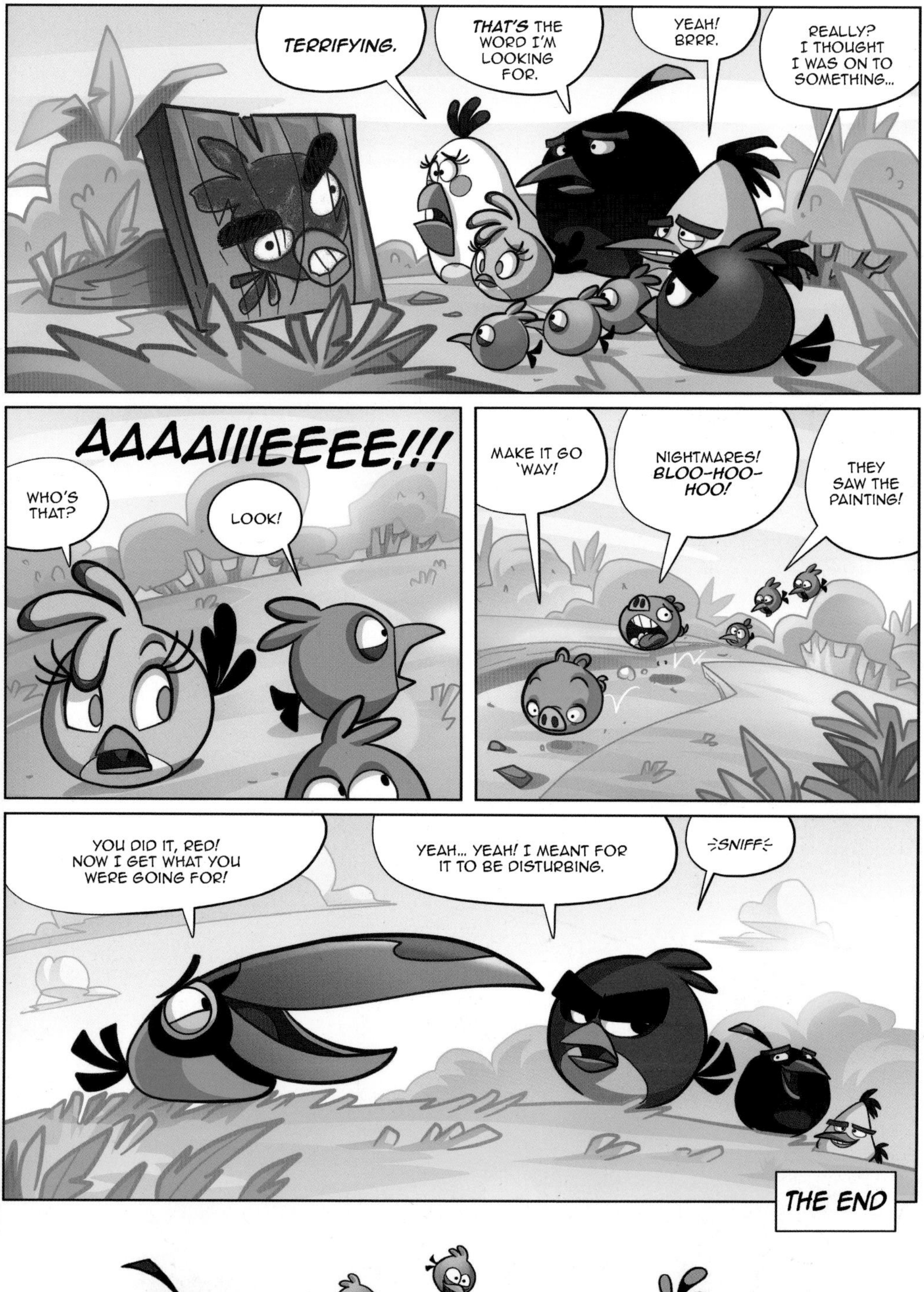
TERRIFYING.
THAT'S THE WORD I'M LOOKING FOR.
YEAH! BRRR.
REALLY? I THOUGHT I WAS ON TO SOMETHING...
AAAAIIIEEEEE!!!
WHO'S THAT?
LOOK!
MAKE IT GO 'WAY!
NIGHTMARES! BLOO-HOO-HOO!
THEY SAW THE PAINTING!
YOU DID IT, RED! NOW I GET WHAT YOU WERE GOING FOR!
YEAH... YEAH! I MEANT FOR IT TO BE DISTURBING.
SNIFF
THE END

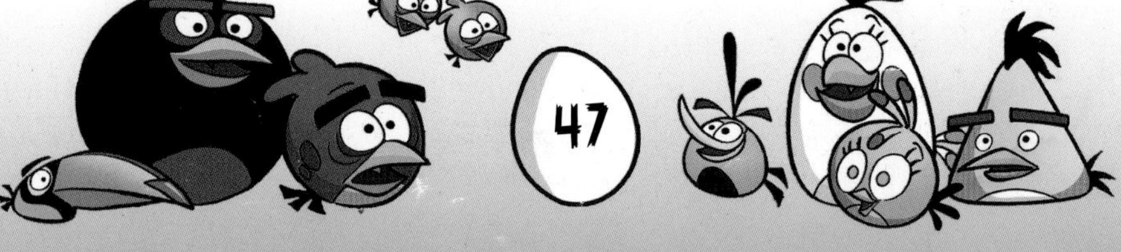

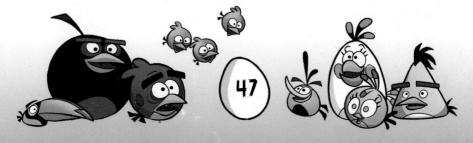

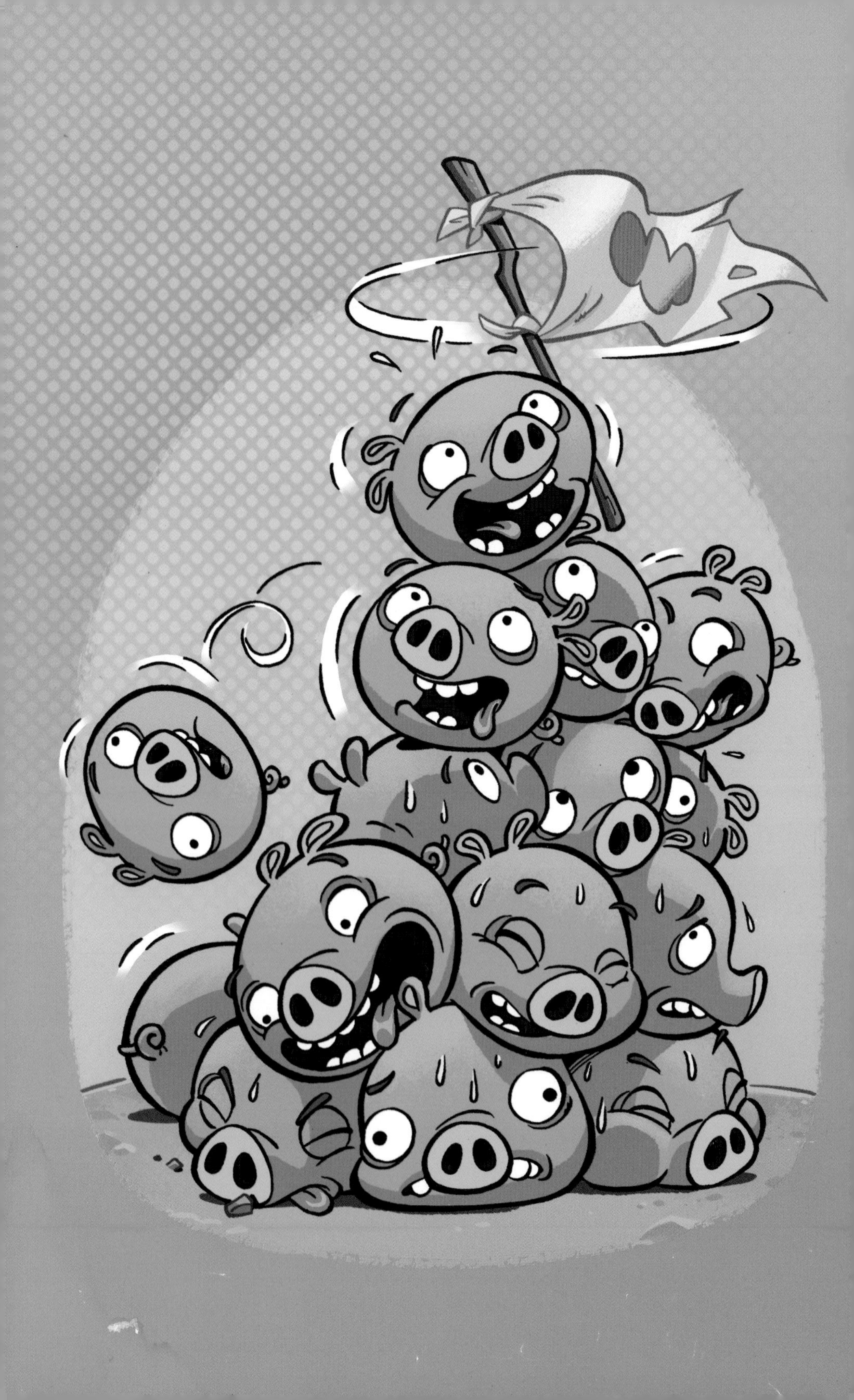

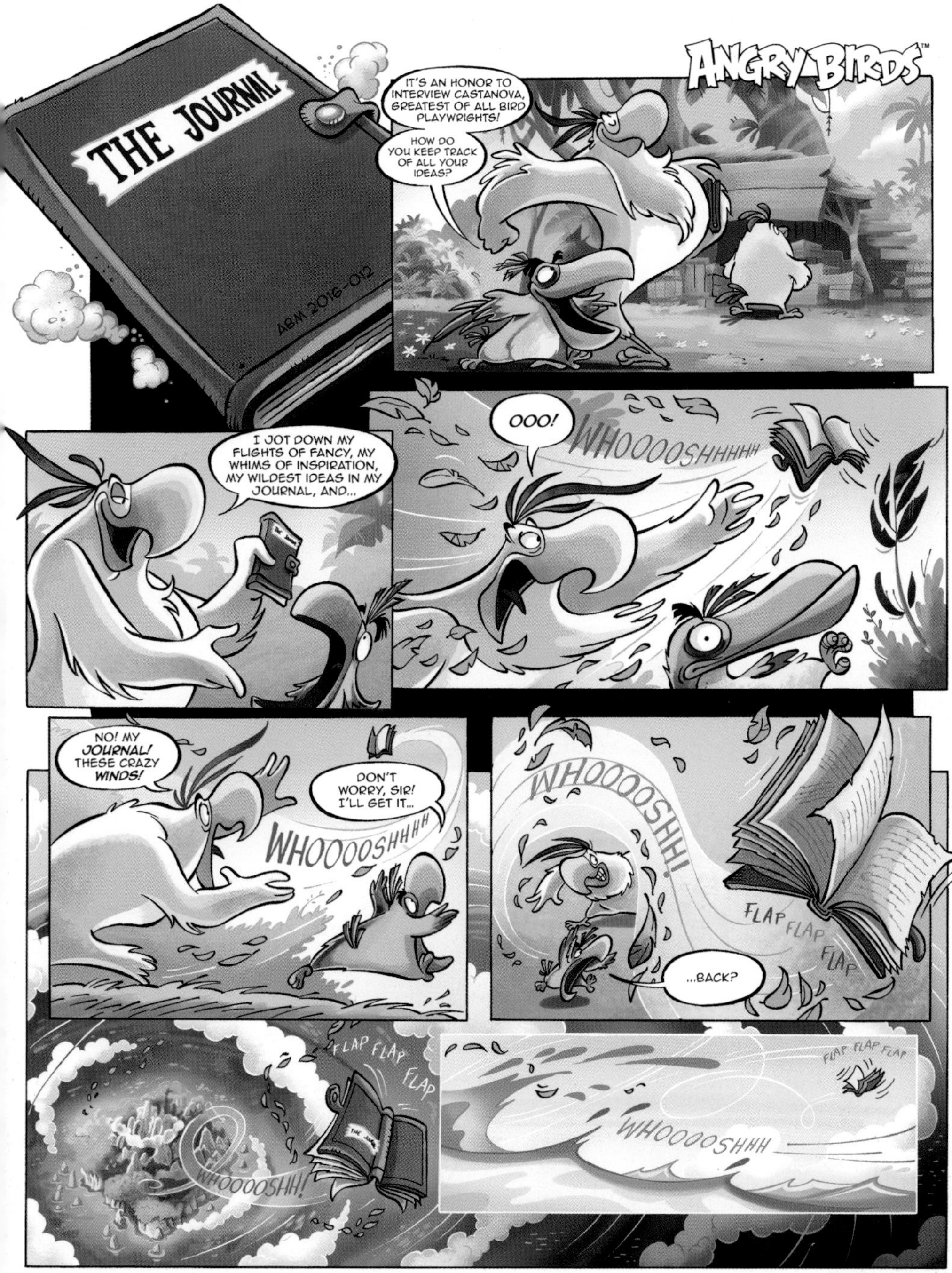
THE JOURNAL
ABM 2016-012
ANGRY BIRDS™
IT'S AN HONOR TO INTERVIEW CASTANOVA, GREATEST OF ALL BIRD PLAYWRIGHTS!
HOW DO YOU KEEP TRACK OF ALL YOUR IDEAS?
I JOT DOWN MY FLIGHTS OF FANCY, MY WHIMS OF INSPIRATION, MY WILDEST IDEAS IN MY JOURNAL, AND...
OOO!
WHOOOOSHHHHH
NO! MY JOURNAL! THESE CRAZY WINDS!
DON'T WORRY, SIR! I'LL GET IT...
WHOOOOSHHHH
WHOOOOSHH!
FLAP FLAP FLAP
...BACK?
FLAP FLAP FLAP
WHOOOOSHH!
FLAP FLAP FLAP
WHOOOOSHHH

ANGRY BIRDS™
FURIOUS FOWL

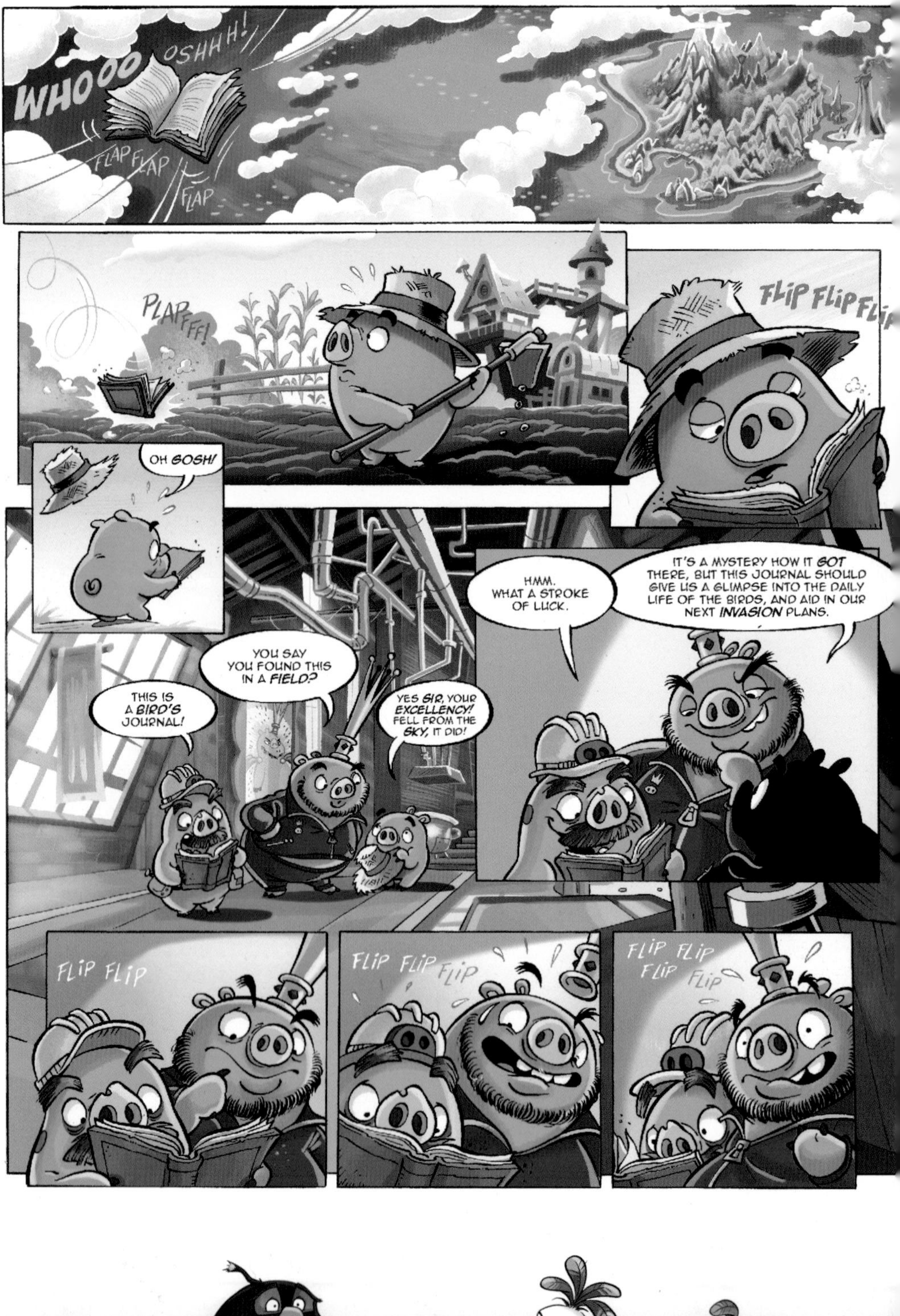
WHOOOOSHHH!
FLAP FLAP
FLAP
PLAPFFF!
FLIP FLIP
OH GOSH!
THIS IS A BIRD'S JOURNAL!
YOU SAY YOU FOUND THIS IN A FIELD?
YES SIR, YOUR EXCELLENCY! FELL FROM THE SKY, IT DID!
HMM. WHAT A STROKE OF LUCK.
IT'S A MYSTERY HOW IT GOT THERE, BUT THIS JOURNAL SHOULD GIVE US A GLIMPSE INTO THE DAILY LIFE OF THE BIRDS, AND AID IN OUR NEXT INVASION PLANS.
FLIP FLIP
FLIP FLIP FLIP
FLIP FLIP FLIP FLIP

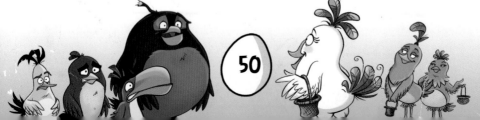

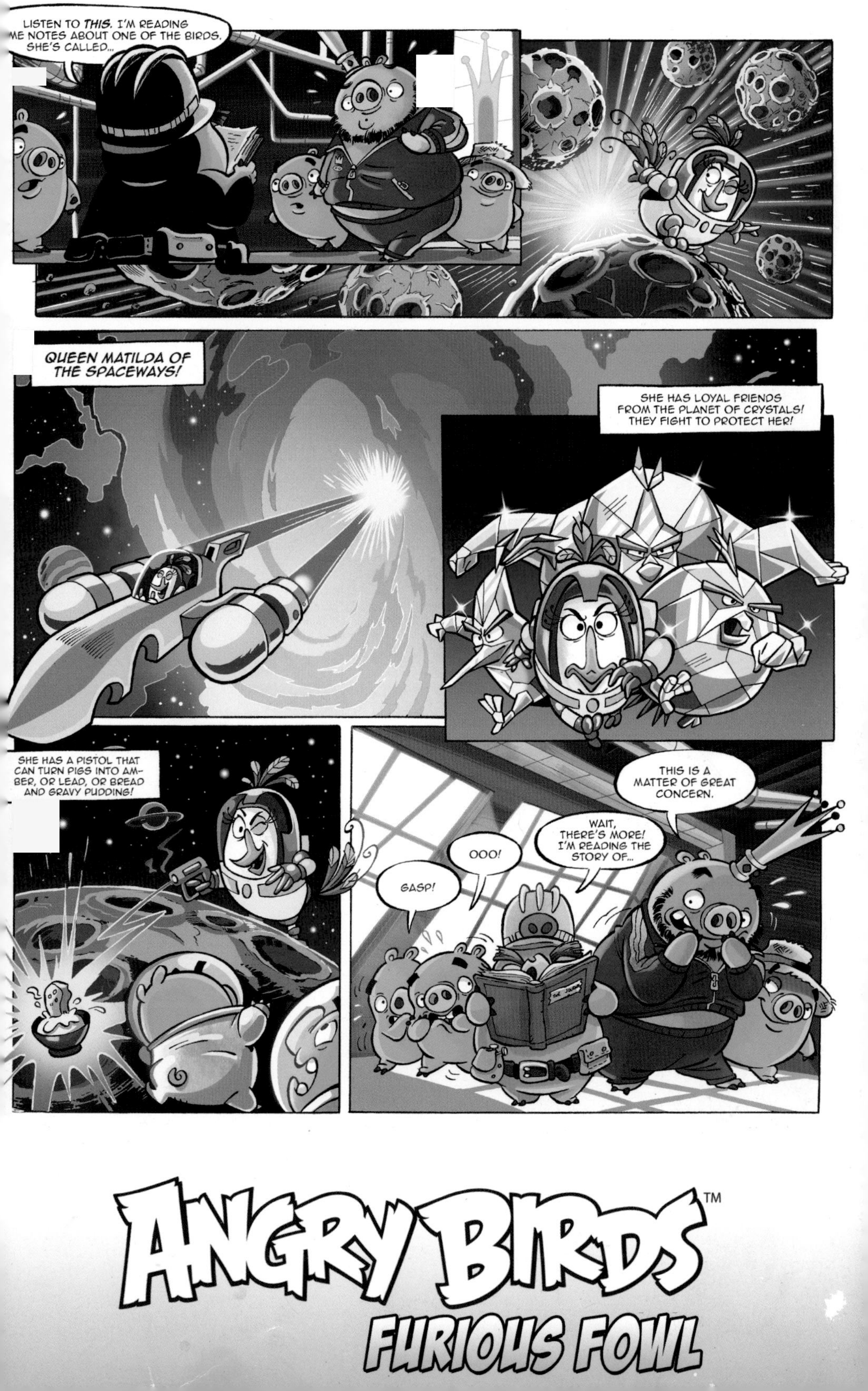
LISTEN TO *THIS.* I'M READING
ME NOTES ABOUT ONE OF THE BIRDS.
SHE'S CALLED...
QUEEN MATILDA OF THE SPACEWAYS!
SHE HAS LOYAL FRIENDS FROM THE PLANET OF CRYSTALS! THEY FIGHT TO PROTECT HER!
SHE HAS A PISTOL THAT CAN TURN PIGS INTO AMBER, OR LEAD, OR BREAD AND GRAVY PUDDING!
THIS IS A MATTER OF GREAT CONCERN.
WAIT, THERE'S MORE! I'M READING THE STORY OF...
OOO!
GASP!

ANGRY BIRDS™
FURIOUS FOWL

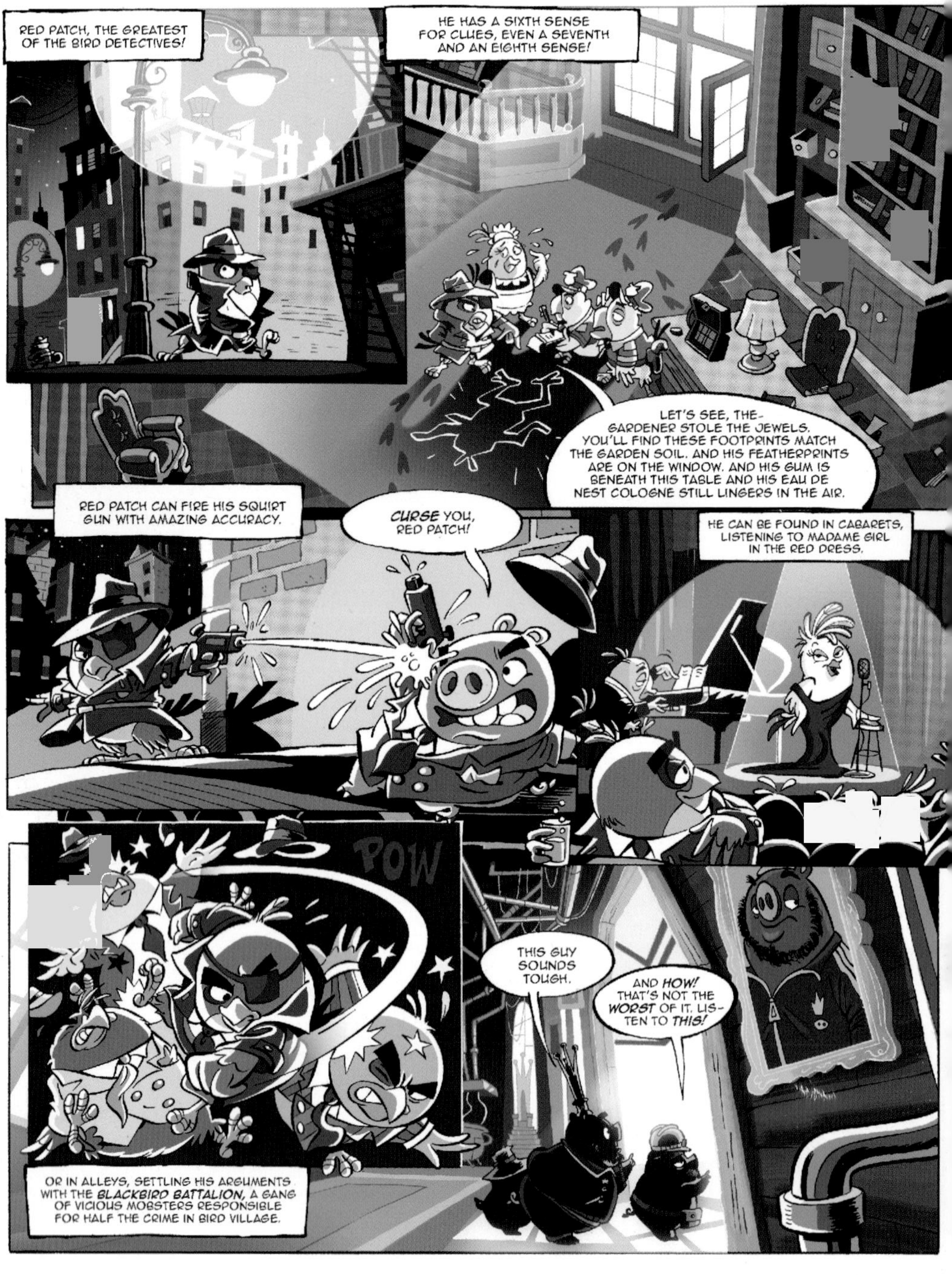
RED PATCH, THE GREATEST OF THE BIRD DETECTIVES!
HE HAS A SIXTH SENSE FOR CLUES, EVEN A SEVENTH AND AN EIGHTH SENSE!
LET'S SEE, THE-GARDENER STOLE THE JEWELS. YOU'LL FIND THESE FOOTPRINTS MATCH THE GARDEN SOIL. AND HIS FEATHERPRINTS ARE ON THE WINDOW. AND HIS GUM IS BENEATH THIS TABLE AND HIS EAU DE NEST COLOGNE STILL LINGERS IN THE AIR.
RED PATCH CAN FIRE HIS SQUIRT GUN WITH AMAZING ACCURACY.
CURSE YOU, RED PATCH!
HE CAN BE FOUND IN CABARETS, LISTENING TO MADAME GIRL IN THE RED DRESS.
POW
THIS GUY SOUNDS TOUGH.
AND HOW! THAT'S NOT THE WORST OF IT. LISTEN TO THIS!
OR IN ALLEYS, SETTLING HIS ARGUMENTS WITH THE BLACKBIRD BATTALION, A GANG OF VICIOUS MOBSTERS RESPONSIBLE FOR HALF THE CRIME IN BIRD VILLAGE.

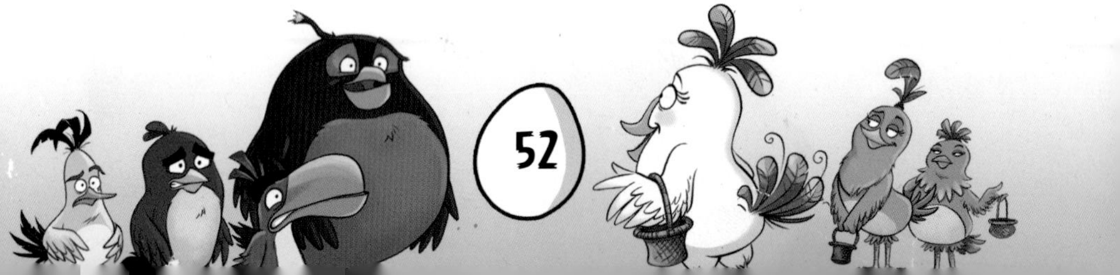

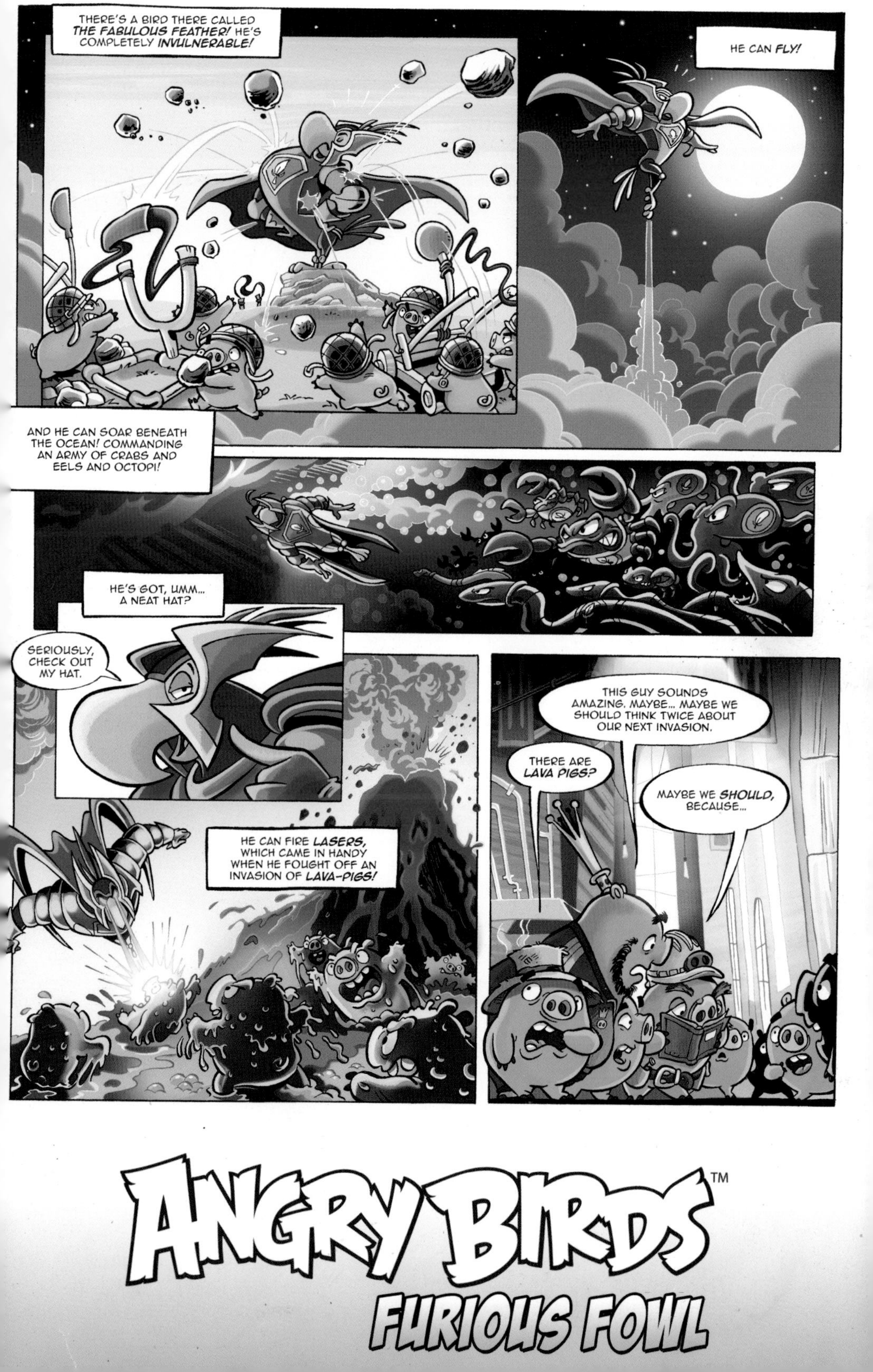
THERE'S A BIRD THERE CALLED THE FABULOUS FEATHER! HE'S COMPLETELY INVULNERABLE!
HE CAN FLY!
AND HE CAN SOAR BENEATH THE OCEAN! COMMANDING AN ARMY OF CRABS AND EELS AND OCTOPI!
HE'S GOT, UMM... A NEAT HAT?
SERIOUSLY, CHECK OUT MY HAT.
HE CAN FIRE LASERS, WHICH CAME IN HANDY WHEN HE FOUGHT OFF AN INVASION OF LAVA-PIGS!
THIS GUY SOUNDS AMAZING. MAYBE... MAYBE WE SHOULD THINK TWICE ABOUT OUR NEXT INVASION.
THERE ARE LAVA PIGS?
MAYBE WE SHOULD, BECAUSE...

ANGRY BIRDS™
FURIOUS FOWL

...ACCORDING TO THIS, THERE'S A WOMAN NAMED SALLY THAT GOES TO A SCHOOL CALLED "ROMANCE HIGH SCHOOL."

SHE'S GOT A FRIEND NAMED CATHY WHO'S DATING A BOY NAMED JIM AND SALLY IS IN LOVE WITH JIM BUT CATHY DOESN'T KNOW.

Romance High School

AND THE SCHOOL PRINCIPAL HAS AMNESIA AND THINKS HE'S ONE OF THE STUDENTS, AND THAT HE'S THE CAPTAIN OF THE FOOTBALL TEAM, BUT THE REAL CAPTAIN OF THE FOOTBALL TEAM IS SALLY, BECAUSE SHE'S DISGUISED HERSELF AS A MAN NAMED GREGOR, AND...

...CATHY IS ALSO IN LOVE WITH GREGOR, BECAUSE SHE DOESN'T KNOW IT'S ACTUALLY HER ROOM-MATE IN DISGUISE...

AND THEN THERE WAS A PROBLEM WITH THE FLOWERS GETTING DELIVERED TO THE WRONG ADDRESS, SO THAT BELINDA THINKS JIM SENT HER FLOWERS.

WAIT. WHO'S BELINDA?

NO! DON'T ANSWER!

HE'S RIGHT! IF WE GOT CAUGHT UP IN THIS, THE PLOT WILL GET SO TANGLED THAT WE'LL NEVER BE ABLE TO ESCAPE.

BIRD VILLAGE IS SOUNDING FAR MORE DANGEROUS THAN I EVER THOUGHT.

BY IMPERIAL DECREE... LET BELINDA REMAIN A MYSTERY!

I'M AFRAID THERE ARE OTHER MYSTERIES ON BIRD ISLAND. MONSTROUS MYSTERIES.

WHAT DO YOU MEAN?

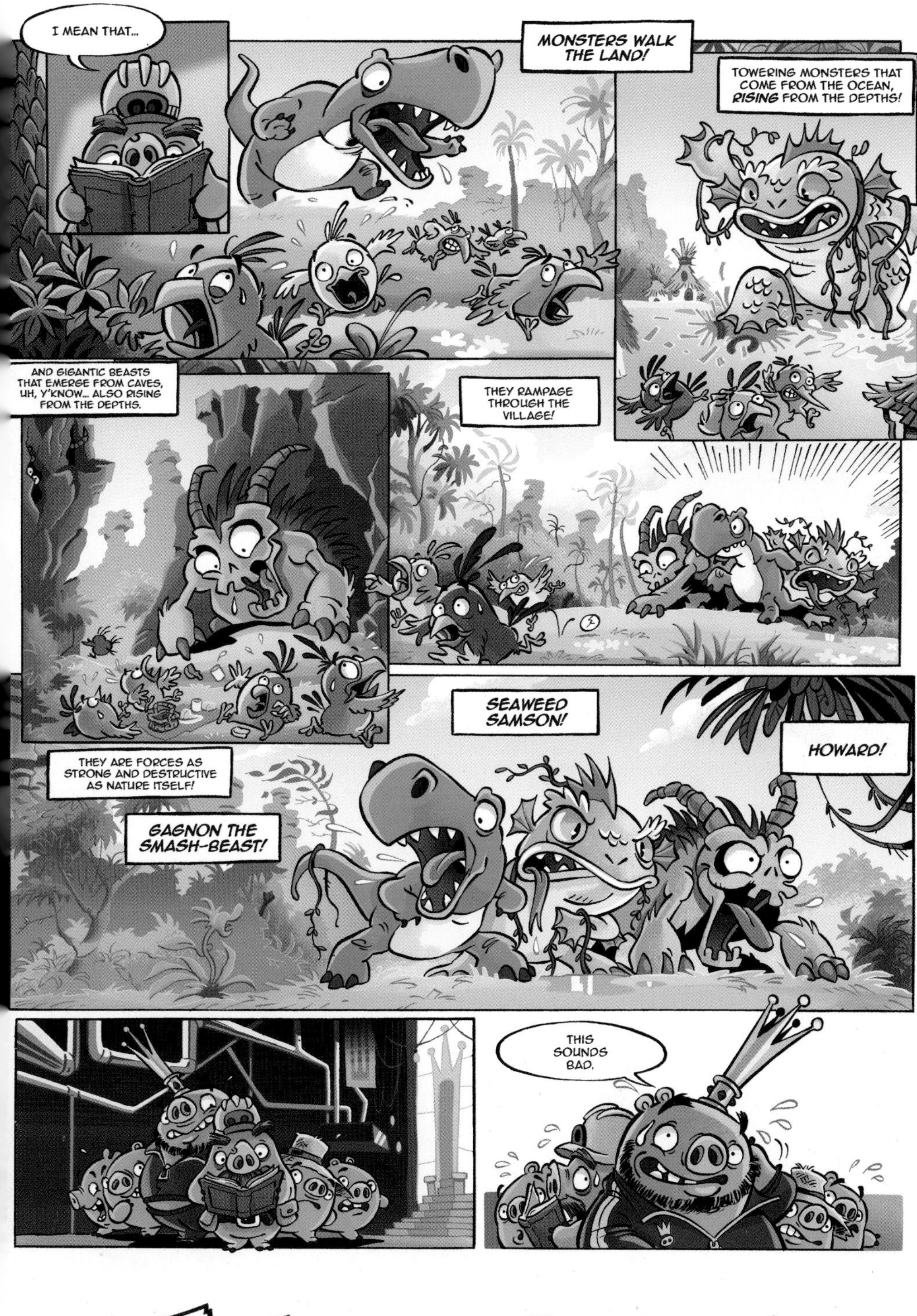
I MEAN THAT...
MONSTERS WALK THE LAND!
TOWERING MONSTERS THAT COME FROM THE OCEAN, RISING FROM THE DEPTHS!
AND GIGANTIC BEASTS THAT EMERGE FROM CAVES, UH, Y'KNOW... ALSO RISING FROM THE DEPTHS.
THEY RAMPAGE THROUGH THE VILLAGE!
THEY ARE FORCES AS STRONG AND DESTRUCTIVE AS NATURE ITSELF!
SEAWEED SAMSON!
GAGNON THE SMASH-BEAST!
HOWARD!
THIS SOUNDS BAD.

ANGRY BIRDS™
FURIOUS FOWL

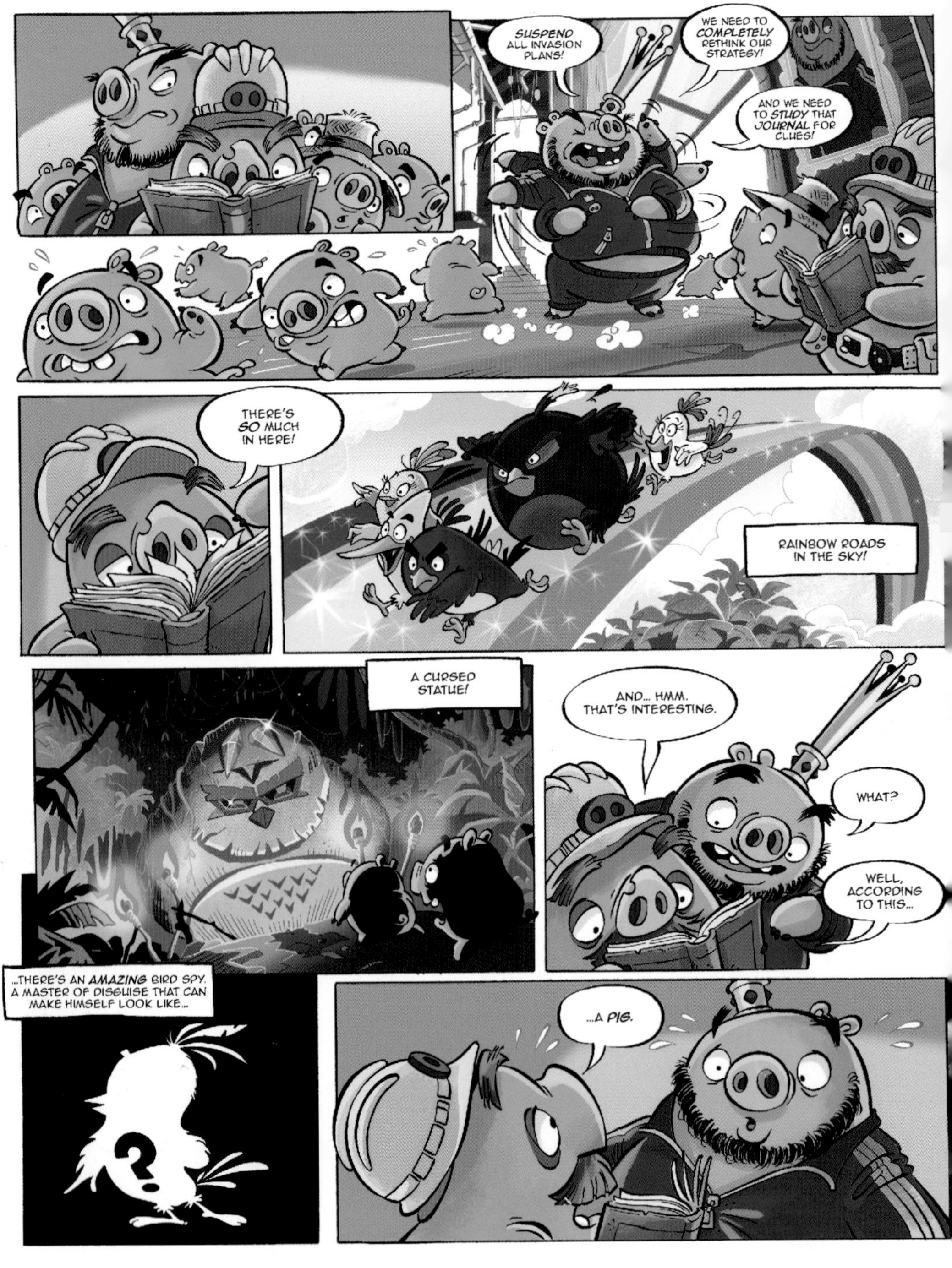
SUSPEND ALL INVASION PLANS!
WE NEED TO COMPLETELY RETHINK OUR STRATEGY!
AND WE NEED TO STUDY THAT JOURNAL FOR CLUES!
THERE'S SO MUCH IN HERE!
RAINBOW ROADS IN THE SKY!
A CURSED STATUE!
AND... HMM. THAT'S INTERESTING.
WHAT?
WELL, ACCORDING TO THIS...
...THERE'S AN AMAZING BIRD SPY. A MASTER OF DISGUISE THAT CAN MAKE HIMSELF LOOK LIKE...
...A PIG.

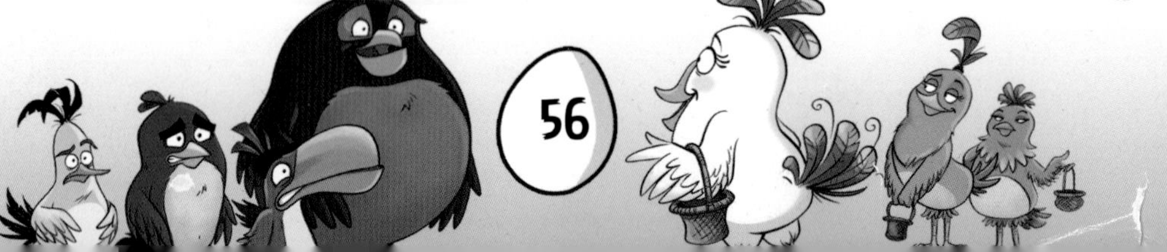

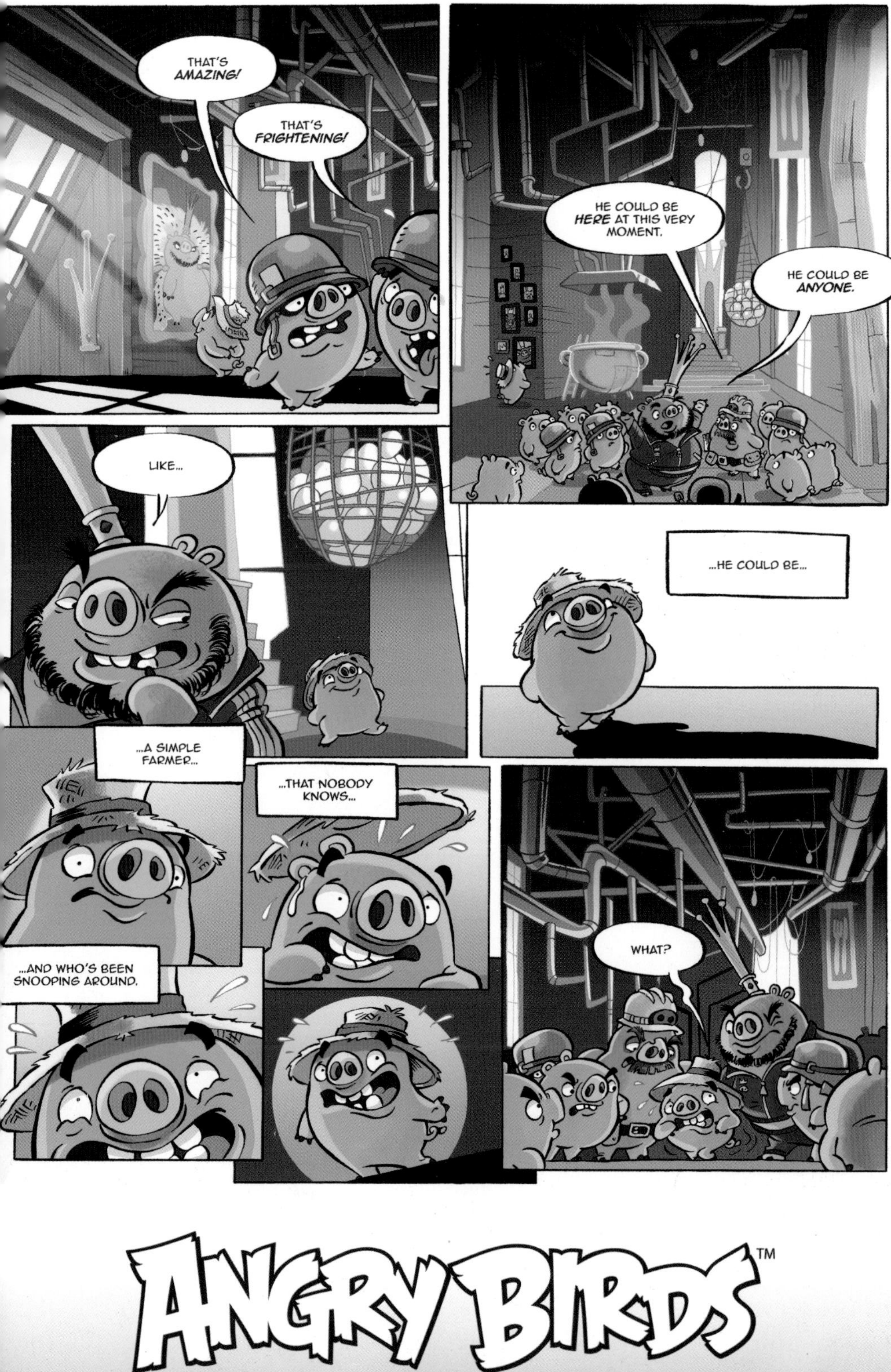
THAT'S AMAZING!
THAT'S FRIGHTENING!
HE COULD BE HERE AT THIS VERY MOMENT.
HE COULD BE ANYONE.
LIKE...
...HE COULD BE...
...A SIMPLE FARMER...
...THAT NOBODY KNOWS...
...AND WHO'S BEEN SNOOPING AROUND.
WHAT?

ANGRY BIRDS™
FURIOUS FOWL

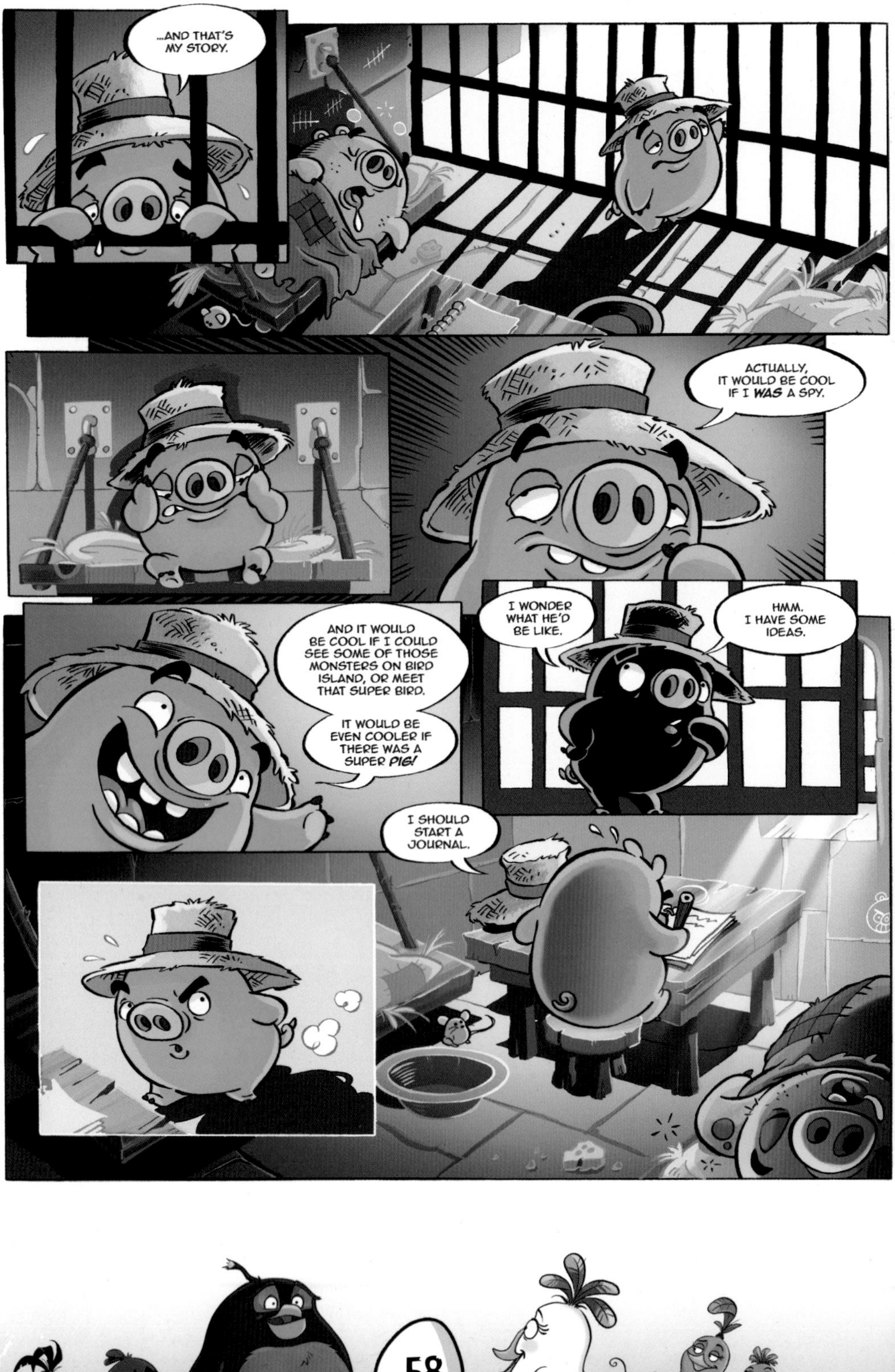
...AND THAT'S MY STORY.
ACTUALLY, IT WOULD BE COOL IF I WAS A SPY.
AND IT WOULD BE COOL IF I COULD SEE SOME OF THOSE MONSTERS ON BIRD ISLAND, OR MEET THAT SUPER BIRD.
IT WOULD BE EVEN COOLER IF THERE WAS A SUPER PIG!
I WONDER WHAT HE'D BE LIKE.
HMM. I HAVE SOME IDEAS.
I SHOULD START A JOURNAL.

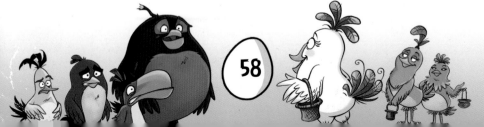

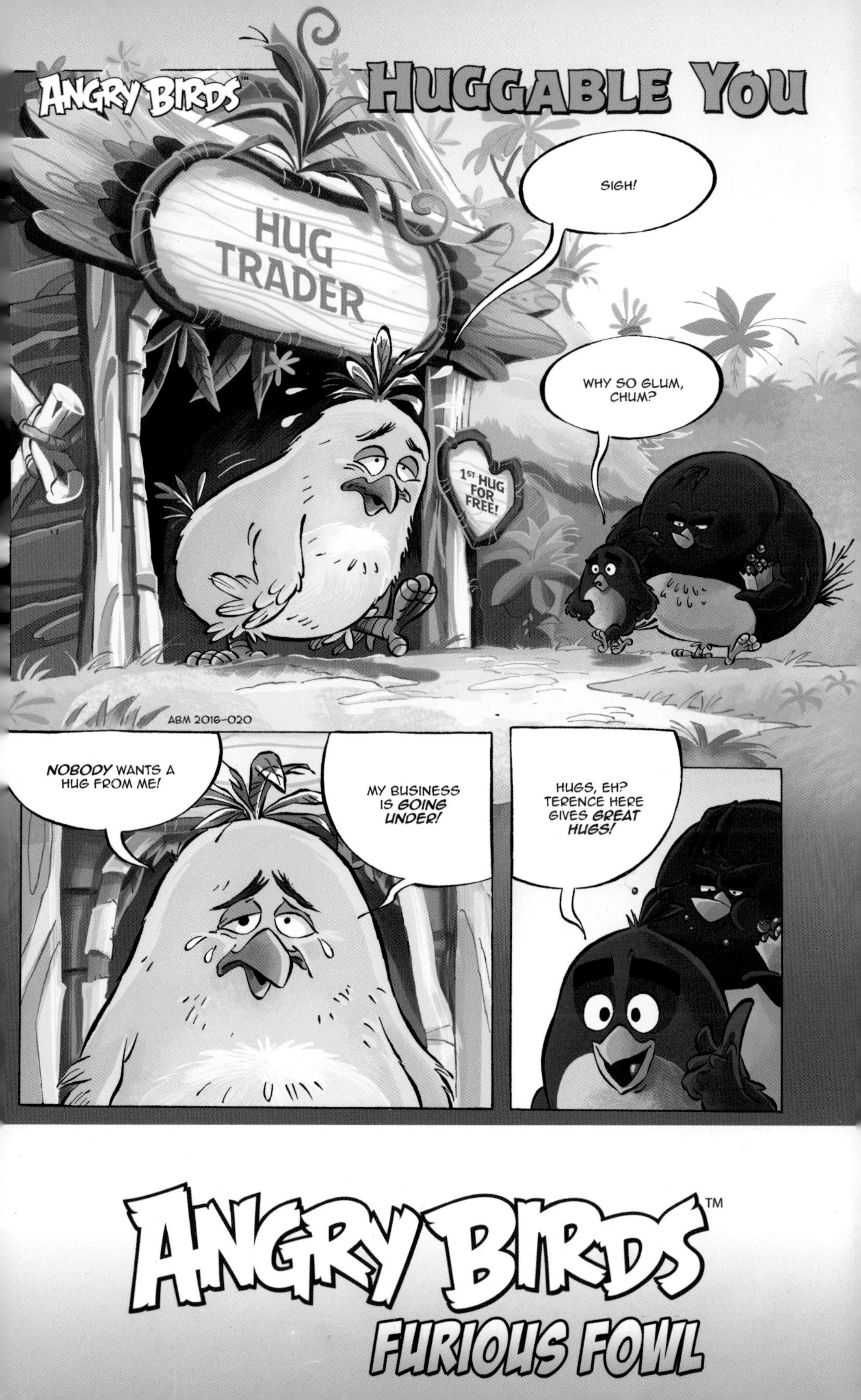
ANGRY BIRDS™
HUGGABLE YOU
HUG TRADER
SIGH!
WHY SO GLUM, CHUM?
1ST HUG FOR FREE!
ABM 2016-020
NOBODY WANTS A HUG FROM ME!
MY BUSINESS IS GOING UNDER!
HUGS, EH? TERENCE HERE GIVES GREAT HUGS!

ANGRY BIRDS™
FURIOUS FOWL

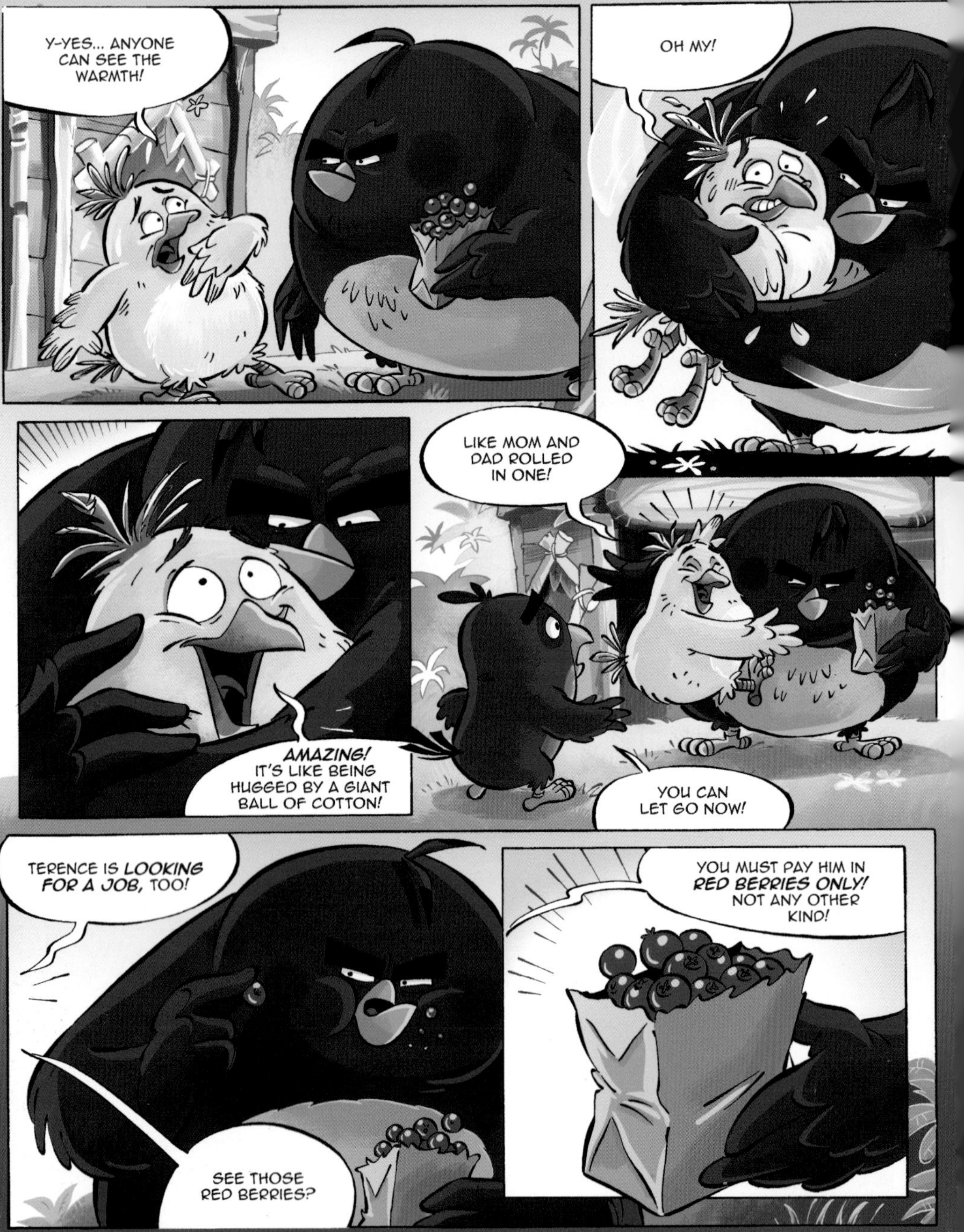
Y-YES... ANYONE CAN SEE THE WARMTH!
OH MY!
AMAZING! IT'S LIKE BEING HUGGED BY A GIANT BALL OF COTTON!
LIKE MOM AND DAD ROLLED IN ONE!
YOU CAN LET GO NOW!
TERENCE IS LOOKING FOR A JOB, TOO!
SEE THOSE RED BERRIES?
YOU MUST PAY HIM IN RED BERRIES ONLY! NOT ANY OTHER KIND!

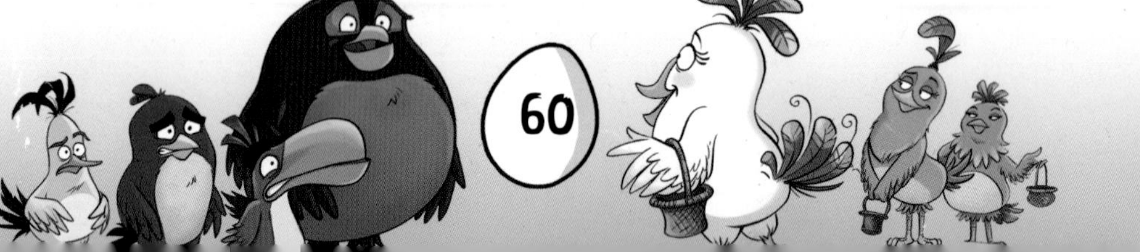

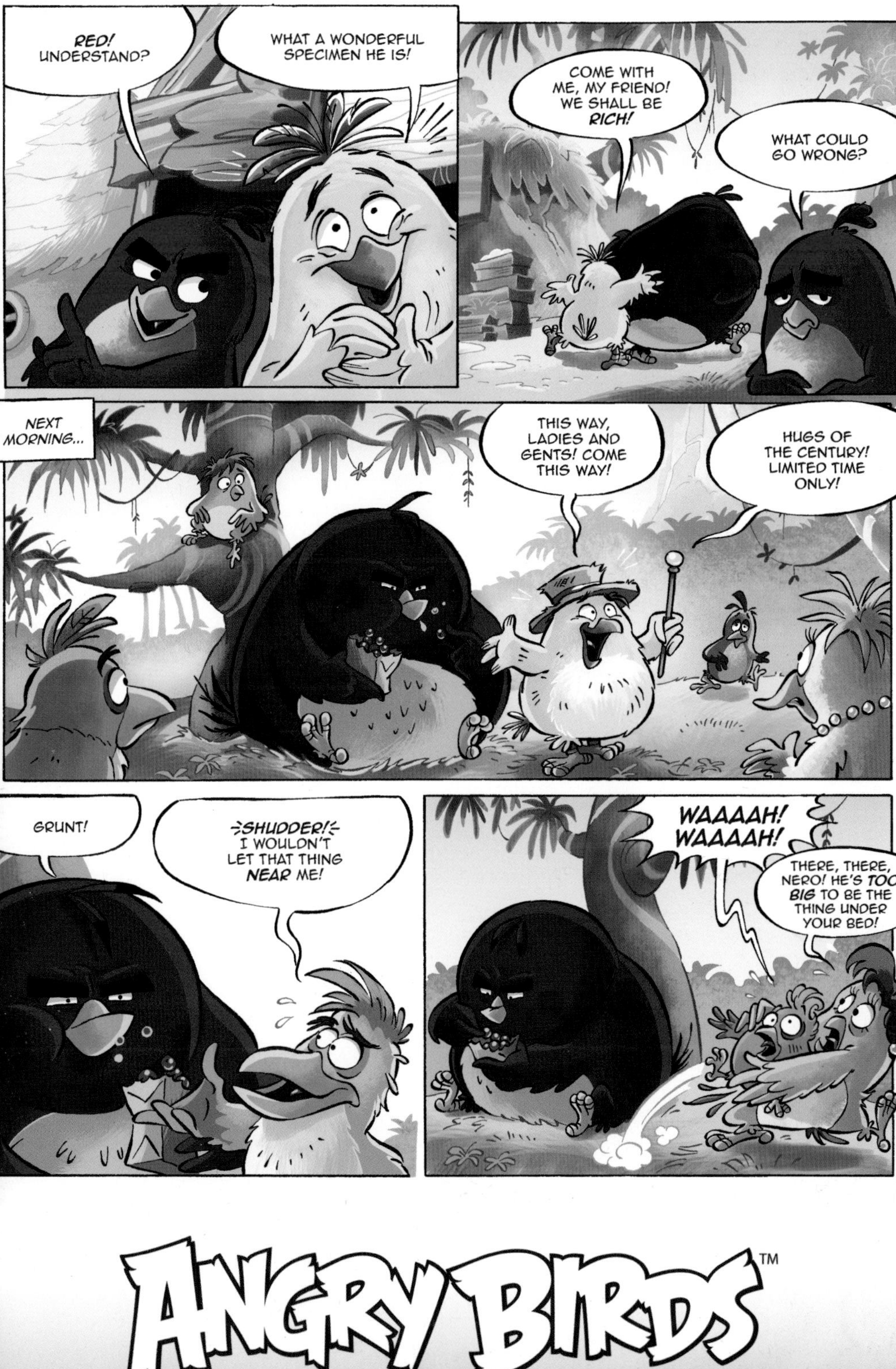
RED! UNDERSTAND?
WHAT A WONDERFUL SPECIMEN HE IS!
COME WITH ME, MY FRIEND! WE SHALL BE RICH!
WHAT COULD GO WRONG?
NEXT MORNING...
THIS WAY, LADIES AND GENTS! COME THIS WAY!
HUGS OF THE CENTURY! LIMITED TIME ONLY!
GRUNT!
SHUDDER! I WOULDN'T LET THAT THING NEAR ME!
WAAAAH! WAAAAH!
THERE, THERE, NERO! HE'S TOO BIG TO BE THE THING UNDER YOUR BED!

ANGRY BIRDS™
FURIOUS FOWL

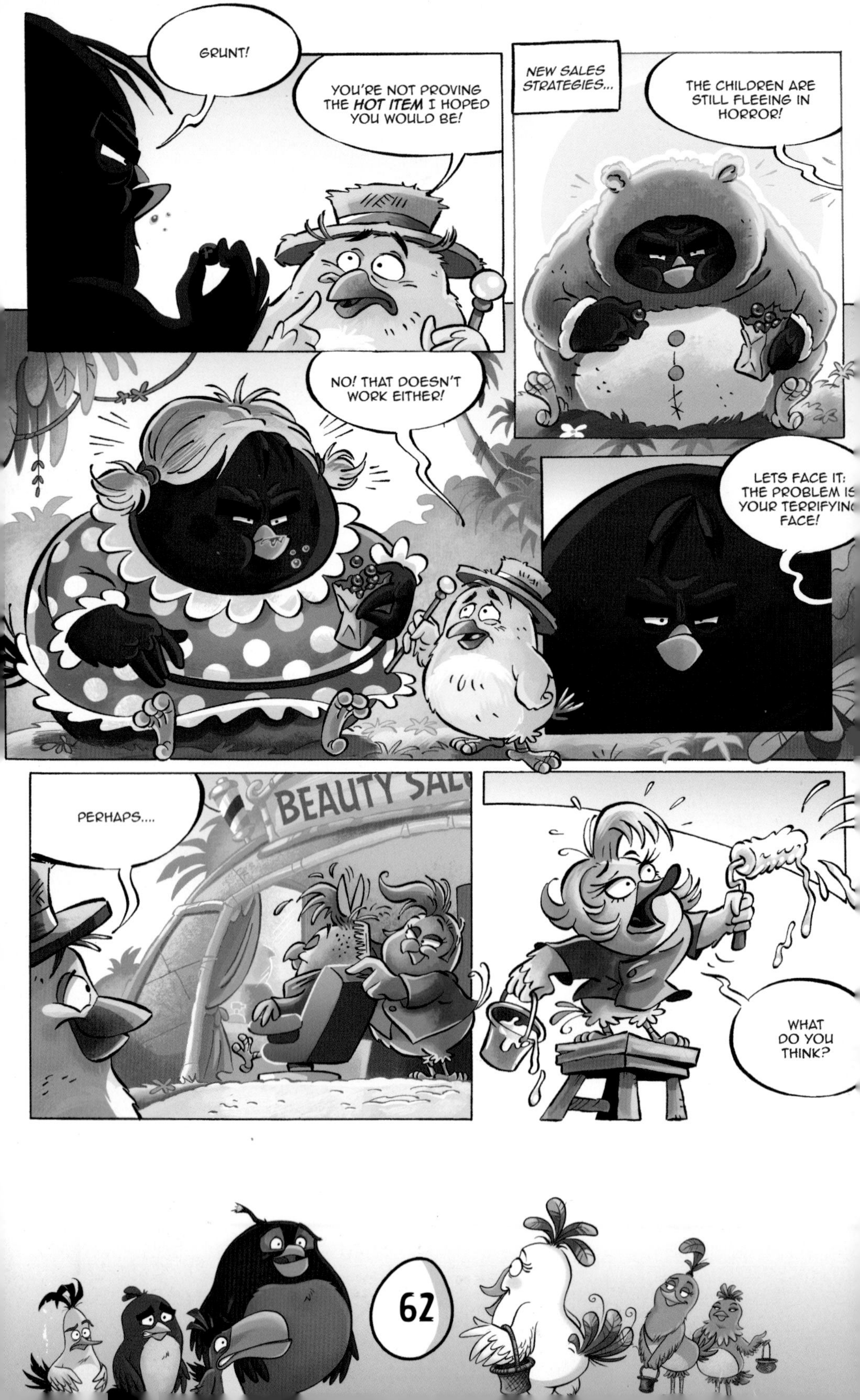
GRUNT!
YOU'RE NOT PROVING THE **HOT ITEM** I HOPED YOU WOULD BE!
NEW SALES STRATEGIES...
THE CHILDREN ARE STILL FLEEING IN HORROR!
NO! THAT DOESN'T WORK EITHER!
LETS FACE IT: THE PROBLEM IS YOUR TERRIFYING FACE!
PERHAPS....
BEAUTY SAL
WHAT DO YOU THINK?

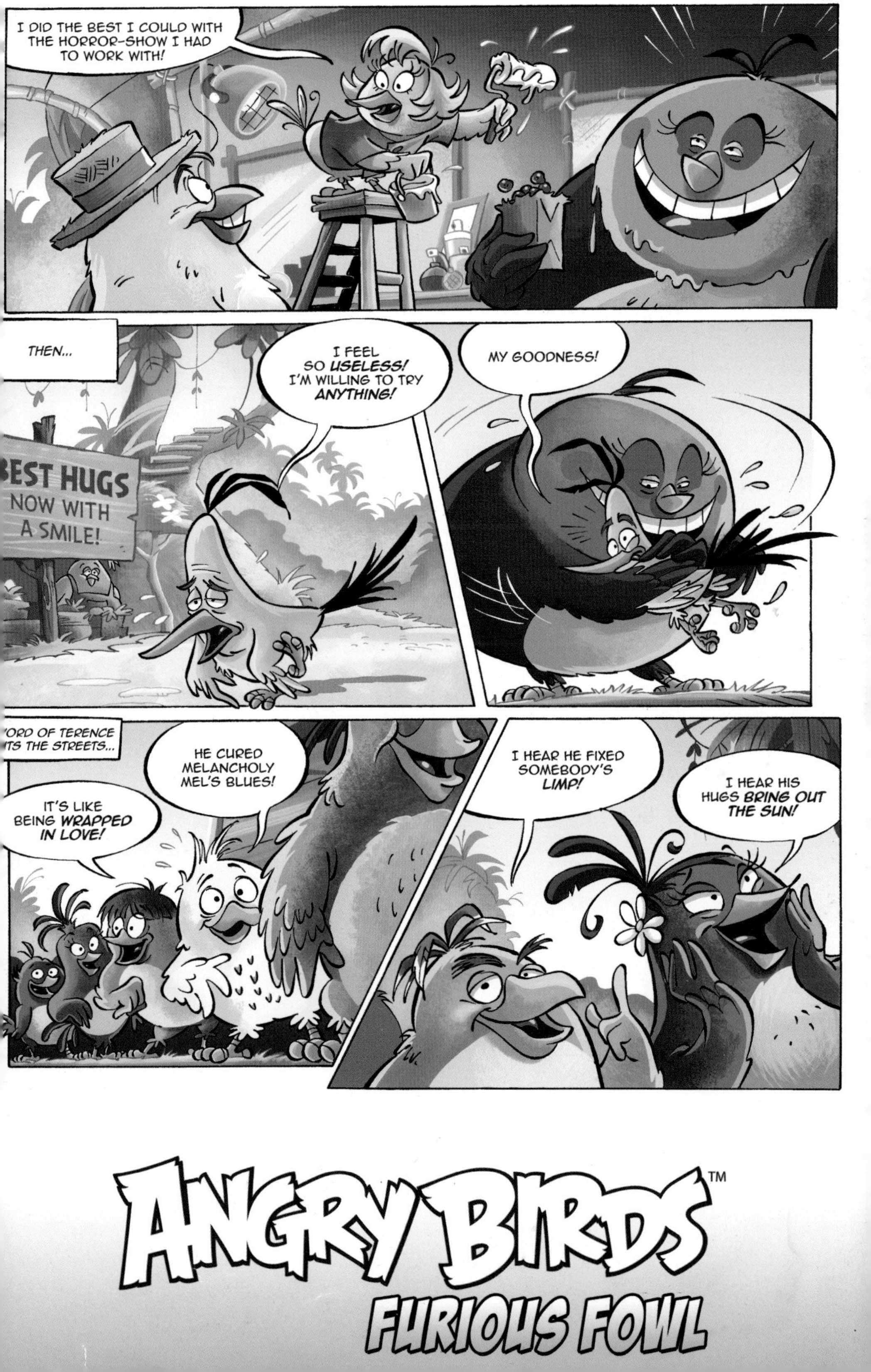
I DID THE BEST I COULD WITH THE HORROR-SHOW I HAD TO WORK WITH!
THEN...
I FEEL SO USELESS! I'M WILLING TO TRY ANYTHING!
EST HUGS
NOW WITH A SMILE!
MY GOODNESS!
ORD OF TERENCE
ITS THE STREETS...
IT'S LIKE BEING WRAPPED IN LOVE!
HE CURED MELANCHOLY MEL'S BLUES!
I HEAR HE FIXED SOMEBODY'S LIMP!
I HEAR HIS HUGS BRING OUT THE SUN!

ANGRY BIRDS™
FURIOUS FOWL

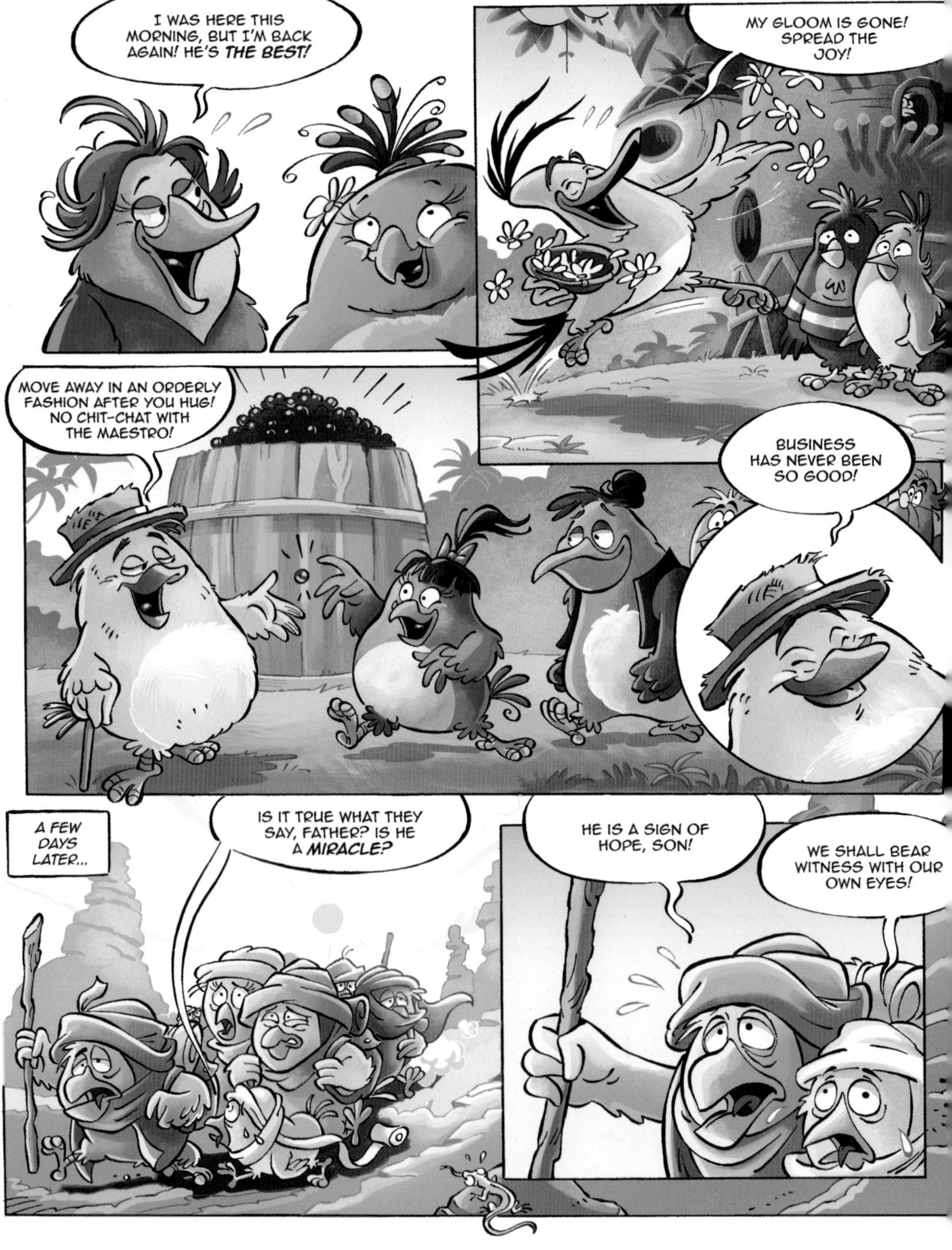
I WAS HERE THIS MORNING, BUT I'M BACK AGAIN! HE'S *THE BEST!*
MY GLOOM IS GONE! SPREAD THE JOY!
MOVE AWAY IN AN ORDERLY FASHION AFTER YOU HUG! NO CHIT-CHAT WITH THE MAESTRO!
BUSINESS HAS NEVER BEEN SO GOOD!
A FEW DAYS LATER...
IS IT TRUE WHAT THEY SAY, FATHER? IS HE A *MIRACLE?*
HE IS A SIGN OF HOPE, SON!
WE SHALL BEAR WITNESS WITH OUR OWN EYES!

PEOPLE COME FROM *FAR AND WIDE* TO GET THE TREATMENT!

DO NOT TOUCH THE MAESTRO'S BERRIES!

NOBODY WANTS A REPEAT OF THE INCIDENT LAST NIGHT!

TERENCE SURE IS *POPULAR!*

I KNOW TERENCE LIKES HIS BERRIES, BUT THAT TRADER MUST BE WORKING HIM TOO HARD!

DUDE! WHERE DO YOU THINK *YOU'RE* GOING?

ANGRY BIRDS™
FURIOUS FOWL

IT'S ALRIGHT! I'M A FRIEND OF HIS! I JUST...
NO CUTS, DUDE! I'VE BEEN HERE SINCE YESTERDAY MORNING!
OKAY, OKAY...
CHUCK! BOMB! WHAT ARE YOU DOING HERE?
WE MISS TERENCE, RED!
THIS IS THE ONLY WAY WE'RE ABLE TO SEE HIM NOW!
A LONG WAIT LATER...
I KNOW THESE PEOPLE HAVE COME A LONG WAY, BUT WE'RE YOUR FRIENDS!
YOU WANT TO BE HERE? YOU LIKE THE BERRIES?

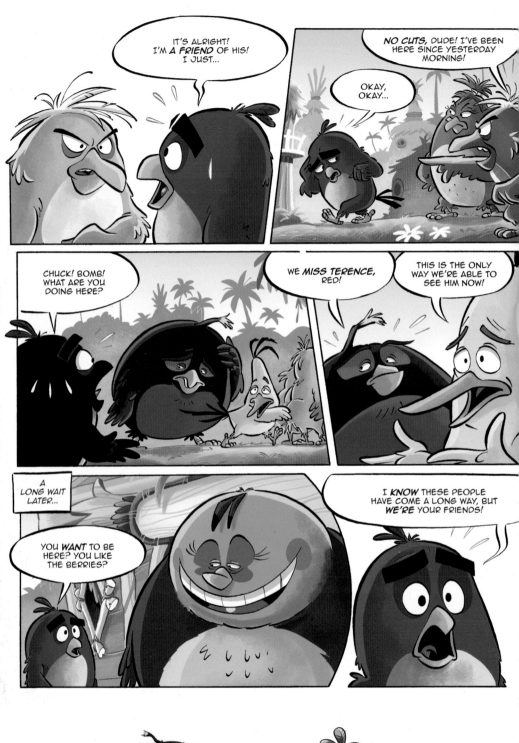

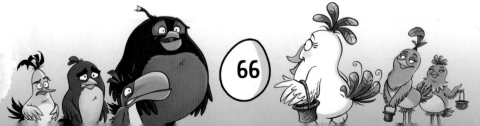

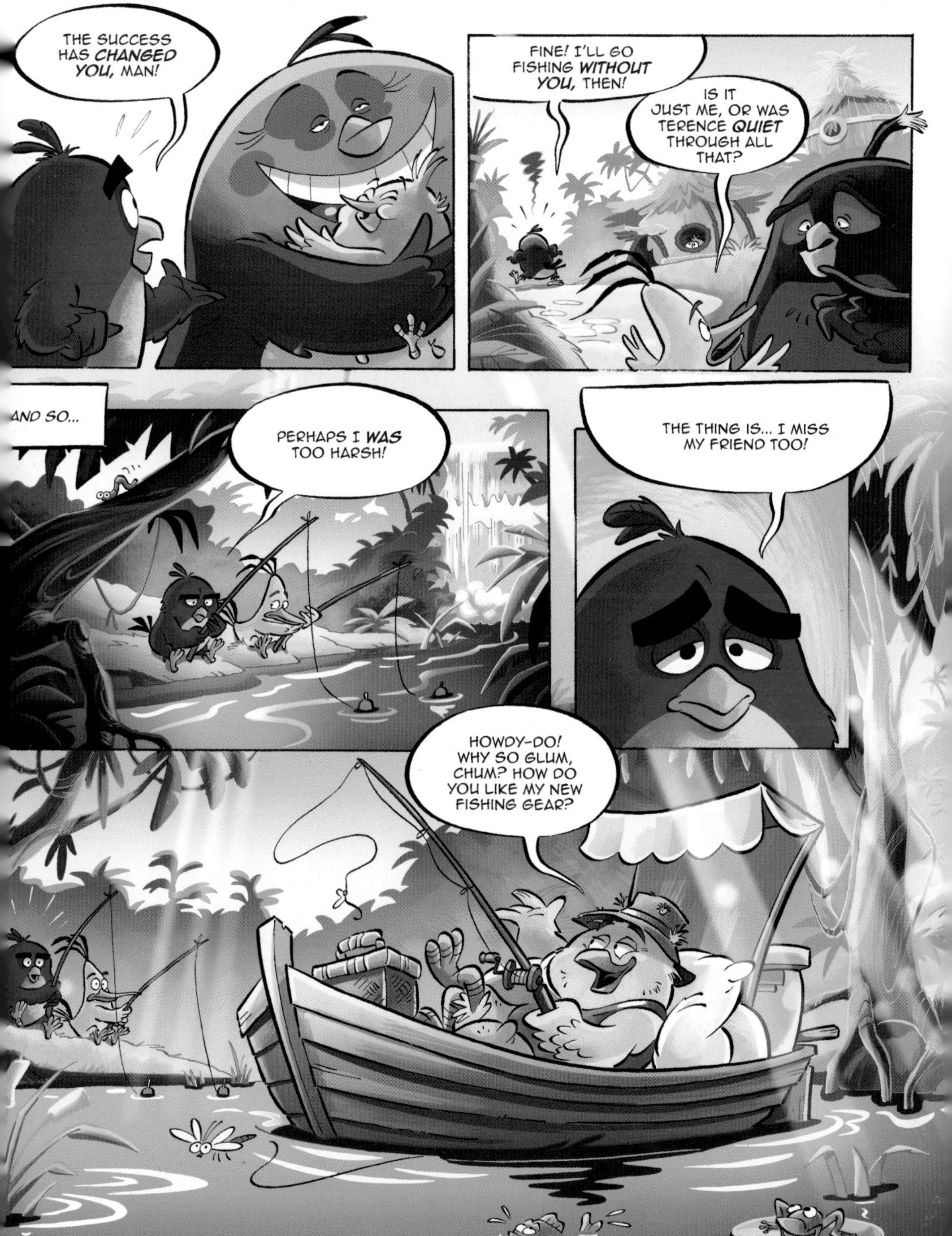
THE SUCCESS HAS CHANGED YOU, MAN!
FINE! I'LL GO FISHING WITHOUT YOU, THEN!
IS IT JUST ME, OR WAS TERENCE QUIET THROUGH ALL THAT?
AND SO...
PERHAPS I WAS TOO HARSH!
THE THING IS... I MISS MY FRIEND TOO!
HOWDY-DO! WHY SO GLUM, CHUM? HOW DO YOU LIKE MY NEW FISHING GEAR?

ANGRY BIRDS™

FURIOUS FOWL

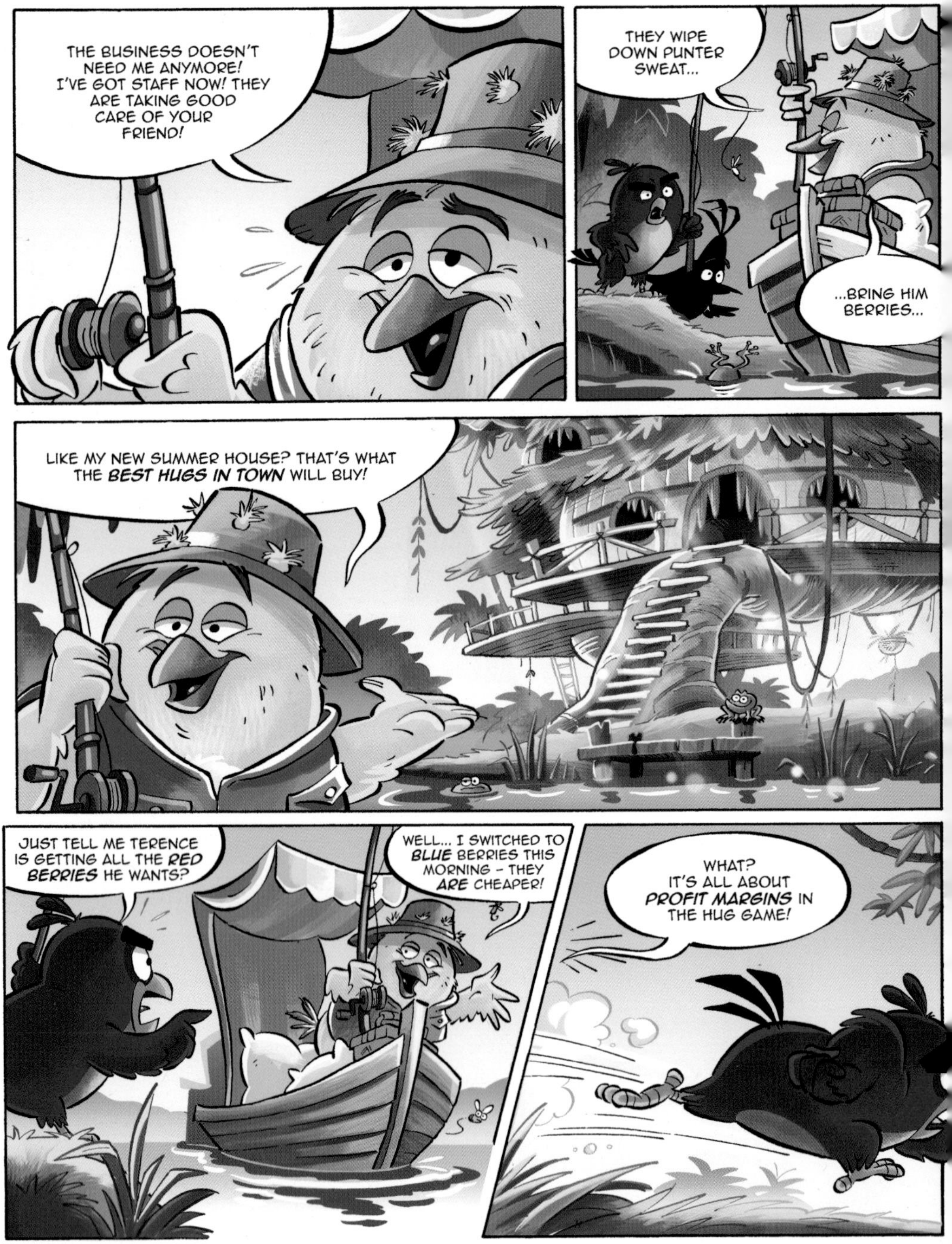
THE BUSINESS DOESN'T NEED ME ANYMORE! I'VE GOT STAFF NOW! THEY ARE TAKING GOOD CARE OF YOUR FRIEND!
THEY WIPE DOWN PUNTER SWEAT...
...BRING HIM BERRIES...
LIKE MY NEW SUMMER HOUSE? THAT'S WHAT THE ***BEST HUGS IN TOWN*** WILL BUY!
JUST TELL ME TERENCE IS GETTING ALL THE ***RED BERRIES*** HE WANTS?
WELL... I SWITCHED TO ***BLUE*** BERRIES THIS MORNING – THEY ***ARE*** CHEAPER!
WHAT? IT'S ALL ABOUT ***PROFIT MARGINS*** IN THE HUG GAME!

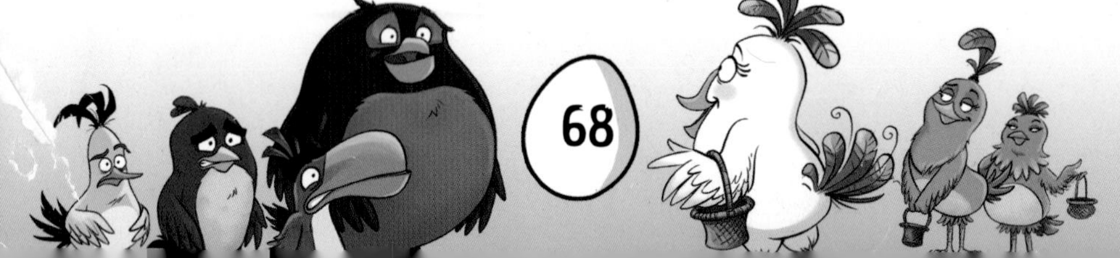

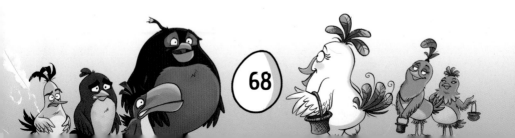

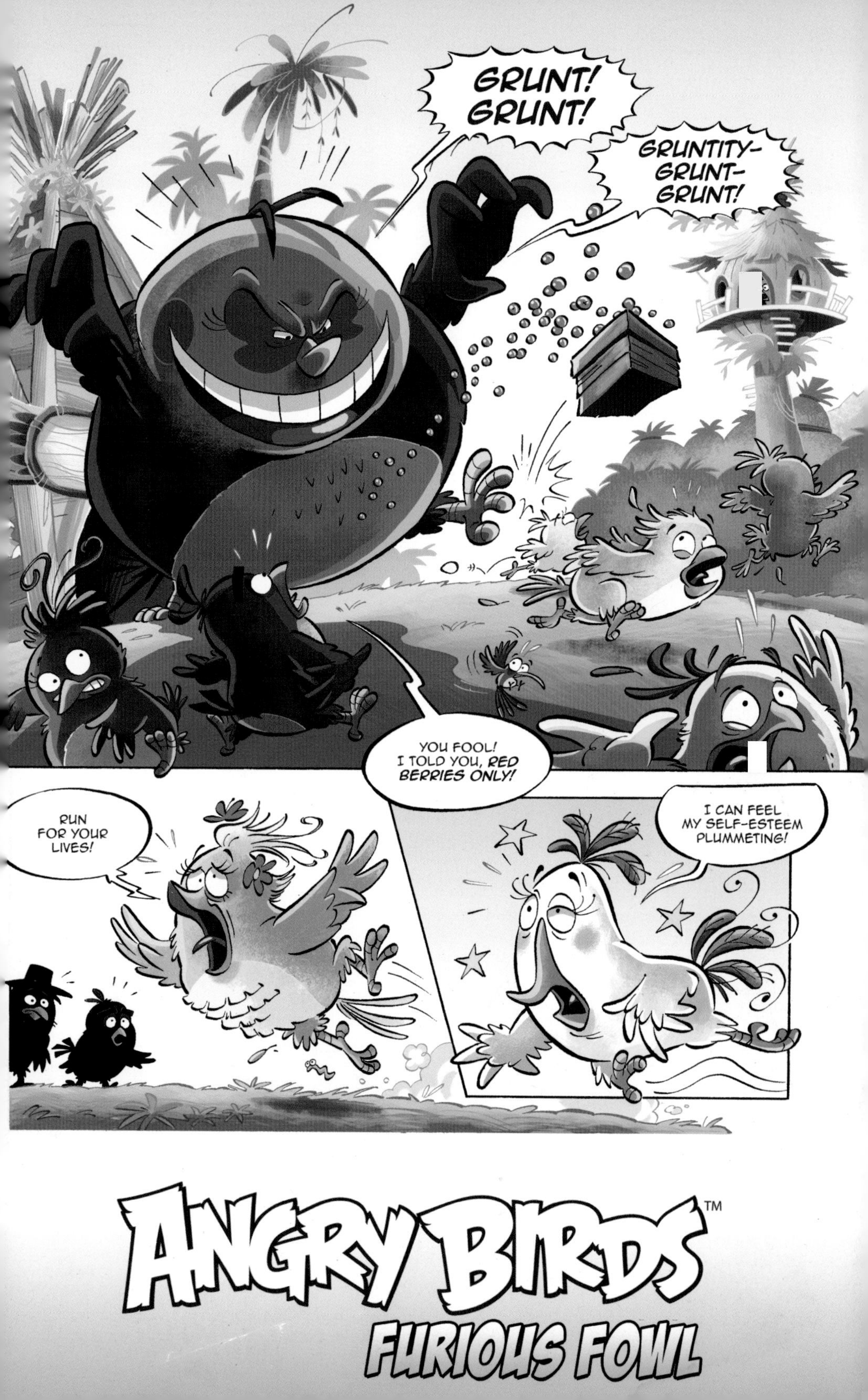
GRUNT! GRUNT!
GRUNTITY-GRUNT-GRUNT!
YOU FOOL! I TOLD YOU, RED BERRIES ONLY!
RUN FOR YOUR LIVES!
I CAN FEEL MY SELF-ESTEEM PLUMMETING!

ANGRY BIRDS™
FURIOUS FOWL

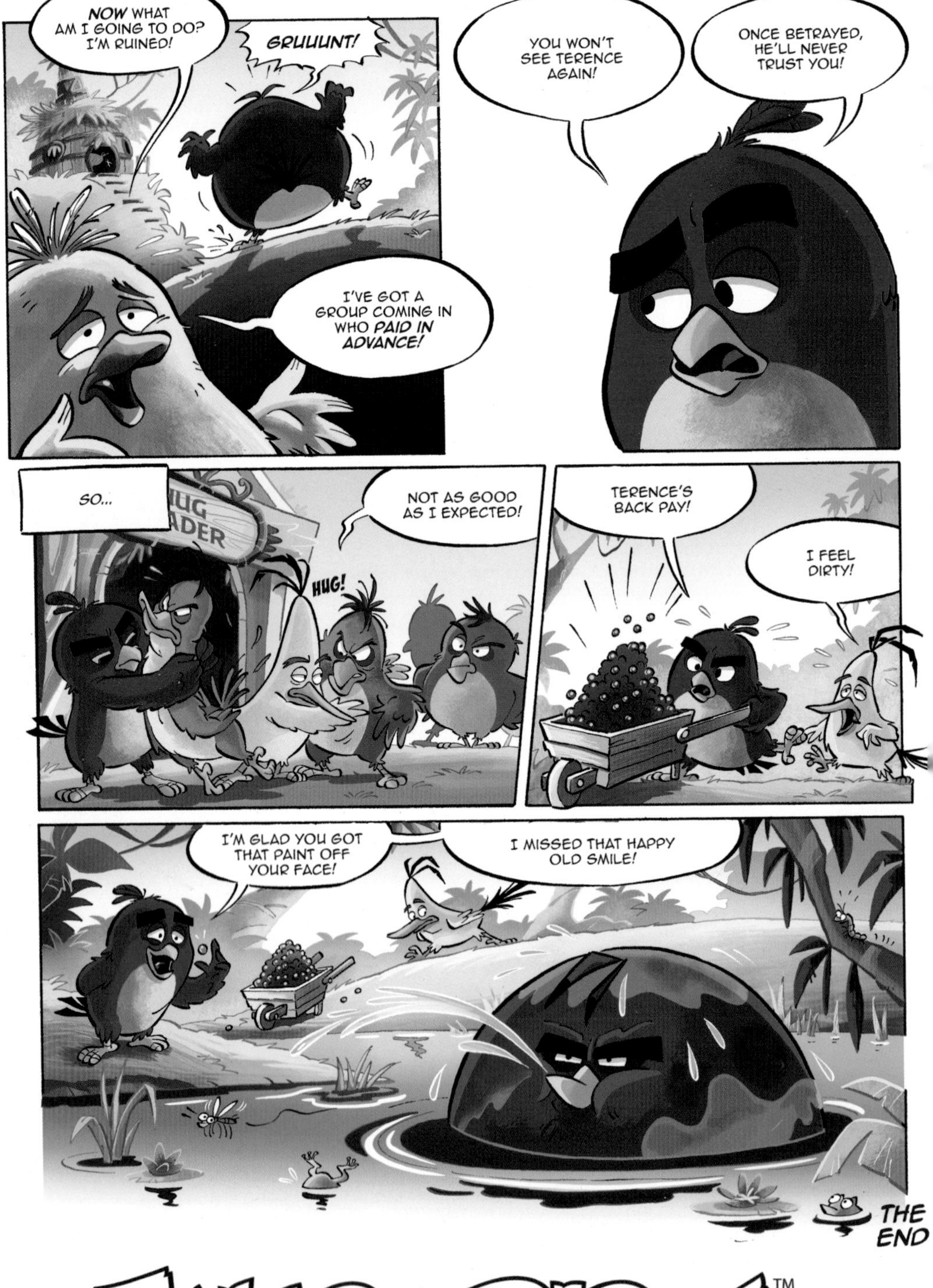

NOW WHAT AM I GOING TO DO? I'M RUINED!
GRUUUNT!
I'VE GOT A GROUP COMING IN WHO PAID IN ADVANCE!
YOU WON'T SEE TERENCE AGAIN!
ONCE BETRAYED, HE'LL NEVER TRUST YOU!
SO...
NOT AS GOOD AS I EXPECTED!
HUG!
TERENCE'S BACK PAY!
I FEEL DIRTY!
I'M GLAD YOU GOT THAT PAINT OFF YOUR FACE!
I MISSED THAT HAPPY OLD SMILE!
THE END

ANGRY BIRDS™

FURIOUS FOWL

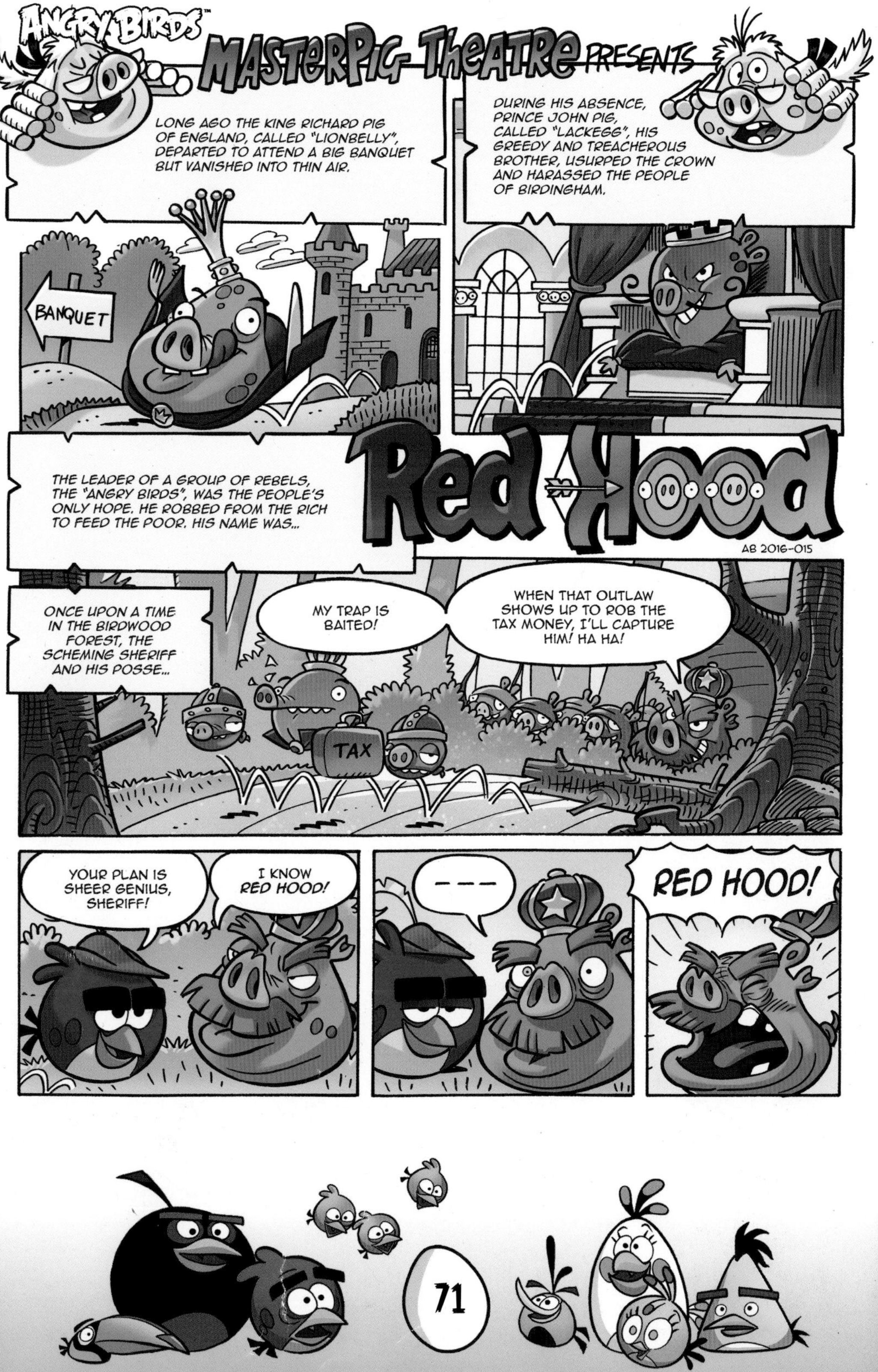
ANGRY BIRDS™
MASTERPIG THEATRE PRESENTS
LONG AGO THE KING RICHARD PIG OF ENGLAND, CALLED "LIONBELLY", DEPARTED TO ATTEND A BIG BANQUET BUT VANISHED INTO THIN AIR.
DURING HIS ABSENCE, PRINCE JOHN PIG, CALLED "LACKEGG", HIS GREEDY AND TREACHEROUS BROTHER, USURPED THE CROWN AND HARASSED THE PEOPLE OF BIRDINGHAM.
BANQUET
THE LEADER OF A GROUP OF REBELS, THE "ANGRY BIRDS", WAS THE PEOPLE'S ONLY HOPE. HE ROBBED FROM THE RICH TO FEED THE POOR. HIS NAME WAS...
Red Hood
AB 2016-015
ONCE UPON A TIME IN THE BIRDWOOD FOREST, THE SCHEMING SHERIFF AND HIS POSSE...
MY TRAP IS BAITED!
WHEN THAT OUTLAW SHOWS UP TO ROB THE TAX MONEY, I'LL CAPTURE HIM! HA HA!
TAX
YOUR PLAN IS SHEER GENIUS, SHERIFF!
I KNOW RED HOOD!
– – –
RED HOOD!

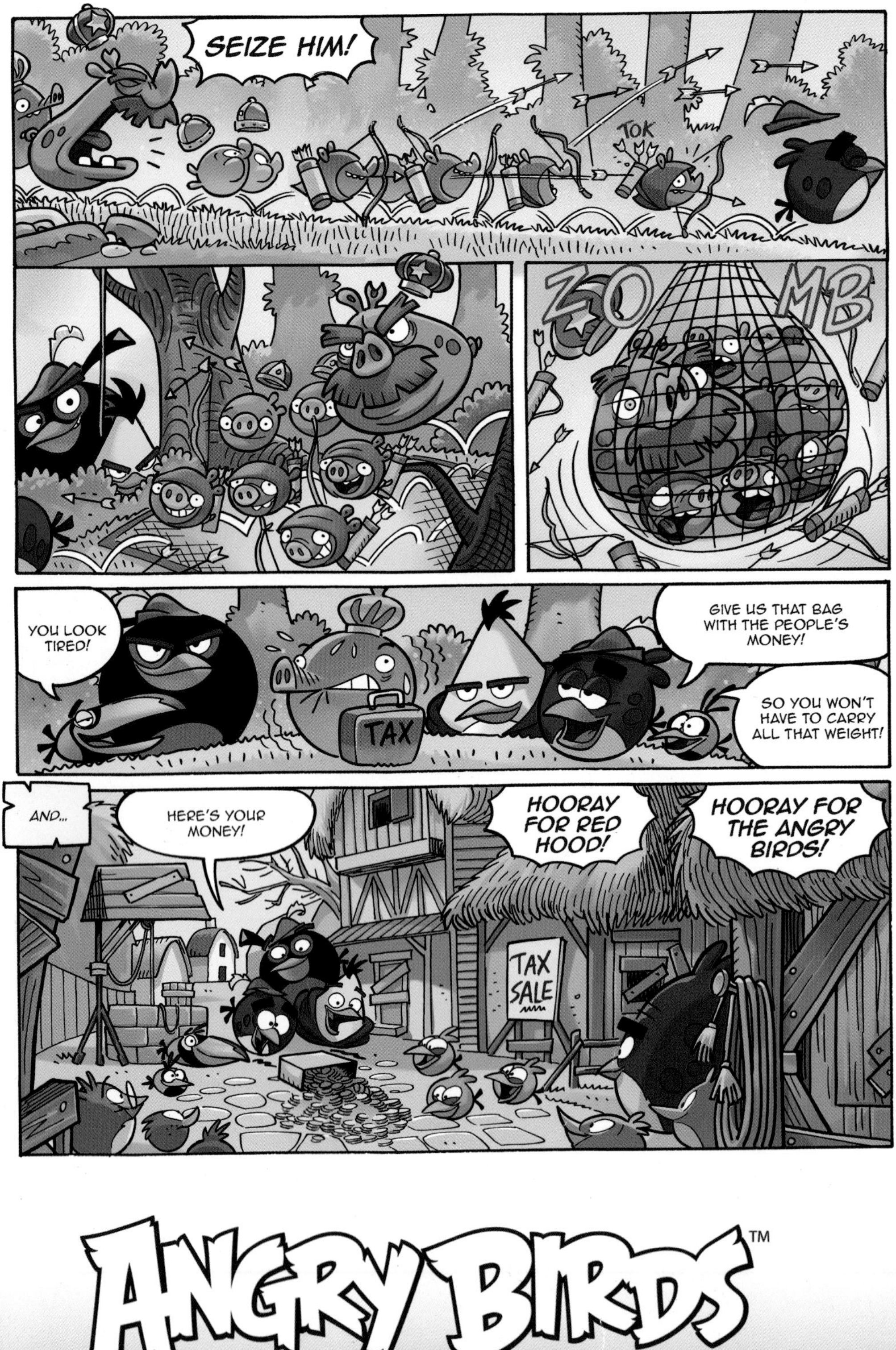
SEIZE HIM!
TOK
ZO
MB
YOU LOOK TIRED!
TAX
GIVE US THAT BAG WITH THE PEOPLE'S MONEY!
SO YOU WON'T HAVE TO CARRY ALL THAT WEIGHT!
AND...
HERE'S YOUR MONEY!
TAX SALE
HOORAY FOR RED HOOD!
HOORAY FOR THE ANGRY BIRDS!

ANGRY BIRDS™
FURIOUS FOWL

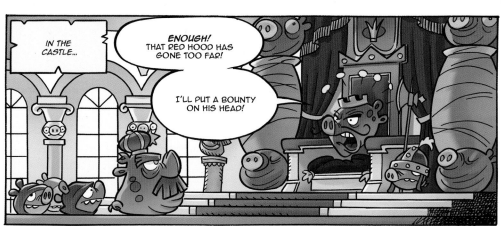

IN THE CASTLE...

ENOUGH! THAT RED HOOD HAS GONE TOO FAR!

I'LL PUT A BOUNTY ON HIS HEAD!

REWARD

10000 INGOTS FOR THE CAPTURE OF THE OUTLAW Red HOOD

BAM BAM BAM

?

BAM BAM BAM

TIT FOR TAT! GIVE OUR REGARDS TO THE PHONY KING OF ENGLAND!

AH! AH! AH!

REWARD

PIG LACKEGG THE PHONY KING OF ENGLAND

Red HOOD

!

THE PHONY KING OF ENGLAND! HA HA!

EH! EH!

AH!

73

...AND THE WHOLE VILLAGE IS SCREAMING IT, SIRE!
PIG LACKEGG THE PHONY KING OF ENGLAND
OH, THEY ARE, ARE THEY?
WELL! THEY'LL BE SCREAMING TO A DIFFERENT TUNE!
DOUBLE THE TAXES! TRIPLE THE TAXES!
AND IF YOU CANNOT PAY YOUR TAXES, YOU GO TO JAIL!
PRINCE JOHN SURE MADE GOOD ON HIS THREAT! THE POOR PEOPLE OF BIRDINGHAM WERE IN DEEP TROUBLE!
EH HEH!

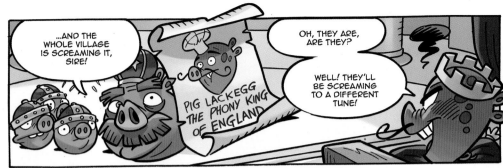

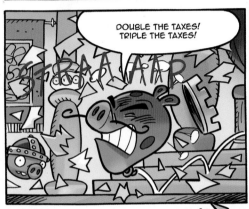

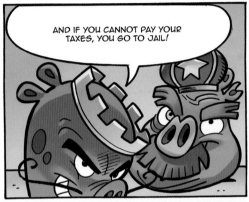

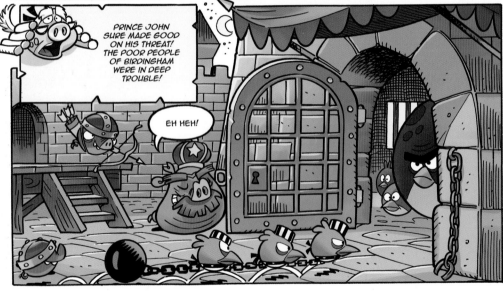

ANGRY BIRDS™

FURIOUS FOWL

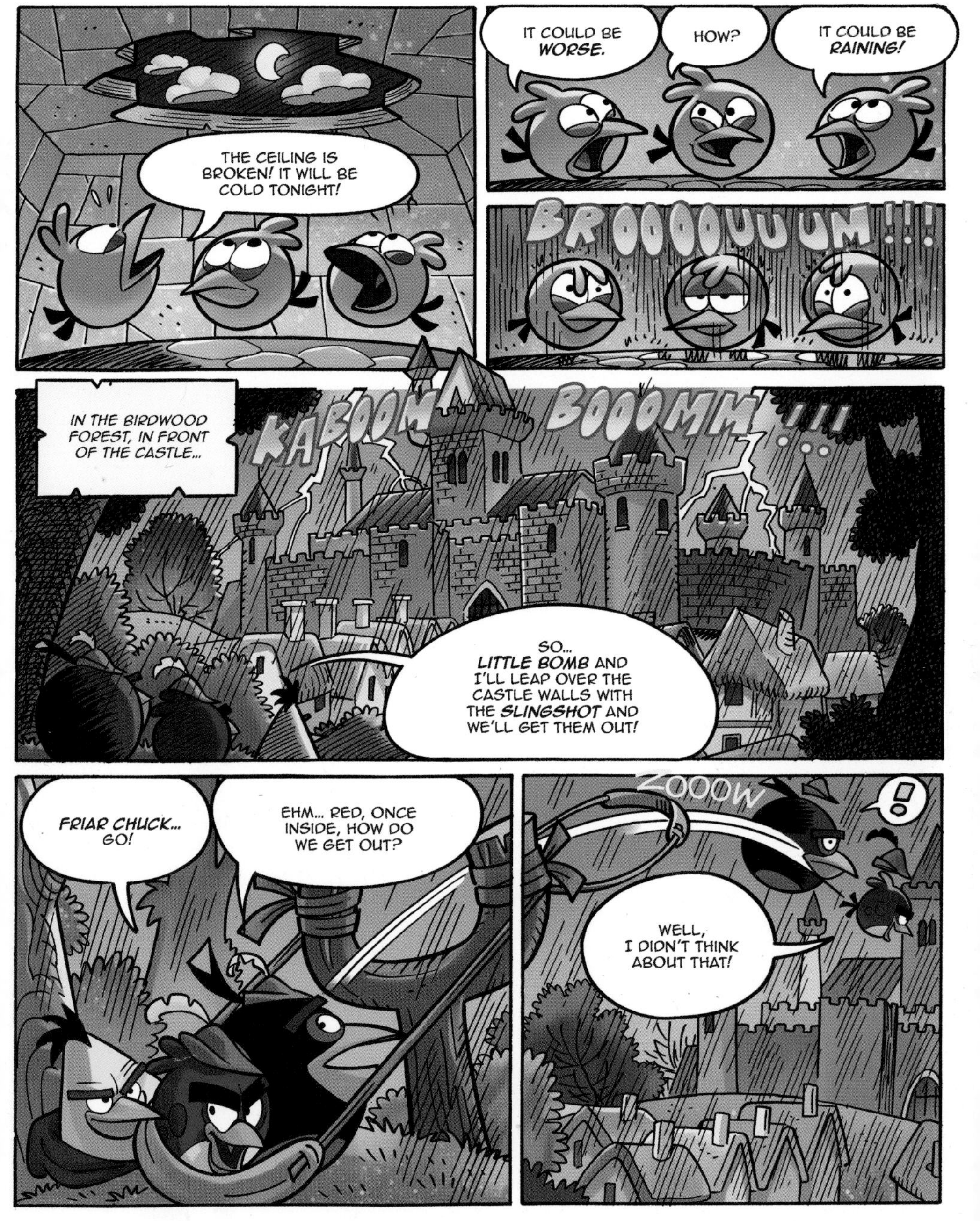
THE CEILING IS BROKEN! IT WILL BE COLD TONIGHT!
IT COULD BE WORSE.
HOW?
IT COULD BE RAINING!
BROOOOUUUUM!!!
IN THE BIRDWOOD FOREST, IN FRONT OF THE CASTLE...
KABOOM
BOOOMM!!!
SO... LITTLE BOMB AND I'LL LEAP OVER THE CASTLE WALLS WITH THE SLINGSHOT AND WE'LL GET THEM OUT!
FRIAR CHUCK... GO!
EHM... RED, ONCE INSIDE, HOW DO WE GET OUT?
ZOOOW
!
WELL, I DIDN'T THINK ABOUT THAT!

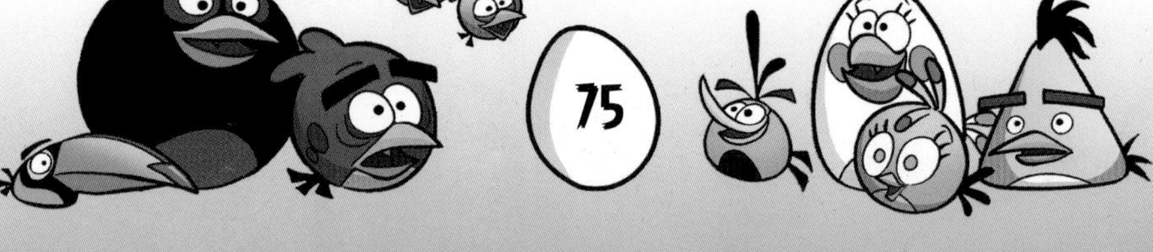

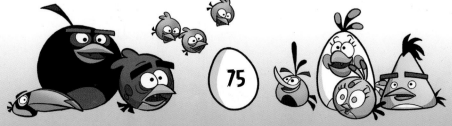

OH, MATILDA, WILL I EVER FIND SOMEONE WHO LOVES ME?
BUT, OF COURSE, MY DEAR MAID STELLA!
BUT WHEN? WHEN?
OH, PATIENCE, MY DEAR! PATIENCE!
YOUR PRINCE CHARMING WILL LEAP IN THROUGH THE WINDOW WHEN YOU LEAST EXPECT HIM...
OUT OF THE WAY!
!
?

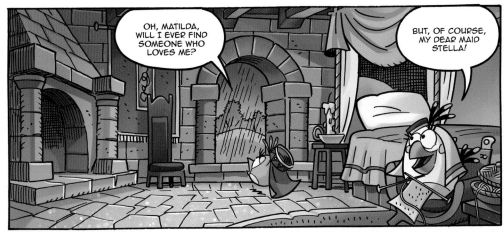

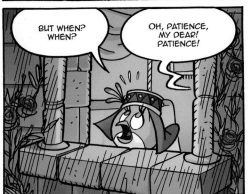

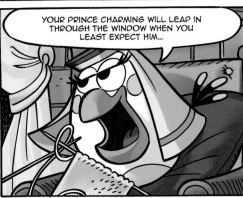

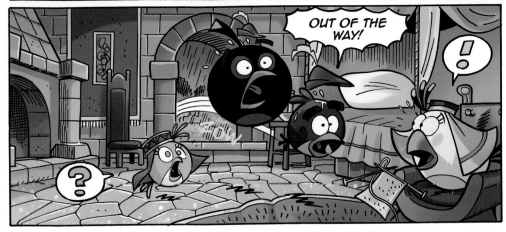

ANGRY BIRDS™
FURIOUS FOWL

BAMM
BOOM
OH, MY PRINCE CHARMING!!!
EHM... RED!
AND YOUR NAME, PRINCE BLACK?
BOMB, LITTLE BOMB!
ARE YOU MARRIED?
EH? OH... NOT... BUT...
SORRY, NOW WE HAVE TO LEAVE, DON'T WE, RED?
RED?
RED?
RED!
YEP! WE HAVE TO GO...
PLEASE, LADY MATILDA, BOMB WOULD LIKE YOUR VEIL AS THE TOKEN OF YOUR LOVE!
WHAT? NO, I DON'T!

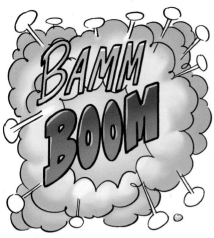

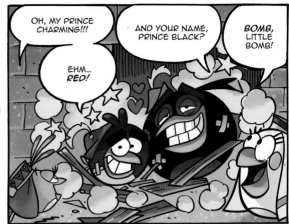

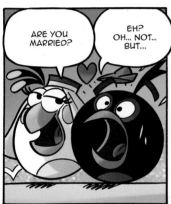

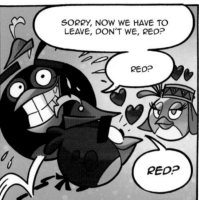

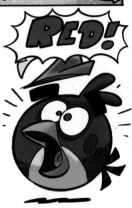

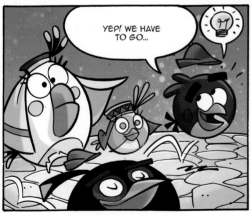

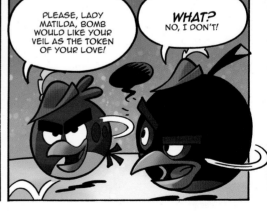

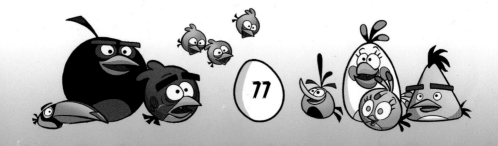

OH, SHERIFF, MAID STELLA FEARS FOR A JAILBREAK TONIGHT!
RED HOOD SURE WILL TRY TO GET HIS FRIENDS OUT!
ZZZ... WHY, LADY MATILDA?
BUT THE SHERIFF IS TOO CRAFTY, TOO CLEVER AND TOO SMART FOR THE LIKES OF HIM, SAY I!
YA HEAR THAT, BIRDS? SHE SURE KNOWS A GOOD PIG WHEN SHE SEES ONE!
SPLOSH
RED HOOD WON'T HAVE A CHANCE IF HE SHOWS UP!

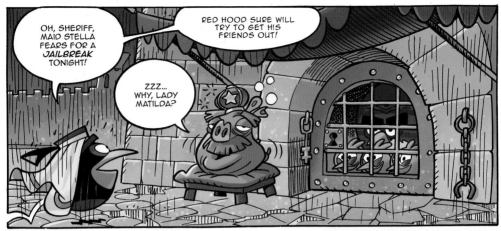

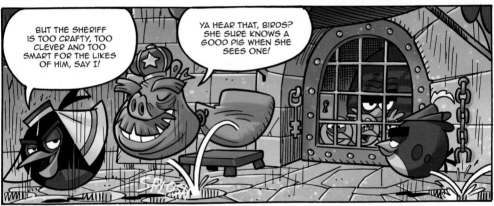

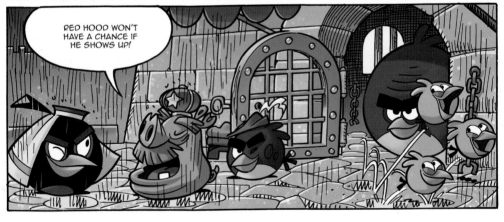

ANGRY BIRDS™
FURIOUS FOWL

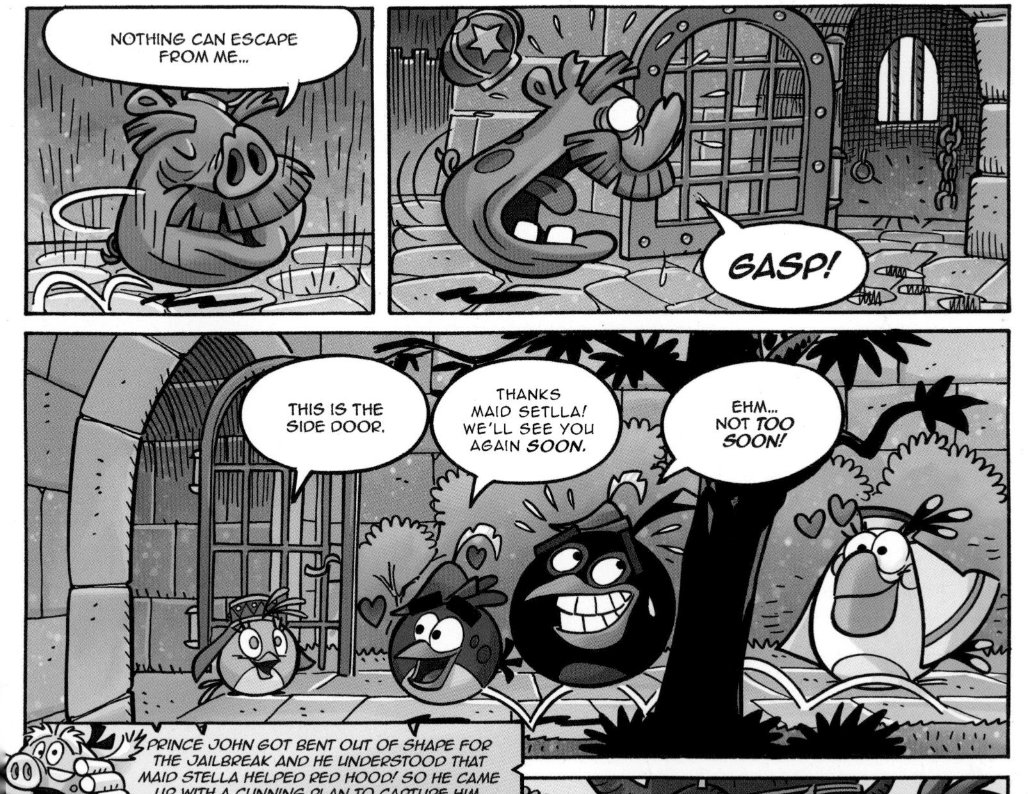
NOTHING CAN ESCAPE FROM ME...
GASP!
THIS IS THE SIDE DOOR.
THANKS MAID SETLLA! WE'LL SEE YOU AGAIN SOON.
EHM... NOT TOO SOON!
PRINCE JOHN GOT BENT OUT OF SHAPE FOR THE JAILBREAK AND HE UNDERSTOOD THAT MAID STELLA HELPED RED HOOD! SO HE CAME UP WITH A CUNNING PLAN TO CAPTURE HIM.
RED! RED!
WHAT'S HAPPENED, FRIAR CHUCK?
CHEF

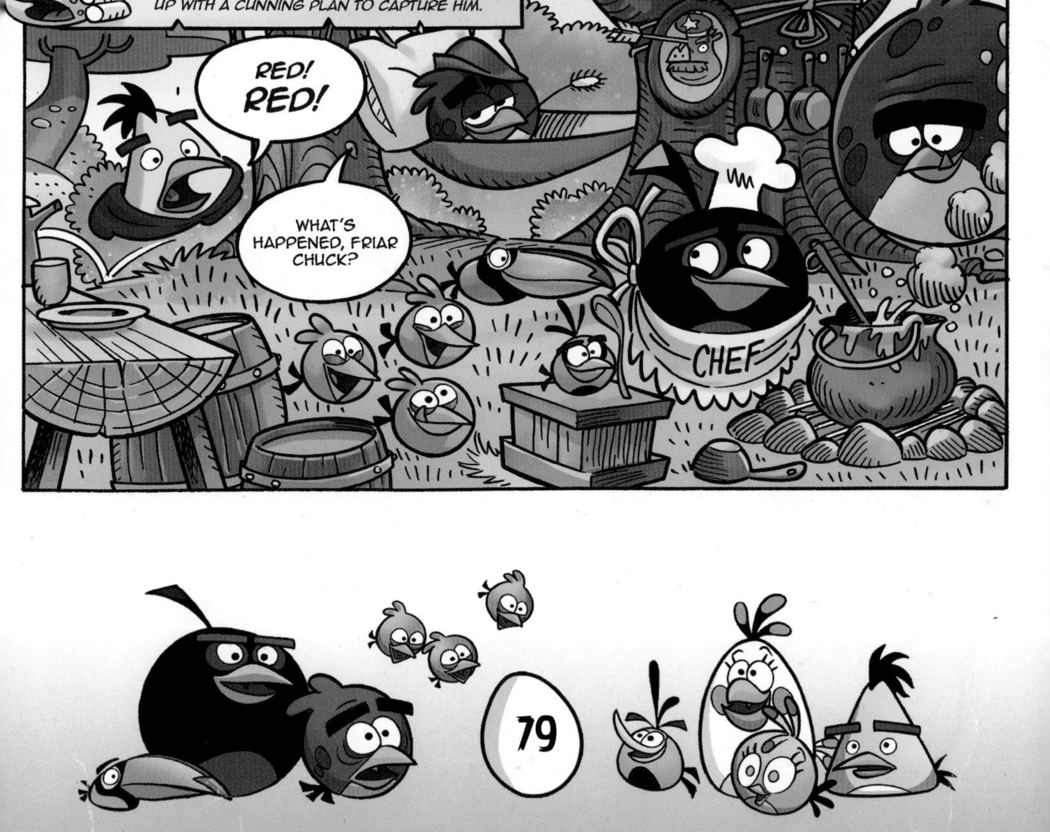

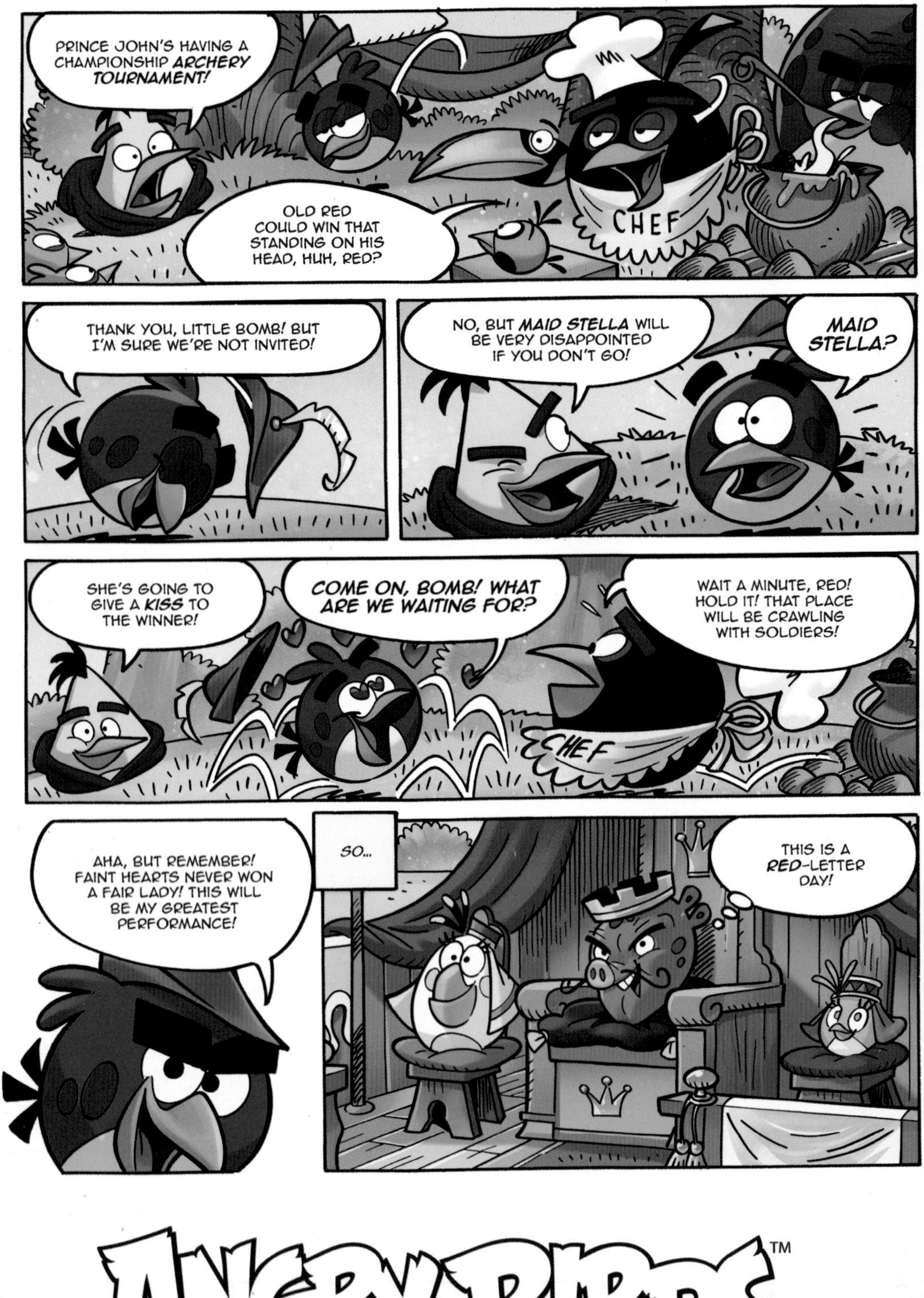
PRINCE JOHN'S HAVING A CHAMPIONSHIP ARCHERY TOURNAMENT!
OLD RED COULD WIN THAT STANDING ON HIS HEAD, HUH, RED?
CHEF
THANK YOU, LITTLE BOMB! BUT I'M SURE WE'RE NOT INVITED!
NO, BUT MAID STELLA WILL BE VERY DISAPPOINTED IF YOU DON'T GO!
MAID STELLA?
SHE'S GOING TO GIVE A KISS TO THE WINNER!
COME ON, BOMB! WHAT ARE WE WAITING FOR?
WAIT A MINUTE, RED! HOLD IT! THAT PLACE WILL BE CRAWLING WITH SOLDIERS!
CHEF
AHA, BUT REMEMBER! FAINT HEARTS NEVER WON A FAIR LADY! THIS WILL BE MY GREATEST PERFORMANCE!
SO...
THIS IS A RED-LETTER DAY!

ANGRY BIRDS™

FURIOUS FOWL

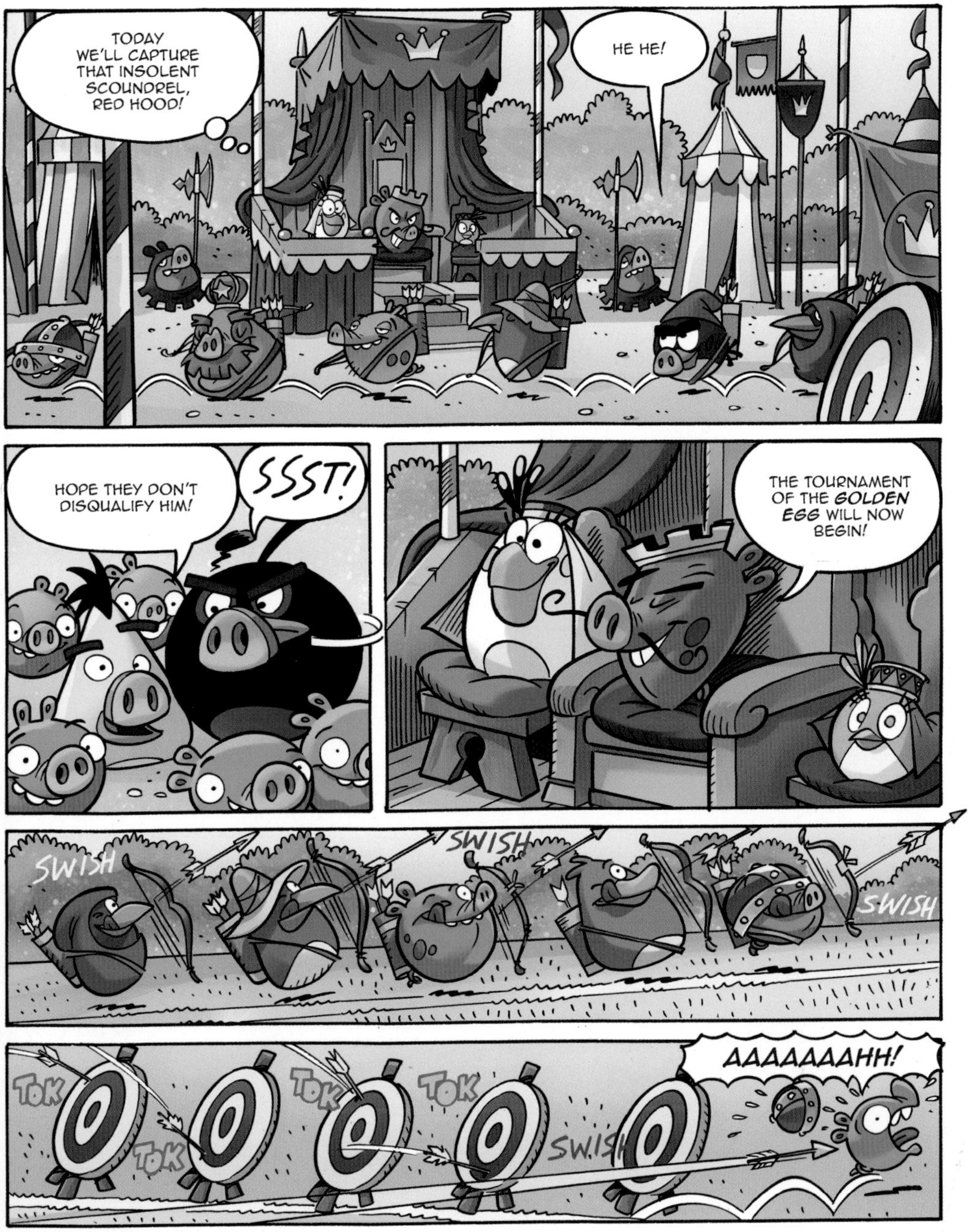
TODAY WE'LL CAPTURE THAT INSOLENT SCOUNDREL, RED HOOD!
HE HE!
HOPE THEY DON'T DISQUALIFY HIM!
SSST!
THE TOURNAMENT OF THE GOLDEN EGG WILL NOW BEGIN!
SWISH
SWISH
SWISH
TOK
TOK
TOK
TOK
SWISH
AAAAAAAHH!

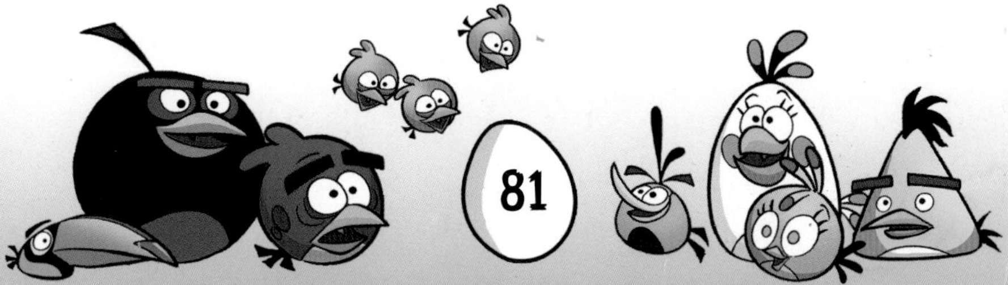

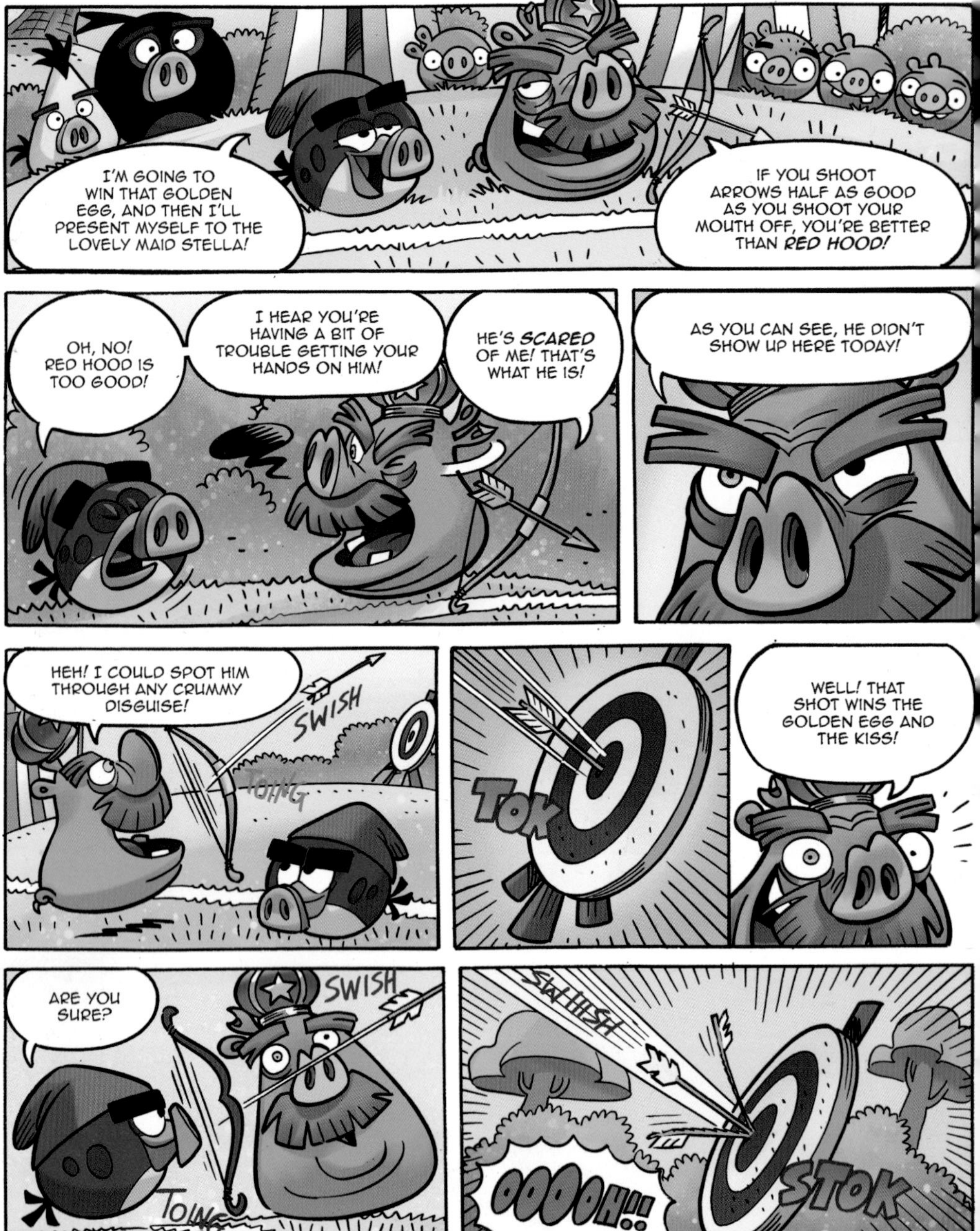
I'M GOING TO WIN THAT GOLDEN EGG, AND THEN I'LL PRESENT MYSELF TO THE LOVELY MAID STELLA!
IF YOU SHOOT ARROWS HALF AS GOOD AS YOU SHOOT YOUR MOUTH OFF, YOU'RE BETTER THAN RED HOOD!
OH, NO! RED HOOD IS TOO GOOD!
I HEAR YOU'RE HAVING A BIT OF TROUBLE GETTING YOUR HANDS ON HIM!
HE'S SCARED OF ME! THAT'S WHAT HE IS!
AS YOU CAN SEE, HE DIDN'T SHOW UP HERE TODAY!
HEH! I COULD SPOT HIM THROUGH ANY CRUMMY DISGUISE!
SWISH
TOING
TOK
WELL! THAT SHOT WINS THE GOLDEN EGG AND THE KISS!
ARE YOU SURE?
SWISH
TOING
SWIIISH
OOOOH!!
STOK

ANGRY BIRDS™
FURIOUS FOWL

YEAH! *RED* DID IT! HE DID IT! HE DID IT!

SHUSH!

AND NOW, I NAME YOU THE *WINNER!*

OR MORE APPROPRIATELY... THE *LOSER!*

ZAK

SEIZE HIM!

POM!
BOM!
THUMP!
BAM!

HERE'S HOW THE TRAITORS TO THE CROWN WILL END!

THAT CROWN BELONGS TO *KING RICHARD PIG!*

LONG BINGE KING RICHARD!

LONG BINGE KING RICHARD!

ENOUGH! I AM THE KING!

I AM THE KING!

RED HOOD WAS IMPRISONED IN THE LOWEST, FARTHEST PRISON CELL IN THE CASTLE, BUT HE WASN'T ALONE!

COUGH! COUGH!

UH? WHO'S THAT?

I'M *KING RICHARD!* HAVE YOU GOT ANYTHING TO EAT?

PRINCE JOHN IMPRISONED ME *BEFORE* THE BANQUET! SIGH!

OH! NOW WE GET OUT, YOUR MAJESTY!

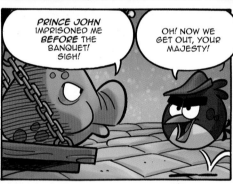

PIG, DO YOU LIKE BEING IN *JAIL?*

I'M NOT IN JAIL! YOU ARE!

ARE YOU SURE? I CAN'T GET OUT, BUT YOU CAN'T COME IN, SO YOU ARE IN JAIL TOO!

— — —

AH! I CAN COME IN! I HAVE *THE KEY!*

SCREEK

HERE!

ANGRY BIRDS™
FURIOUS FOWL

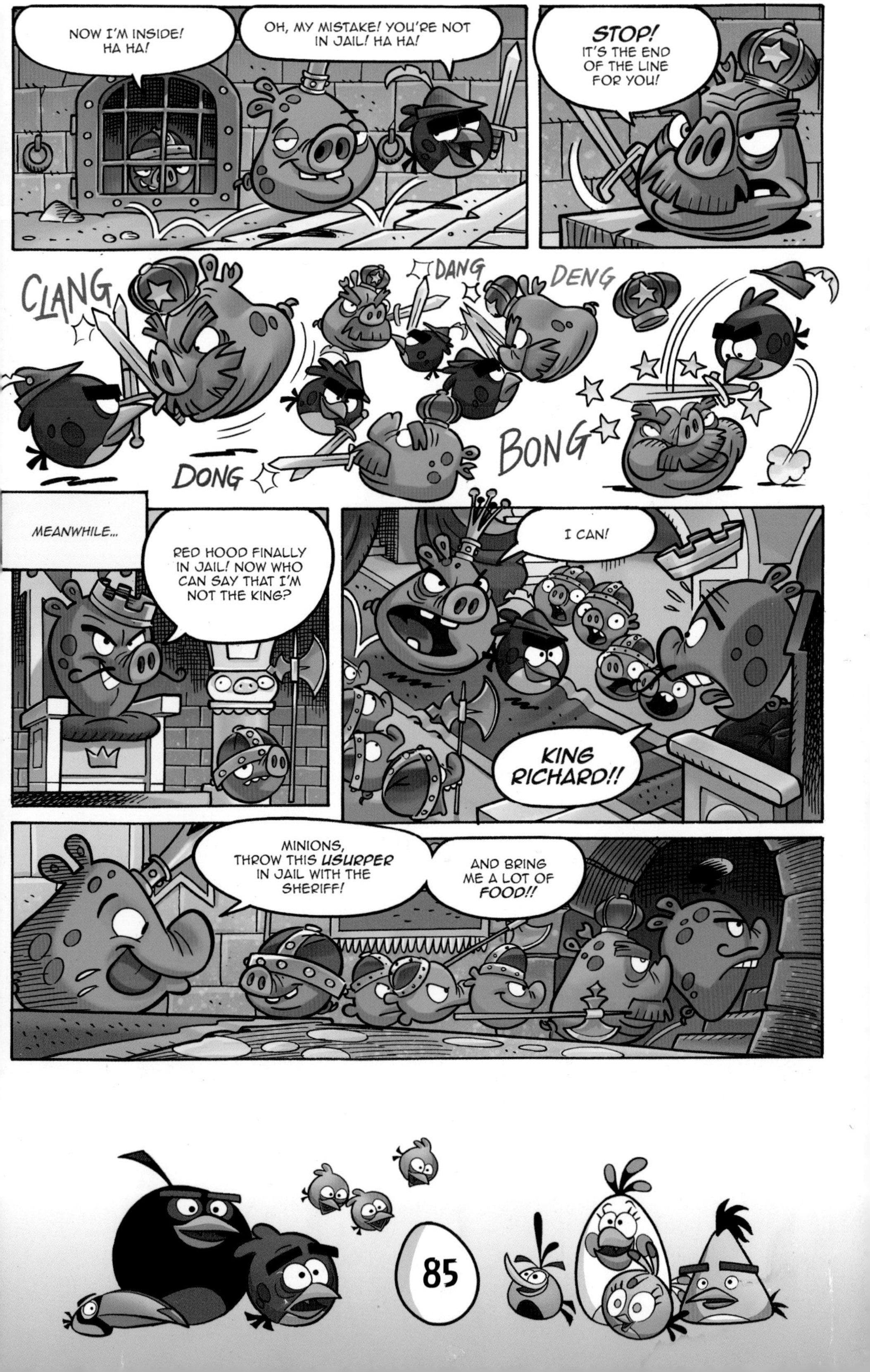
NOW I'M INSIDE! HA HA!
OH, MY MISTAKE! YOU'RE NOT IN JAIL! HA HA!
STOP! IT'S THE END OF THE LINE FOR YOU!
CLANG
DANG
DENG
DONG
BONG
MEANWHILE...
RED HOOD FINALLY IN JAIL! NOW WHO CAN SAY THAT I'M NOT THE KING?
I CAN!
KING RICHARD!!
MINIONS, THROW THIS USURPER IN JAIL WITH THE SHERIFF!
AND BRING ME A LOT OF FOOD!!

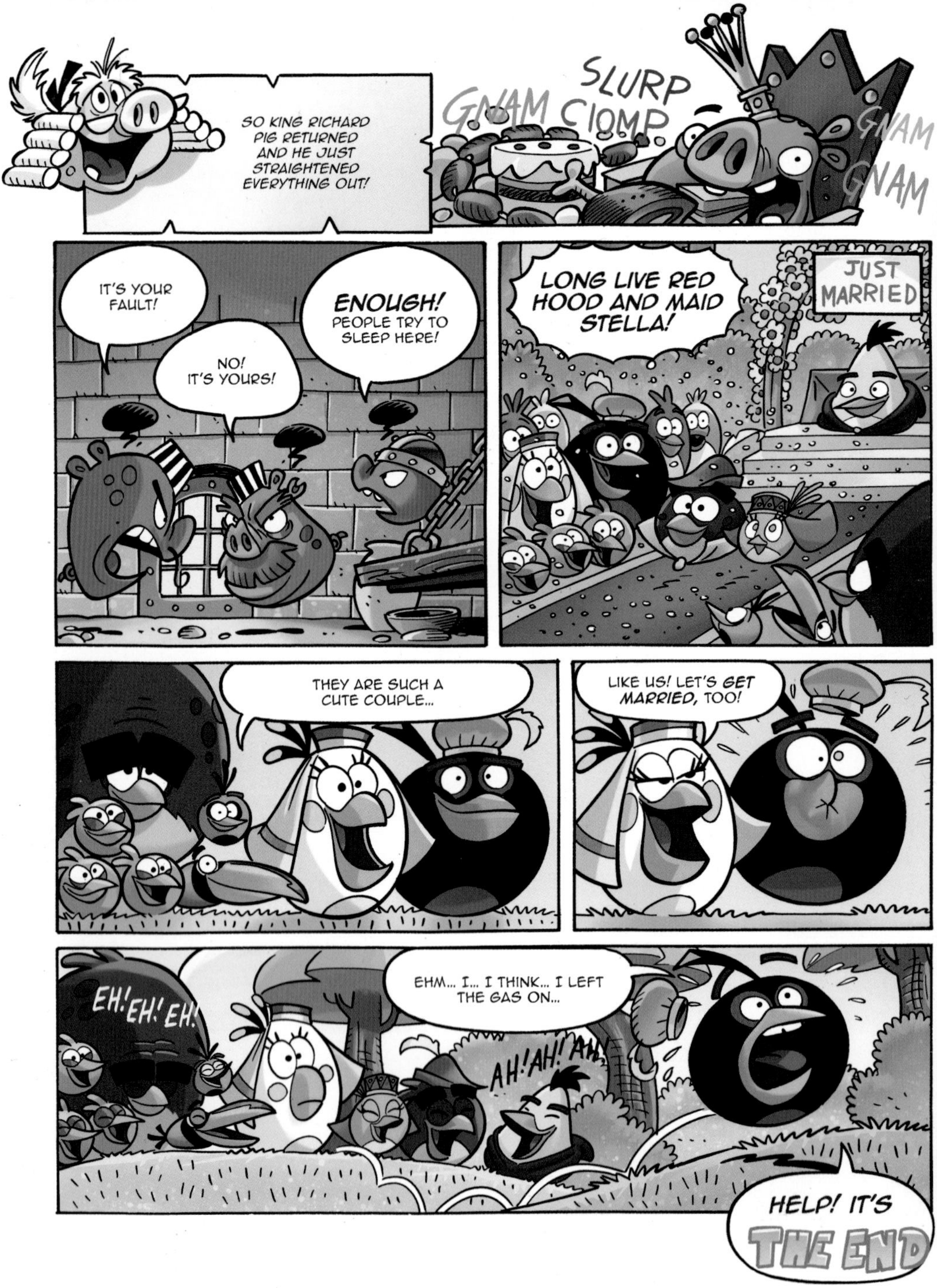
SO KING RICHARD PIG RETURNED AND HE JUST STRAIGHTENED EVERYTHING OUT!
GNAM CIOMP
SLURP
GNAM GNAM
IT'S YOUR FAULT!
NO! IT'S YOURS!
ENOUGH! PEOPLE TRY TO SLEEP HERE!
LONG LIVE RED HOOD AND MAID STELLA!
JUST MARRIED
THEY ARE SUCH A CUTE COUPLE...
LIKE US! LET'S GET MARRIED, TOO!
EH! EH! EH!
EHM... I... I THINK... I LEFT THE GAS ON...
AH! AH! AH!
HELP! IT'S
THE END

ANGRY BIRDS™
FURIOUS FOWL

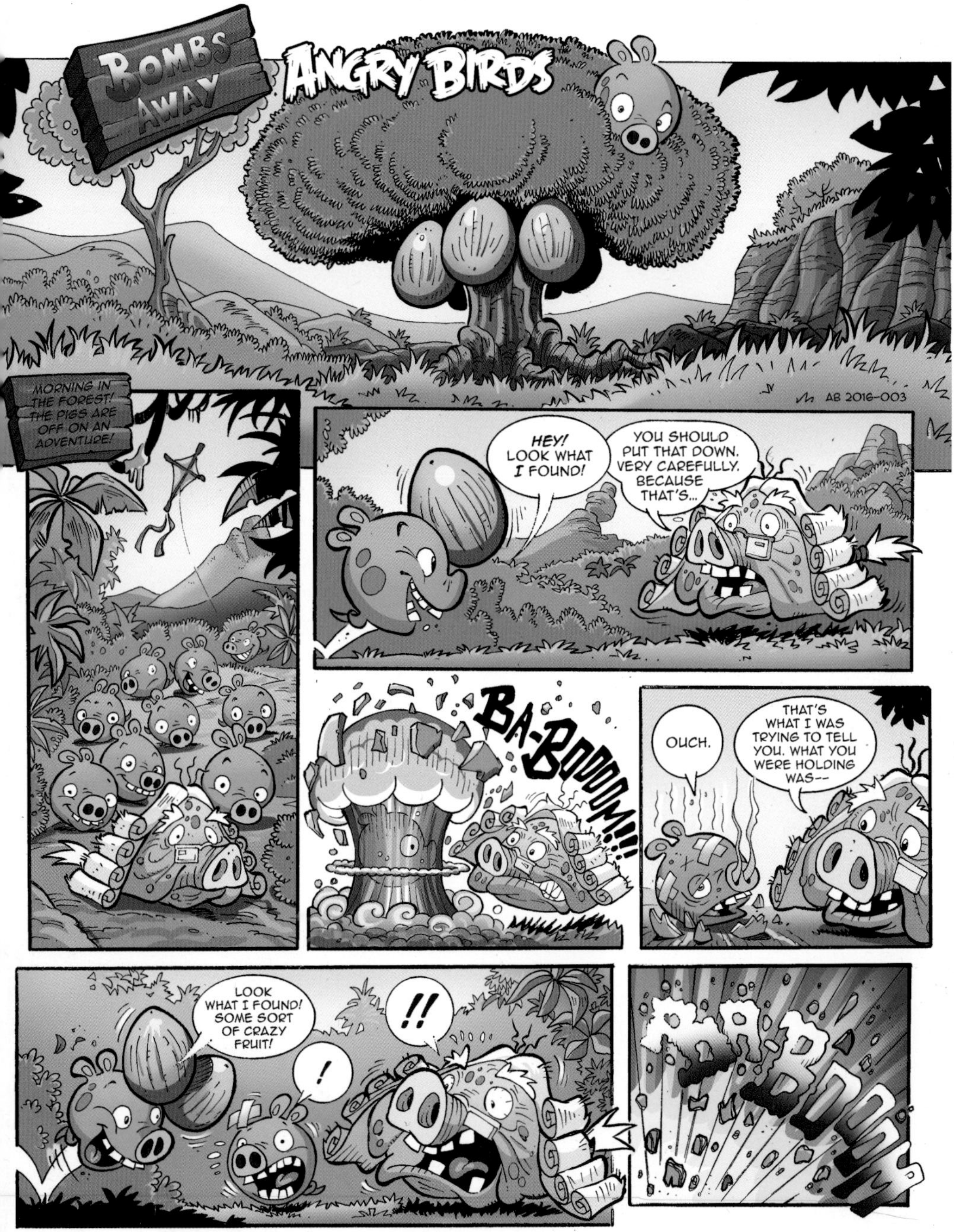
BOMBS AWAY
ANGRY BIRDS
AB 2016-003
MORNING IN THE FOREST! THE PIGS ARE OFF ON AN ADVENTURE!
HEY! LOOK WHAT I FOUND!
YOU SHOULD PUT THAT DOWN. VERY CAREFULLY. BECAUSE THAT'S...
BA-BOOOOM!!!
OUCH.
THAT'S WHAT I WAS TRYING TO TELL YOU. WHAT YOU WERE HOLDING WAS--
LOOK WHAT I FOUND! SOME SORT OF CRAZY FRUIT!
!
!!
KA-BOOOM

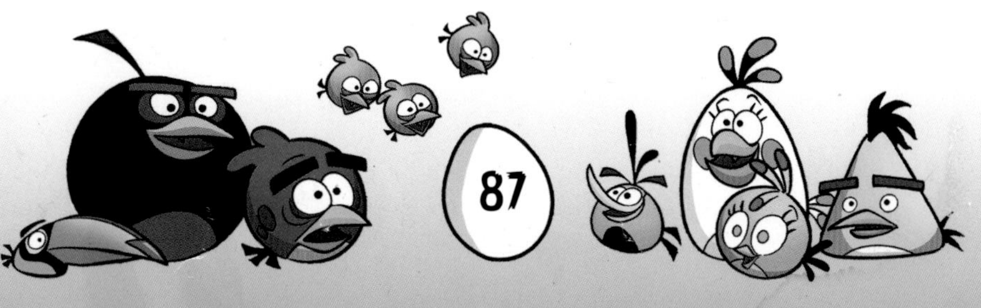

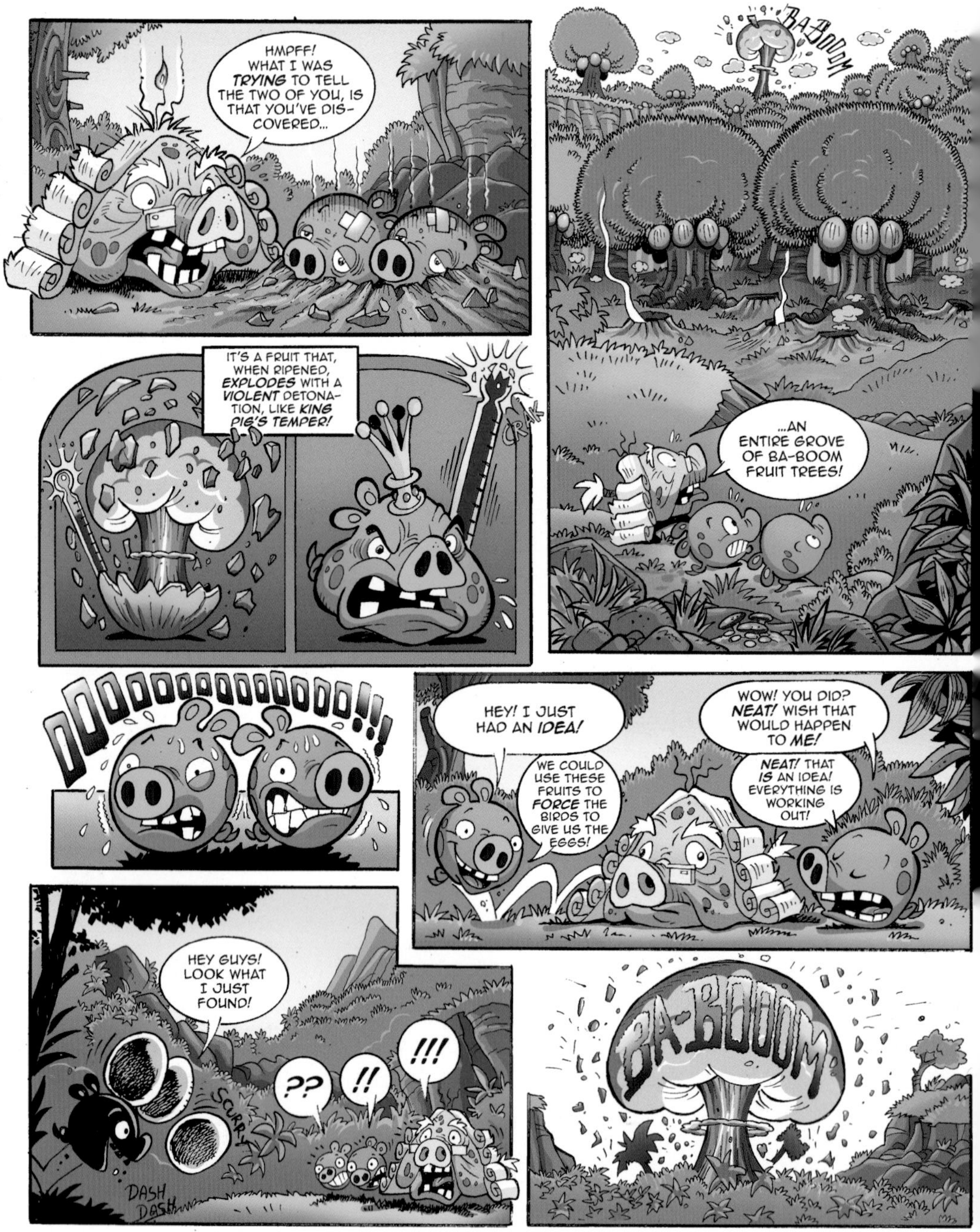
HMPFF! WHAT I WAS TRYING TO TELL THE TWO OF YOU, IS THAT YOU'VE DISCOVERED...
BA-BOOM
...AN ENTIRE GROVE OF BA-BOOM FRUIT TREES!
IT'S A FRUIT THAT, WHEN RIPENED, EXPLODES WITH A VIOLENT DETONATION, LIKE KING PIG'S TEMPER!
CRAK
OOOOOOOOOOOOOOO!!!
HEY! I JUST HAD AN IDEA!
WOW! YOU DID? NEAT! WISH THAT WOULD HAPPEN TO ME!
WE COULD USE THESE FRUITS TO FORCE THE BIRDS TO GIVE US THE EGGS!
NEAT! THAT IS AN IDEA! EVERYTHING IS WORKING OUT!
HEY GUYS! LOOK WHAT I JUST FOUND!
SCURRY
DASH DASH
??
!!
!!!
BA-BOOOM

ANGRY BIRDS™
FURIOUS FOWL

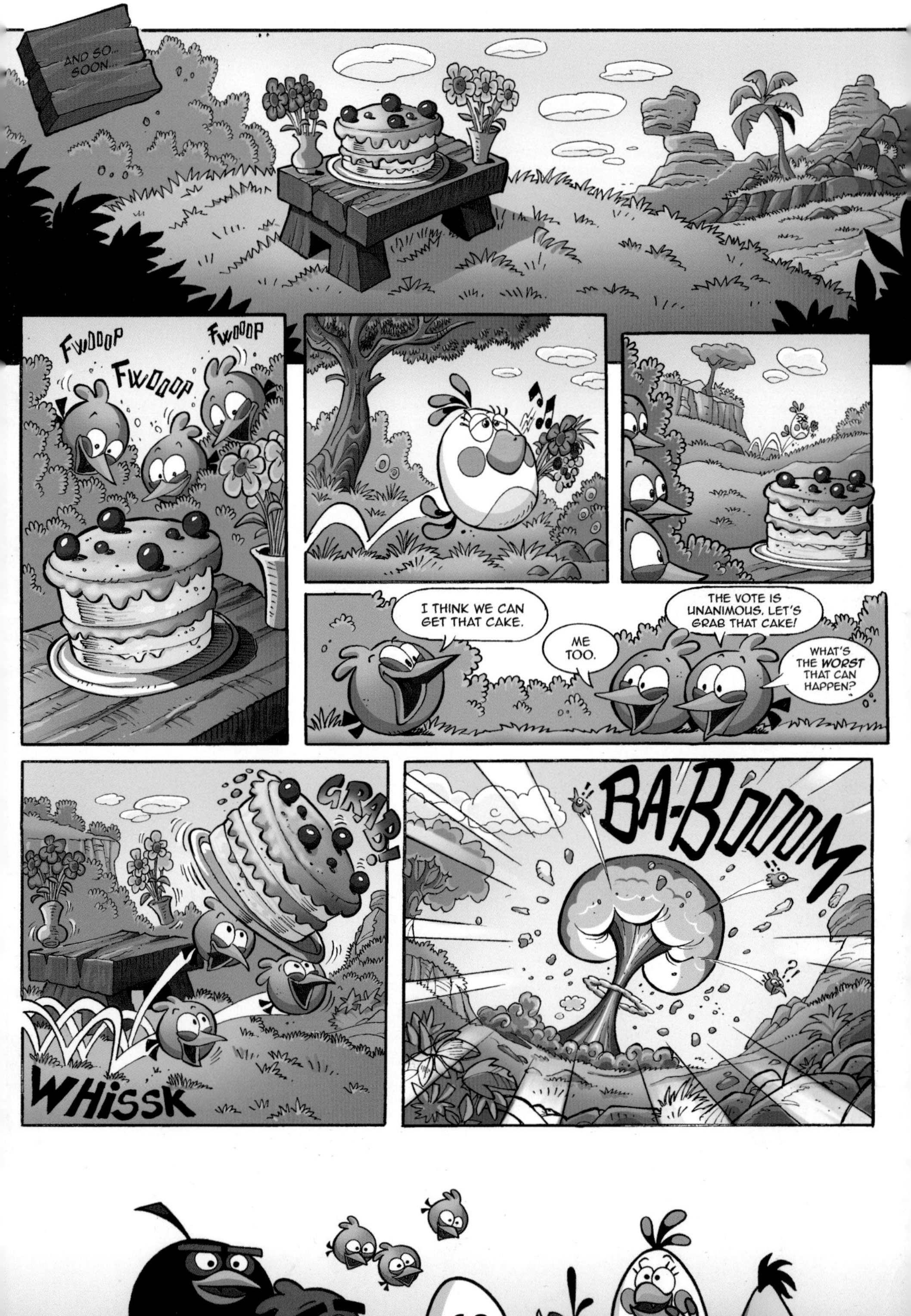
AND SO... SOON...
FWOOOP
FWOOOP
FWOOOP
I THINK WE CAN GET THAT CAKE.
ME TOO.
THE VOTE IS UNANIMOUS. LET'S GRAB THAT CAKE!
WHAT'S THE *WORST* THAT CAN HAPPEN?
GRAB!
WHISSK
BA-BOOOM

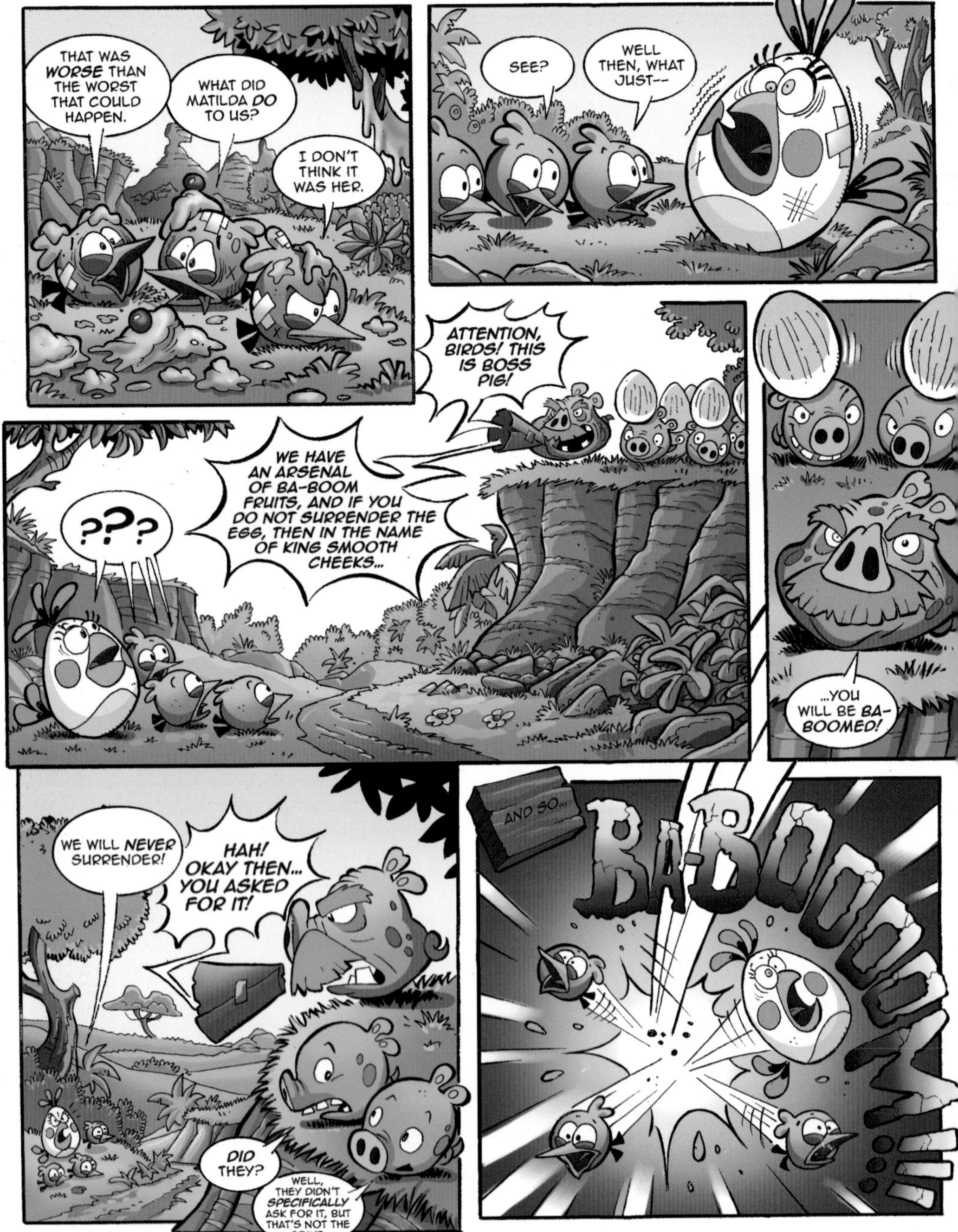

THAT WAS WORSE THAN THE WORST THAT COULD HAPPEN.
WHAT DID MATILDA DO TO US?
I DON'T THINK IT WAS HER.
SEE?
WELL THEN, WHAT JUST--
ATTENTION, BIRDS! THIS IS BOSS PIG!
WE HAVE AN ARSENAL OF BA-BOOM FRUITS, AND IF YOU DO NOT SURRENDER THE EGG, THEN IN THE NAME OF KING SMOOTH CHEEKS...
???
...YOU WILL BE BA-BOOMED!
WE WILL NEVER SURRENDER!
HAH! OKAY THEN... YOU ASKED FOR IT!
DID THEY?
WELL, THEY DIDN'T SPECIFICALLY ASK FOR IT, BUT THAT'S NOT THE POINT.
AND SO...
BA-BOOOOOM!!

ANGRY BIRDS™
FURIOUS FOWL

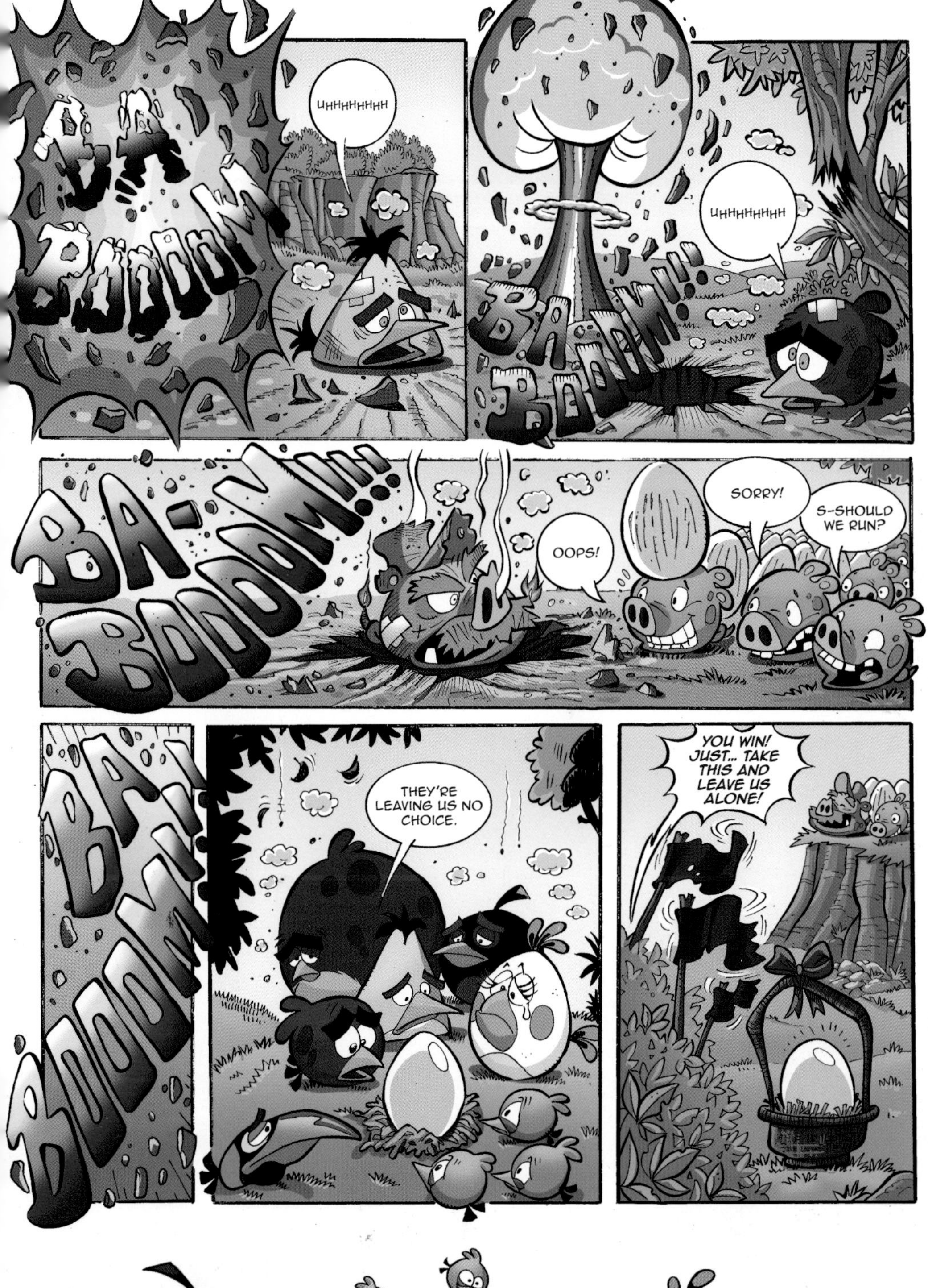
BA-BOOOOM!
UHHHHHHHHH
BA-BOOOM!!
UHHHHHHHHH
BA-BOOOOM!!!
OOPS!
SORRY!
S-SHOULD WE RUN?
BA-BOOOOM!!
THEY'RE LEAVING US NO CHOICE.
YOU WIN! JUST... TAKE THIS AND LEAVE US ALONE!

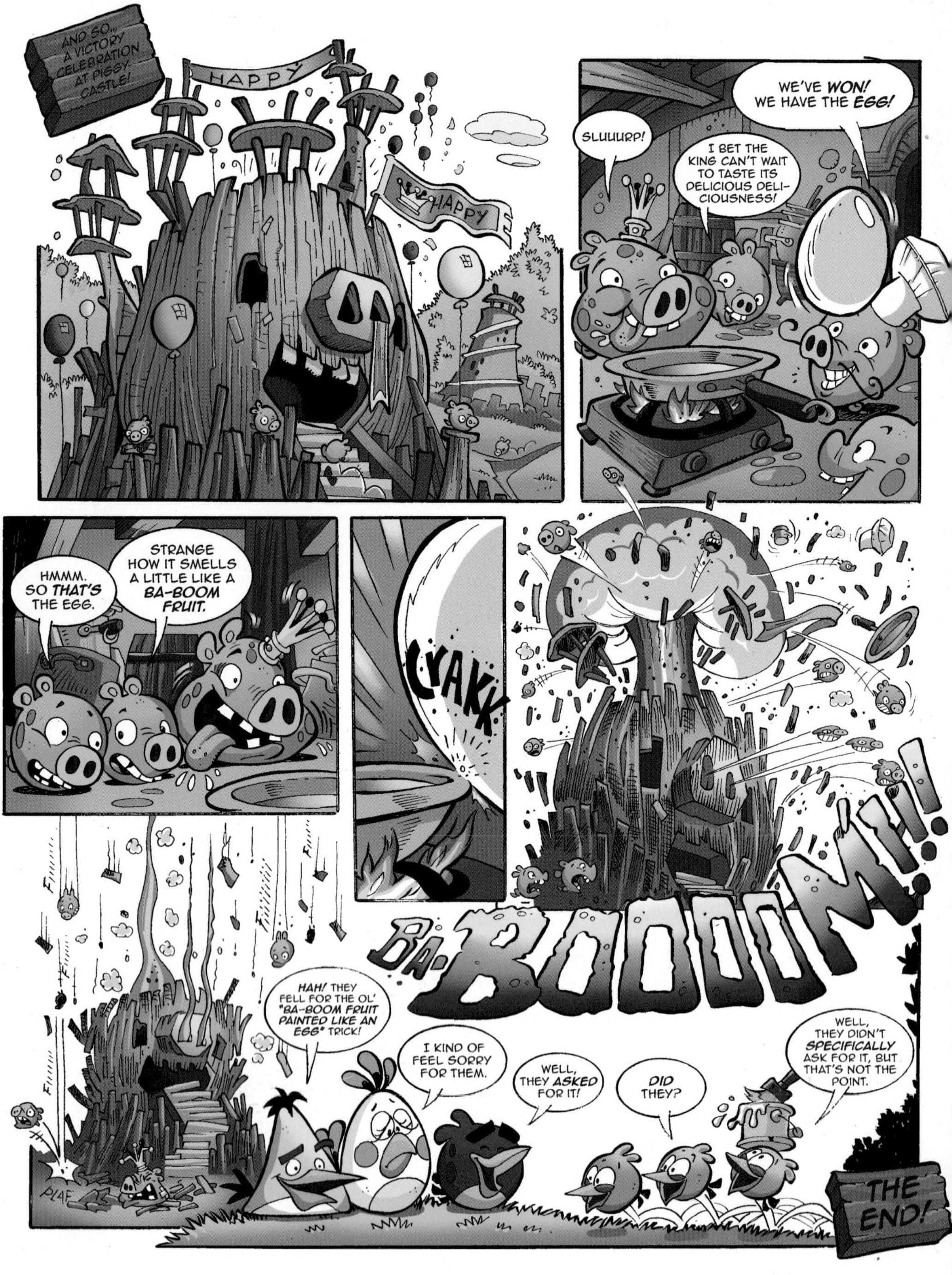
AND SO... A VICTORY CELEBRATION AT PIGGY CASTLE!
HAPPY
HAPPY
SLUUURP!
WE'VE WON! WE HAVE THE EGG!
I BET THE KING CAN'T WAIT TO TASTE ITS DELICIOUS DELI-CIOUSNESS!
HMMM. SO THAT'S THE EGG.
STRANGE HOW IT SMELLS A LITTLE LIKE A BA-BOOM FRUIT.
CYAKK
BA-BOOOOM!!!
HAH! THEY FELL FOR THE OL' "BA-BOOM FRUIT PAINTED LIKE AN EGG" TRICK!
I KIND OF FEEL SORRY FOR THEM.
WELL, THEY ASKED FOR IT!
DID THEY?
WELL, THEY DIDN'T SPECIFICALLY ASK FOR IT, BUT THAT'S NOT THE POINT.
PLAF
THE END!

ANGRY BIRDS™

FURIOUS FOWL

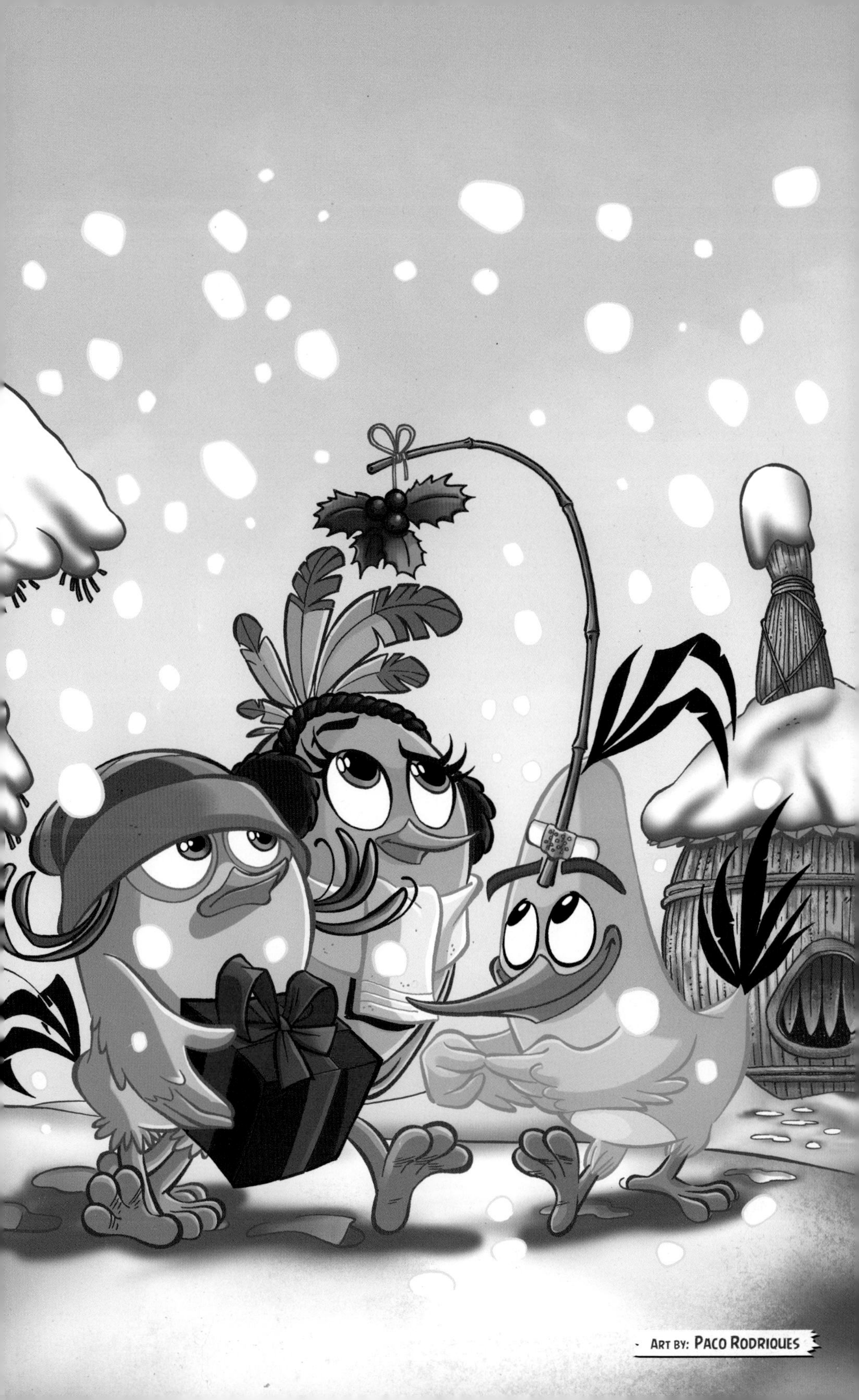

ART BY: PACO RODRIQUES

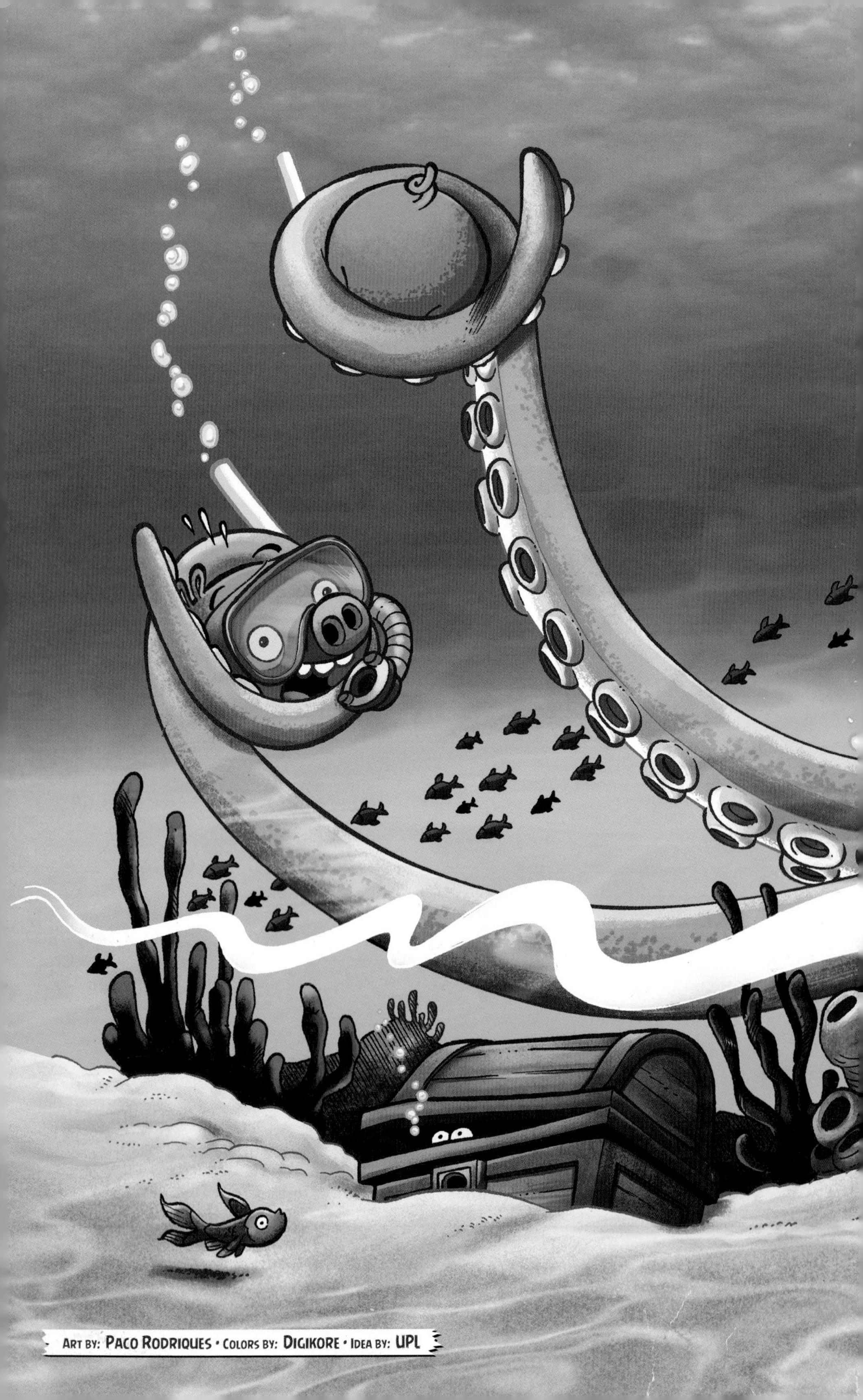
Art by: Paco Rodriques • Colors by: Digikore • Idea by: UPL

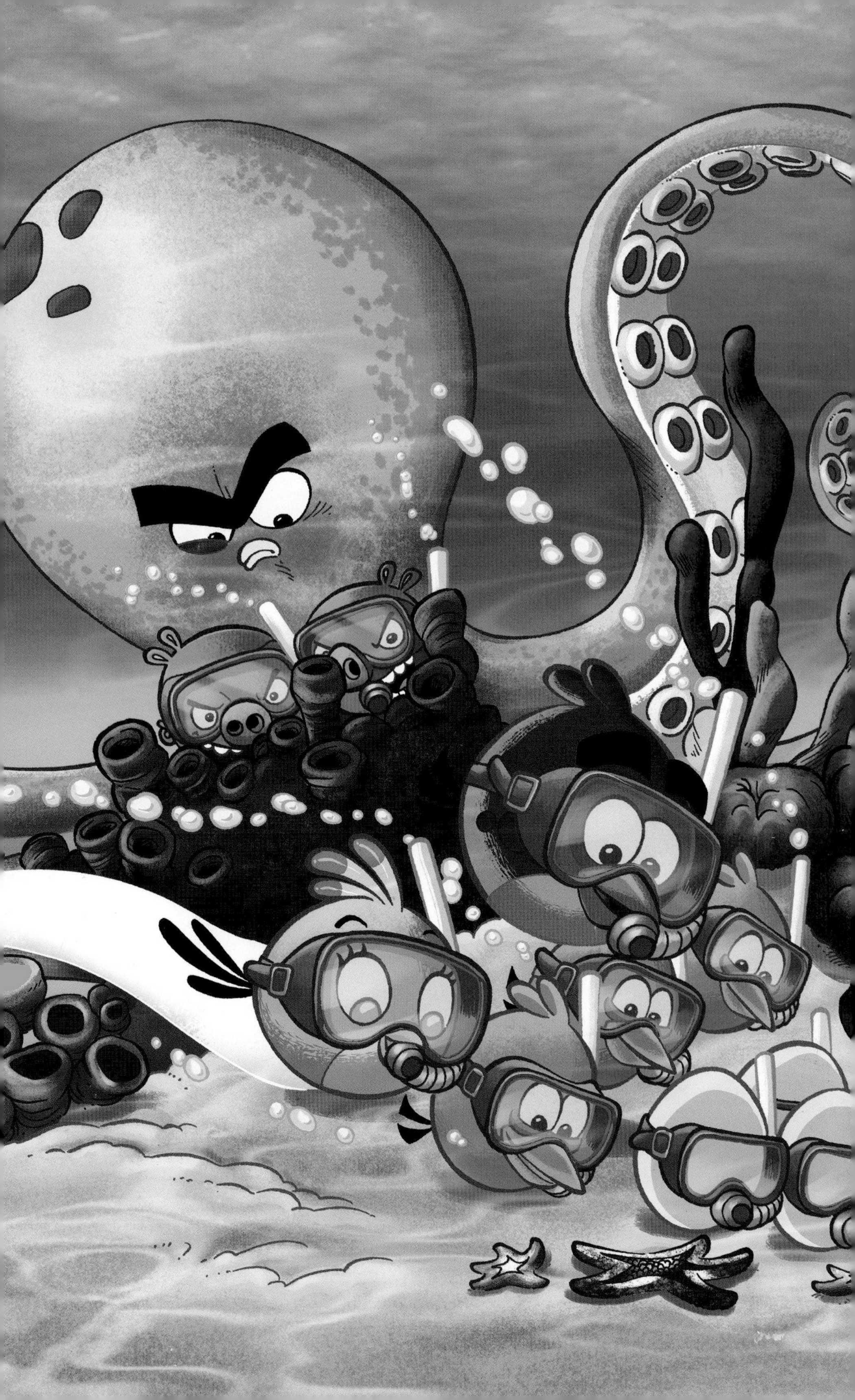

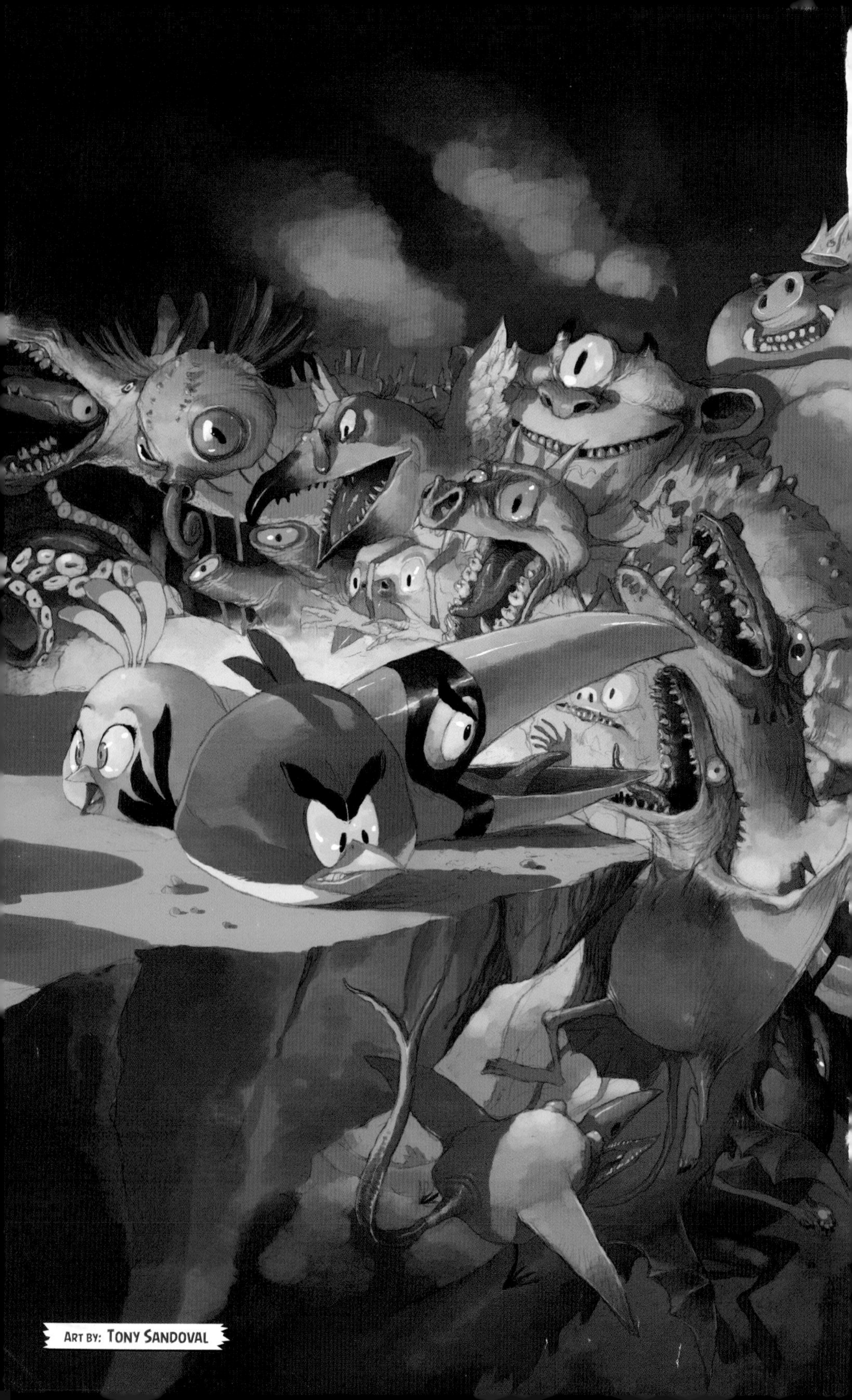

Art by: Tony Sandoval